Praise for the Midnight Breed series by LARA ADRIAN

BOUND TO DARKNESS

"While most series would have ended or run out of steam, the Midnight Breed series seems to have picked up steam. Lara Adrian has managed to keep the series fresh by adding new characters . . . without having to say goodbye to the original ones that made the series so popular to begin with. Bound to Darkness has all the passion, danger and unique appeal of the original ten books but also stands on its own as a turning point in the entire series with new pieces to a larger puzzle, new friends and old enemies."

—*Adria's Romance Reviews*

"Lara Adrian always manages to write great love stories, not only emotional but action packed. I love every aspect of (Bound to Darkness). I also enjoyed how we get a glimpse into the life of the other characters we have come to love. There is always something sexy and erotic in all of Adrian's books, making her one of my top 5 paranormal authors."

—*Reading Diva*

CRAVE THE NIGHT

"Nothing beats good writing and that is what ultimately makes Lara Adrian stand out amongst her peers.... Crave the Night is stunning in its flawless execution. Lara Adrian has the rare ability to lure readers right into her books, taking them on a ride they will never forget."

—*Under the Covers*

"...Steamy and intense. This installment is sure to delight established fans and will also be accessible to new readers."

—*Publishers Weekly*

Look for these titles in the *New York Times*
and #1 international bestselling

Midnight Breed series

. . . and more to come!

Other books by Lara Adrian

Contemporary Romance

100 Series
For 100 Days
For 100 Nights (forthcoming)
For 100 Reasons (forthcoming)

Historical Romance

Dragon Chalice Series
Heart of the Hunter
Heart of the Flame
Heart of the Dove

Warrior Trilogy
White Lion's Lady
Black Lion's Bride
Lady of Valor

Lord of Vengeance

Romantic Suspense and Paranormal Romance

Phoenix Code Series
(with Tina Folsom)
Cut and Run
Hide and Seek

Masters of Seduction Series
Merciless: House of Gravori (novella)
Priceless: House of Ebarron (novella)

DEFY THE
DAWN

A Midnight Breed Novel

(

NEW YORK TIMES BESTSELLING AUTHOR

LARA ADRIAN

ISBN: 1939193109
ISBN-13: 978-1939193100

DEFY THE DAWN
© 2016 by Lara Adrian, LLC
Cover design © 2016 by CrocoDesigns

www.LaraAdrian.com

Available in ebook and trade paperback. Unabridged audiobook edition forthcoming.

DEFY THE
DAWN

CHAPTER 1

London, England

Brynne Kirkland threw her head back and downed the shot of premium whisky in one throat-scalding gulp. Being Breed, alcohol wasn't her typical drink of choice. This noisy bar and strobe-lit dance club in Cheapside wasn't her usual after-hours hangout either. On those rare occasions when she socialized, the staid taverns and social clubs on the other side of the Thames were more her speed.

Then again, that was precisely why she was here.

She needed to decompress, let off some steam.

Get a little wild for once in her life.

Ah, to hell with the pretense of decorum. After the lousy day she'd just had, what she really needed was to get drunk and get laid.

Preferably in that order.

She also needed to feed. Although quenching that other self-inflicted dry spell was a problem she was hardly prepared to deal with on a good day, let alone now.

Setting the shot glass down on the mirrored surface of the sleek bar, she licked her lips and blew out a heavy sigh. The bartender was right there with the bottle of Glenmorangie as soon as she lifted her finger to beckon him over.

Ginger-haired, broad-shouldered, with a pair of sweet dimples bracketing his friendly smile, the twenty-something human wasn't hard to look at in the least. And given his firm, muscular body, obviously honed by years of dedicated work in the gym, he looked reasonably able to withstand the intense cardiovascular workout he'd get from taking a Breed female into his bed.

Which is more than she could say for most of the other human men in the place tonight. She had already sized up and mentally discarded a dozen potential candidates for a variety of reasons, not the least of which being the fear that sex with one of her kind was liable to kill a mere mortal from sheer exhaustion alone. She already had one dead human on her record this week; she damned well didn't need to add another.

The bartender took in her conservative white silk button-down and dark navy slacks as he refilled her shot glass. She'd come straight from work, hadn't even bothered to pull her hair loose from its tidy twist at the back of her head.

"Rough day at the office, luv?" The bartender asked over the throbbing pulse of the club music.

Brynne arched a brow at his unwitting remark. "You have no idea."

She'd spent the past decade building her career as an investigator at the London branch of JUSTIS—the

Breed/human law enforcement organization more formally known as the Joint Urban Security Taskforce Initiative Squad. She'd worked hard, devoted her life to her job. Hell, the job *was* her life.

Or, rather, it had been until a few hours ago.

Everything she'd worked for had gone down in flames—all the worse because she had no one to blame but herself.

Two nights ago, she'd secretly assisted a covert mission with Lucan Thorne and the Order, willfully withholding information about that mission from her colleagues and superiors at JUSTIS, well aware that in so doing she was gambling with her career. Thankfully, the Order mission had been a success. They'd struck a major blow against the terror group Opus Nostrum, taking out a key player in Dublin and unmasking another in London. Brynne's cooperation had been instrumental in making that happen.

Unfortunately, JUSTIS didn't see it that way.

Her superiors had no quibble with the Order exterminating the Breed male in Ireland. Fineas Riordan was a known criminal and underworld figure, but the human councilman who killed himself in London rather than fall into the hands of the Order was a scandal that JUSTIS could not afford.

Never mind that Neville Fielding had been corrupt and secretly on the take with Opus Nostrum. Never mind that the two men, along with the deadly cabal they belonged to, had declared themselves in war against the rest of the civilized world.

And never mind that Brynne had done what she believed was right—the result being two fewer problems for the world to worry about later.

None of that mattered, because in aiding the Order on their clandestine operation, she had willfully defied JUSTIS command. She'd broken the organization's trust.

For the first time ever, she had followed her heart instead of her head.

Unfortunately, the price was her career.

If that didn't call for a few shots of single malt and a rare, blindingly hot one-night-stand with someone she'd never see again, she didn't know what did.

Wrapping her fingers around the small glass the bartender had generously filled to the rim, Brynne tossed it back. She felt his heated gaze on her, felt the ripple of his sexual interest thicken the air as he watched her swallow the fiery liquor then wipe the back of her hand across her parted lips.

"Another, please."

His answering smile was slow, charmingly crooked. Framed by those endearing twin dimples. "Careful now, luv. Take things too fast here tonight, and you'll leave me no choice but to carry you home."

Was he serious? She stared at him, realizing he had no idea what she was. To anyone who looked at her now, she wasn't identifiable as Breed. At a glance, she was merely a tall, athletically built, green-eyed brunette.

Her fangs only appeared when she was emotionally provoked in some way, be it hunger, anger, or desire. That was when her other Breed characteristics manifested too, from the fiery amber glow of her irises and the vertical narrowing of her pupils, to the awakening of her *dermaglyphs*—color-changing skin markings that every member of the Breed had on their bodies to varying degrees.

Right now, she felt nothing but the pleasant buzz of the alcohol seeping into her bloodstream. Well, that, and the lingering sting of useless, self-directed anger. What she wanted was to feel less sting and more buzz, thank you very much.

"I'd like another shot, please."

"Jamie," the bartender said, still holding on to the bottle. "And you are?"

Brynne smiled. "Thirsty."

He chuckled as he leaned in close and poured more liquor into her glass. "All right, but don't say I didn't warn you. Not that I'd mind carrying a pretty lady like you home. In fact, I'd consider it my chivalrous duty."

Flirting. God, he was flirting with her. Or trying to, at any rate.

She had no skill in that area, had never imagined she'd have a use for it until this very moment. She licked her lips, casting about for a witty comeback or better yet, something to show him that she was ready, willing, and able to take him up on whatever he had in mind.

Except she couldn't.

She *wasn't*—interested in him, that is.

And that was a shame, because none of the other men leering at her in the club stirred anything more than shades of boredom in her.

Lamely, she thanked Jamie for the further shot, then breathed a sigh of relief when he was summoned down to the other end of the bar to wait on other patrons. The place was crowded, practically elbow-to-elbow with people jockeying for spots at the bar or at the twenty-odd pub tables in the area at Brynne's back. Out on the dance floor, bodies bounced and gyrated and swayed to the relentless thump of the music.

With the bartender swamped by customers placing drink orders, Brynne sipped her shot and tried to convince herself she was there to have a good time. She may not have much experience with flirting or seduction—and okay, maybe that was putting it mildly—but she could do this. She wanted to do this.

God knew, she needed some kind of outlet tonight or she was going to lose her mind.

Still nursing her drink, she pivoted around in her seat to watch the crowd. Not long afterward, a waitress carrying a long-stemmed martini glass approached her from the other side of the club. The bright blue cocktail glowed like neon and had some kind of lacy sugar stick of candy resting in it.

Brynne frowned when the server stopped right in front of her.

"This is from the gentleman across the room."

The waitress gestured to a group of young men—some of them with visible *glyphs* on their arms. The Breed youths were civilians from the area Darkhavens, no doubt on the prowl for human blood Hosts before the nightly feeding curfew went into effect.

While most of the little pack were chatting up human women, one of them stared directly at Brynne. Dark-haired, serious, the Breed male nodded in acknowledgment as the waitress started to hand her the frou-frou cocktail.

Brynne shook her head. "Please tell the gentleman thanks, but no thanks. I prefer whisky, and I prefer to drink it alone."

The waitress shrugged. "Whatever."

Just brilliant, Kirkland. That's two for two on failed attempts to engage.

No wonder she sucked at sex.

Growing more frustrated with herself by the moment, she swung back around in her seat and slammed the shot—her fourth tonight, but who was counting?—then set the glass down on the bar.

That's it. No more dragging her feet about this.

She'd come here to self-medicate and forget the empty mess she was making of her life, and that meant she wasn't leaving this club alone.

Time to check her excuses and her conscience into her panties for the night.

As the Glenmorangie burned a soothing trail of fire down her throat, Brynne made a promise to herself.

She was going to scratch her itch on the first viable man to approach her.

It didn't take long. No sooner had she made her ridiculous vow than a wave of heat moved in beside her at the bar. Awareness prickled along her nerve endings like electricity, lifting the fine hairs on her arms and at her nape, making her nipples tighten in immediate response.

"This seat taken?"

The low, aggravatingly confident voice was familiar to her.

As was the pair of unearthly cerulean blue eyes that arrested her gaze and didn't let go as she turned her head to look at the man who'd just arrived.

No, not a man.

An immortal male.

Atlantean.

Golden-haired. Handsome. Arrogant beyond compare.

Easily the last person she wanted to see, especially

tonight.

He grinned at her, that broad, sensual mouth of his sending a spike of outrage—and something far more troubling—through her veins.

"Hello, Brynne."

"Zael," she all but growled. "What the hell are you doing here?"

CHAPTER 2

E kizael had walked this earth for thousands of years, every last one of them lived with the full awareness of what his sculpted, ageless face and sun-kissed, chiseled body did to the sensibilities of the fairer sex. His flawless Atlantean looks and preternatural sensuality had always been part of his charm.

Or so he'd thought.

Until he met Brynne Kirkland.

As she had several days ago in D.C. when they'd first laid eyes on each other, the gorgeous, but pitifully uptight, Breed female seemed utterly unimpressed.

She glowered at him as he slid onto the barstool beside her. A seat he'd ensured would be vacated when he mentally sent its previous occupant away a moment ago.

"What are you drinking, beautiful?"

She didn't answer, and he knew the casual endearment annoyed her as much as his presence. Her forest green eyes narrowed on him pointedly as he picked up her empty glass. He sniffed the smoky, peat-laced fragrance of the top shelf whisky she'd been hammering back one after the other like shots of cheap tequila.

"You know, the real pleasure of a single malt is in its nuances. Like a lot of other pleasurable pursuits, if you rush through it, you miss the best part." He smiled. "Didn't anyone ever tell you that?"

Frowning, she took the glass away from him and set it down on the mirrored bar in front of her. "I prefer to do my own thing."

Zael chuckled. "Yeah, so I'm gathering. Is that why you're sitting here all by your lonesome tonight, pounding down shots and driving every red-blooded male in the place crazy?"

He should know; he was one of them. It had taken every ounce of his restraint to keep from stalking over to stake his claim until now. Not that he had a claim to stake where she was concerned. Brynne could have her pick of any man she set her sights on, though whether she understood that or not, he wasn't sure. She'd made a point of letting him know back in D.C. that he would never be in the running.

And damned if that didn't make Zael even more determined to find out why.

She let out an indignant snort as she swiveled on her stool to face him. "I'm not lonesome. I *was* trying to have a good time. Until you showed up, that is. How long have you been here?"

"Long enough to see you have a couple of close calls with some poor decision-making."

She snorted. "Spying on me, you mean?"

Zael grinned. "How is that any different from when

you crept out onto the terrace at the Order's headquarters to lurk in the bushes and check me out while I did my sunrise workout?"

She gave him an outraged look. "I did *not* creep out there, and I most certainly didn't lurk."

"But you do admit you were checking me out?"

"Only in your deluded dreams, Atlantean."

Her tone was defensive, though whether out of habit or the alcohol buzz she must be feeling, he wasn't sure. She crossed her arms over her breasts, drawing his attention to her hardened nipples beneath the satiny fabric of her prim white button-down shirt. Her scowl and closed body language might be telling him she wasn't interested, but the pretty flush of her cheeks— and the blood he could hear racing through her veins— were saying something far different.

As were the tiny amber sparks that kindled in her stormy irises.

The no-nonsense law enforcement agent may want to pretend the attraction between them wasn't real, the way she had when they met for the first time last week, but he hadn't been fooled then and he wasn't fooled now. Whether Brynne wanted to admit it or not, the truth was right in front of him.

She cleared her throat and hiked up her chin. "You haven't answered my question, Zael. What the hell are you doing in London? For that matter, what the hell are you doing in this club?"

"Looking for you."

Well, that certainly got her attention. She went silent, her lips slack. The frown that seemed permanently creased into her forehead now faltered, though only for a moment.

"Looking for me." She sounded surprised, her words guarded. "Whatever for?"

He knew he could play it smooth with her right now, use his charm and her physical, if slightly inebriated, reaction to him to his ultimate advantage. He had to admit, it was tempting.

Despite the fact that she was still dressed for a day in the office, from her sensible heels to the careful updo that corralled her thick mane of sable waves, Brynne had obviously come to this strobe-lit meat market in Cheapside tonight for a reason. Until he saw her shoot down every male who approached her, Zael had wondered if she was there with the intent that she wouldn't be going home alone.

And why that idea should bother him so much, he didn't want to examine.

Personally, he'd be up for the challenge himself, but seducing the prickly daywalker wasn't the reason he was in London. All right, not the sole reason, anyway. He'd actually come out of concern.

He kept his voice low, even though the din in the club assured no one else would overhear. "I heard what happened last night here in London, Brynne."

"Good news certainly travels fast," she said dryly. She gave him a mistrusting look. "I wasn't aware the Order had cleared you for that kind of information, Atlantean."

"What good is an alliance if it's crippled by secrets?" At Brynne's grim nod of acknowledgment, Zael said, "I don't imagine your colleagues at JUSTIS were pleased to find out you were working in secret with the Order."

She groaned. "Your intuitive skills astound."

When she raised her empty glass in plea to the

bartender to come back and refill it, Zael gently caught her wrist and brought her hand back down. She looked too shocked to protest the physical contact, even as he covered her fingers with his on the bar. It took her a moment before she withdrew from his loose grasp.

"I know what you're sacrificing by allying yourself with the Order in this. I also know what it is to be torn between the people you belong to and the ones you know are doing the right thing."

He'd been toeing that same line since Lucan Thorne had summoned him to Washington, D.C., last week with a request to join forces. In truth, it had been something more than a request. A demand. Hell, it had been nothing short of a plea—no doubt, a first for a man like Lucan.

Zael held Brynne's skeptical look. "I just wanted to make sure you were okay."

"Well, I'm fine." She broke his stare on a quiet scoff. "If you came here for a front row seat to watch my career implode, you're too late."

"What do you mean?"

"I was relieved from duty this afternoon." Quiet words, heavy with restraint. For all of this female's cool control and confidence, it was plain enough that the loss of her job had cut her deeply.

"Shit. No wonder you're sitting here trying to drown yourself in whisky and other bad choices."

Her sidelong glance was as dry as her voice. "Let me guess. You're available to be one of them?"

Zael cocked a brow at her. "Are you asking?"

"Never." She gave him an arch look that should have withered him, but instead sent a flare of heat straight to his crotch. "There isn't enough whisky in the world for that."

"Madam, you wound me."

"Ah, now, there's an idea," she said, her lips curving in a smile.

Zael chuckled, not the least dissuaded. He got up from his seat at the bar. "Come on, Brynne."

She stayed put, frowning at his outstretched hand. "Come on where?"

He took her hand, and was surprised that she slid off her stool without a fight. *Score one point for the Glenmorangie.*

Taking the opportunity, and her, in a firmer grasp, he led Brynne away from the bar and through the busy club.

"You're wasting your time with me," she said as they wended between the clusters of human and Breed patrons. "Wouldn't you rather go find a woman who might appreciate your so-called charms?"

"Not especially. I prefer a challenge." He paused with her at the edge of the crowded dance floor. Music vibrated the walls and the floor, throbbing with an energetic beat he felt reverberating in his chest. Multi-hued laser lights swirled in all directions, the flashing colors illuminating Brynne's wary expression.

"What are you doing?"

He gestured to the dance floor. "Helping you have a good time. That is what you said you were trying to do before I showed up, right?"

Her mouth flattened with the beginnings of a protest. "I'm not interested in dancing, Zael."

"Then what are you interested in?"

She fell silent, her gaze holding his as more bodies pushed and jostled their way past them onto the floor. The heavy bass pounded all around them, punctuating the hammer of Zael's pulse as he waited for Brynne to push him away, to deny the attraction he felt crackling like lightning between them.

Damn, she was beautiful.

Color rose in her cheeks. As he watched it bloom, the flush spread down her pretty throat and onto the pale smoothness of her chest. The embers in her Breed irises glittered with more fire—banked but burning. And although she was careful when she spoke to him, more than once he'd seen the delicate tips of her fangs gleaming behind the lush pink line of her mouth.

Finally, she huffed out a resigned sigh. "All right, fine. If you insist, then let's get this over with."

Zael chuckled. "That's the first time a woman's ever said those words to me before."

Brynne pursed her lips. "I'm glad to know I stand out among the throng."

Oh, yeah. Understatement of the century right there. "That you do, Ms. Kirkland. That you do."

He brought her into the center of the floor where he found a small space for them amid the dancing couples, groups, and singles that filled the club. She stood there in front of him, unmoving. The normally cool and confident Breed female suddenly looked as lost and uncertain as a child.

"What's wrong?"

"You should know that I don't..." Her words trailed off, and she slowly shook her head. Then she leaned in close to speak over the noise. "I don't normally do...this." Her confession skated warmly against his skin, her breath laced with the sweetness of the whisky she'd imbibed. "I'm not very good at it, Zael. Not in front of an audience, anyway. And never with a partner."

Fuck. Was she talking about dancing? For a second, he wasn't sure. His mind had blown a circuit while she was explaining, and now all of his blood was rushing south in a hot instant.

He swallowed on a parched throat, wondering if she had any idea what her whispered words had done to him. He had to force himself to remain still, in control, as she listed a little on her heels, one hand coming to rest on his shoulder to hold herself steady.

Her body brushed against his, inflaming him as powerfully as if he was a teenage boy, not a long-lived immortal warrior whose appetite for beauty and pleasure were practically legend among his kind.

"You doing anything alone is a pity for a hundred different reasons," he murmured, his voice rough with desire he could not hide.

To his shock, she didn't resist when he gathered her into his arms to dance. She didn't stiffen or pull away when he began moving with her to his own rhythm, ignoring the frenetic beat of the music and the jostle of the other writhing bodies crushed in around them.

To his utter amazement, she held on to him too. She swayed with him, her breasts brushing against his chest, her thighs woven lightly between his. Her head came to rest lightly on his chest. She felt so warm in his arms. Softer than he'd imagined. Each breath he took filled his senses with Brynne's unique scent—vanilla and rain and an elusive sweetness that seemed at odds with the tough facade she seemed so determined to present to the rest of the world.

Or maybe just toward him.

Zael didn't know. At the moment, he didn't care.

Time slowed. The song blaring over the sound

system was loud and relentless, but the cacophony of the music and the hundreds of other people around them faded into the background as Zael held Brynne in his arms.

He hadn't come to London expecting any of this.

But then, Brynne Kirkland was nothing if not unexpected.

Unpredictable. Unforgettable.

And now he had to add another superlative to the growing list where she was concerned.

Irresistible.

He wanted to kiss her. He wanted to feel her body pressed against him without the barrier of clothing between them. He wanted her so badly, he moaned with the force of his need.

She had to know how she was affecting him. Holy hell, she had to feel it.

She did. He saw the knowledge register in her widened eyes as she lifted her head from his chest. A small crease burrowed between her brows.

But instead of pushing him away or making a break for the nearest door, beautiful, tipsy Brynne did something else he wasn't expecting.

Reaching up to lace her fingers behind his neck, she pulled him into a shocking, mind-blowingly deep kiss.

CHAPTER 3

S he didn't know what had gotten into her.

With her mouth locked on Zael's in a kiss that seemed to stagger them both, Brynne wanted to blame her rash—not to mention mortifying—impulse on the whisky.

It *was* because of the whisky.

Had to be.

How else could she explain the fact that this unwelcome reunion with the Atlantean had been the highlight of her entire day?

What other excuse could she possibly find for the fact that she was currently wrapped within the arms of a man who had done nothing but unsettle and annoy her from the instant they met, and she *liked* it?

God help her, she more than liked it.

Moaning, she speared her fingers deeper into his thick golden hair as she pulled him closer and her tongue dove deeper into his mouth. Her fangs surged, elongating as her desire intensified. Behind her closed eyelids her vision burned blood-red, and beneath her silk blouse and tailored pants, her skin tingled with the awakening of her *dermaglyphs*.

She was overcome with need, no doubt because it had been so long since she'd given in to her body's demands—carnal and otherwise. Surely, that had to be the reason.

Every cell in her body lit up with a sudden and startling current of electricity as she sparred and tangled her tongue with Zael's. Heat licked through her senses, into her veins, with each brush of his lips over hers.

It wasn't as if she'd never kissed a man before. She had—although admittedly, infrequently at most. To her chagrin, kissing Zael made the memory of those other encounters dissolve into oblivion now.

And regardless of the fact that an audience of other clubgoers surrounded Zael and her from all sides, Brynne couldn't get enough of him.

Just how many shots had she drunk tonight?

She couldn't remember, nor did she care. With Zael's mouth moving so hotly over hers, the only thing she could answer to now was her desire.

Wasn't that what she'd wanted? Distraction from her problems. From her failures.

And yes, from her loneliness too. Zael had been right about that. She'd wanted a release from the emptiness of her life.

Just for a little while.

For a night.

With someone who wouldn't judge her, or be inclined to stick around long enough to see just how fucked up she truly was. With her train wreck of an upbringing, she had no experience with emotional bonds, aside from the half-sister she'd met just several years ago.

And if having spent the first twenty-odd years of her life simply trying to survive wasn't bad enough, she also had the added bonus of a cellular metabolism flaw that was slowly tearing her apart. She wasn't wired for relationships. Long-term romantic commitments were not in her DNA—literally.

Which kind of made a player like Zael the perfect sexual outlet she was looking for tonight.

Hell, she was almost halfway there with him already.

Her veins felt like rivers of fire under her skin. The low hum of her need was rising swiftly in her temples, building with each heavy pound of her heart.

Panting as she tore her mouth away from his, Brynne stared up into his heavy-lidded, darkened blue eyes.

"Let's get out of here. My flat is just across the river." She licked her lips, no easy feat when her fangs were fully extended and filling her mouth. "I want to go. Right now. With you."

It was intended as a command, which should have been clear enough to him. But he stood unmoving. His handsome face was taut with desire, his mouth wet and slack from their kissing.

Sexual interest radiated off every hard, golden inch of him. Most obviously in the rigid length of the erection that pressed against her hip.

Yet he slowly shook his head in denial.

"What are you trying to do here, Brynne? You've had too much to drink. I doubt you even know what you're saying."

She reached up, grabbing a fist full of the front of his shirt. "I'm saying I want to have sex with you, Zael. No strings attached, no need to call me in the morning. We don't ever have to see each other again. In fact, I'd prefer that we don't."

She fully expected him to jump on the offer. At the very least, she expected she'd have to endure the Atlantean's self-satisfied grin as he tossed off one of his snappy, arrogant comebacks before dragging her out of the club like the caveman she was certain he was.

Instead, he held her slightly unsteady gaze. His square jaw remained firm, unyielding.

When he spoke, his voice was low, utterly serious. "I should take you to bed, if only because you strike me as a woman who's never been properly fucked in your life. But I won't. Not like this."

He pried her fingers from his shirt and took a step back from her.

Good lord, was he . . . *offended?*

Brynne scowled, weaving slightly on her feet. Her body vibrated with stalled need. "Aren't you the one who's been putting the full court press on me every time I've seen you? I thought you wanted me. It sure as hell felt like you did just now."

His answering grunt was sharp, caustic. "I can have any woman under the terms you just described. And I have."

"Then what's the problem?"

He didn't answer, just started walking away from her. Brynne fell in behind him, hurrying to catch up as he sliced through the crowd. She didn't reach him until they were through the bar and heading for the exit.

"Zael, wait. Please."

He paused just inside the club's vestibule.

"I shouldn't have come." He stared at her as if he

was going to say something more, then changed his mind. He shook his head. "You want to go home, I'll take you home. I'll even put you to bed, Brynne. But I won't fuck you. Not like this. No matter how much I want to."

His toneless reply took her so aback, he might as well have slapped her.

She swallowed back her humiliation, but it sat at the back of her throat, bitter as acid.

"Come on," he said tightly. "I'll hail us a taxi."

As they stepped outside the building, Brynne's apology sat on the very tip of her tongue. All of the alcohol in her bloodstream seemed to dissolve under the weight of her embarrassment, leaving her feeling cold and foolish.

And never more alone.

"Zael, I—"

She didn't know what she could say to fix things. She wasn't even sure she knew how.

But then something bright in the starlit distance caught her eye—something disturbing, setting the skyline across the Thames aglow.

A fire.

No, it was more than a fire.

It was a churning, massive plume of flames and roiling, thick gray smoke. Outside the club, a crowd was gathering to look at the spectacle.

As they all watched in silent horror, a low rumble sounded across the water…followed by the unspeakable crash and roar of crumbling metal, glass, and mortar.

"Oh, my God," Brynne murmured. She glanced over at Zael, feeling all of the blood drain from her face. "That's the government block at Vauxhall Cross. That building that just went down? Zael… It was JUSTIS headquarters."

CHAPTER 4

☾

Order Headquarters
Washington, D.C.

Lucan Thorne had been a warrior far too long and seen too damned much for anything to take him by surprise anymore. Yet as he stood in front of a wall of video monitors in the Order's war room at headquarters, watching with most of his lieutenants and their mates as the heart of London's government district burned, he couldn't deny the cold sense of disbelief that gripped him.

The iconic white building that once housed the famed British MI6, and, for the past twenty years, the global operations headquarters for JUSTIS...*gone*.

Nothing but rubble. The highly secured, impenetrable modern fortress and all who'd been inside it tonight, consumed by the massive cloud of dark ash and searing fire that lit up the London skyline like a volcano.

"Opus Nostrum wasted no time claiming responsibility," Gideon said grimly from beside Lucan. "It's all over the Internet now."

The Order's technology expert had a tablet in hand, scanning underground sites where hackers and other society misfits liked to boast and preen for one another. Gideon was as much a warrior as any of his comrades, but he also had skills that would leave any black hat computer genius in his wake.

Lucan ground out a tight curse. "We should've seen this coming."

"No one saw this coming," Gideon said. "There was no chatter, no posturing. No threats. Nothing but silence leading up to this attack."

"Even so, we should have known they wouldn't let us take out two of their key players without some kind of response."

Sterling Chase, head of the Boston command center, shook his head as he considered. "This kind of assault takes time. It takes planning and coordination. You don't just roll up to a high-security government facility with enough firepower to raze the place."

Dante, another of the longtime Order members, grunted in agreement. "Not without getting your own ass blown to pieces as soon as your toe crosses the property line."

"There were no reports of unusual activity anywhere in the area," added Tegan.

The massive male was first generation Breed, like Lucan—both of them powerful Gen Ones, both of them centuries-old founding members of the Order. They had gone from friends to enemies and back again in the long time they'd known each other. Now, both mated to extraordinary women who'd given them each brave sons who shared their fathers' commitment to the Order, Lucan and Tegan had become as close as kin.

"No one saw this coming," Tegan said, "let alone had time to prevent it."

As much as Lucan wanted to believe that was true, the leader in him didn't feel the weight of the blame on his shoulders any less.

"Is that what we'll tell the public when they ask how this was allowed to happen? That we were all caught unaware and now we're standing around with our dicks in our hands?"

"JUSTIS never wanted our help, Father." Lucan's son, Darion, stared at him from the other side of the room. The adult Breed male stood with a few of the other warriors' grown sons who had gathered in the war room as the first reports were coming in from London.

As he spoke, several heads of the younger recruits nodded.

"Ask anyone in JUSTIS or the Global Nations Council," Dare went on. "They don't trust us and they don't approve of our methods. They haven't from day one."

"Neither did the old guard of the Breed's famously ineffective Enforcement Agency," Rio pointed out. "But we outlasted them too."

The Spanish warrior's statement drew assenting comments from his fellow comrades Brock and Kade. Even Hunter, the formidable former assassin, voiced agreement.

Lucan glanced back to the fiery destruction still filling the video monitors. "I don't give a damn about JUSTIS's approval, or the GNC's, or any other organization that talks a good game right up until a real threat comes around and blows them all to shit. I care about peace. I care about protecting the lives of the innocents who can't do it for themselves."

"We all do, Lucan." His Breedmate, Gabrielle, moved in closer and nestled against him, her voice calm and rational, even in the face of terror like the kind that was dealt tonight. That steadiness was one of the things he'd always admired about her.

But she clung tightly to him as she spoke. Whether she intended the physical contact as a reassurance to herself or to him, Lucan wasn't sure.

Gabrielle looked at Mathias Rowan, who led the Order's command center in London. "Do we know how many people were in the building tonight?"

Mathias might have been home in England tonight himself, but he'd recently come to the States with his newly expecting Breedmate, Nova, to visit his friend Sterling Chase in Boston.

Mathias gave a vague shake of his head, his arm around Nova's shoulder as the pair watched the horror unfold on the monitors. "They're still working to get an accurate count. Given the late hour of the attack, there were few human members of JUSTIS on site." His gaze was as sober as his voice. "My men over there are on the ground as we speak. Thane, the team's captain, says there were no survivors. From the looks of it, he thinks we should expect Breed casualties to be in the high double-digits, possibly a hundred."

A ripple of outrage traveled the gathered warriors. The women's reaction was quieter, a couple of the Breedmates sniffling as they struggled to hold back tears. Most affected of them all was Sterling Chase's mate,

Tavia.

Her half-sister, Brynne Kirkland, worked in London as a JUSTIS investigator. Tavia had been frantically trying to reach her ever since the first news of the attack surfaced.

"Has there still been no word?" Gabrielle asked the other female.

"Nothing yet." Tavia's worry drew her mouth into a flat line. "Brynne emailed me before heading in to JUSTIS headquarters this morning. She said she expected to be in debriefing meetings at least all day about Fielding's death. She said she'd call me after she was out. I've called her several times and emailed, but..." She drew in a shaky breath. "Brynne's flat is in that same neighborhood. If she wasn't still at the JUSTIS building tonight, then she was probably home when..."

Her words trailed off again, her voice constricted. Chase drew her against him and pressed a kiss to the top of her head. He offered no words or false hope, just held his mate as his grim gaze met Lucan's.

"We have to stop Opus before they grow any bolder," the Boston commander said.

Lucan nodded. "Yes, we do. And we will."

He was well aware that this assault would not be the last. Nor would it be the worst still to come, based on their dealings with the cabal whose main goal seemed to be global chaos and terror. The type of kindling that never failed to spark war.

And every man and woman in the room with Lucan now also knew that Opus Nostrum was only one enemy they had to contend with.

The other force that had declared itself the Order's enemy was even worse for the fact that it was unseen—

unknown thus far, except for her name.

Selene.

The exiled queen of the hidden race of immortals whom legend and myth had called Atlanteans.

If the Order's information was to be trusted, Selene was preparing for a strike of her own. According to what they knew, she had been plotting, waiting to make her move. What they didn't know was how or when. Perhaps if they did, they would know how best to stop her. Failing that, Lucan and his warriors would have no choice but to destroy her.

Before she had the chance to destroy them.

And to accomplish that, the Order was prepared to utilize every advantage they had over the Atlanteans and their mad queen.

As Lucan contemplated all of the grave work ahead of him and his warriors, his comm unit vibrated with an incoming call on his private, encrypted line.

He could count on one hand the number of people who had direct access to him—most of them gathered in the war room with him now.

Except for one recent addition.

He put the phone to his ear and heard a deep voice of an individual he'd only come to know a few days ago. A man the Order had little choice but to trust as a much-needed ally.

"Lucan, it's Zael." Sirens screamed in the background, punctuated by the low, distant percussions of explosive aftershocks. "I'm in London with Brynne. We need help."

CHAPTER 5

B rynne wanted to pretend the humiliation of having propositioned Zael—and been rejected—hadn't actually happened. She wanted to pretend a lot of things hadn't truly happened tonight, chief among them the heinous attack on her colleagues at JUSTIS.

But it was impossible to ignore anything that had occurred these past several hours as she sat alone with Zael inside the luxury cabin of the Order's private jet en route to Washington, D.C.

Opus Nostrum had destroyed the entire London headquarters in one fell swoop.

No survivors. Nearly a hundred JUSTIS officers and officials incinerated in the blast, all but a dozen or so of the victims Breed. Men and women Brynne had worked with for the bulk of her career with the organization. People she liked, simply gone in an instant.

The rubble from the explosion was burning as the jet had taken off from outside the city. It would likely take days before the two-block diameter pyre finally cooled.

Her city would never be the same.

Around the whole world, nothing would ever be the same now.

Opus had made that point clear tonight.

Brynne jiggled the ice in her glass then took a long drink of the cold liquid. Water this time, even though her grief and fury called for something stronger. Witnessing the inferno that had devoured her longtime workplace—*former workplace,* she reminded herself grimly—had been enough to sober her on the spot. The way she felt after tonight, she might never touch another drop.

Zael was watching her from his seat across the cabin. He'd been uncharacteristically reserved since they boarded the jet. Even now, he kept his tongue and his distance, allowing her much needed space to process and reflect.

She set her empty glass on the console next to her. "I keep picturing myself walking those networks of corridors," she murmured softly. "I keep seeing their faces—the other officers and investigators I worked with on a daily basis at that building. I can't stop running through their names in my mind, doing a mental body count."

Zael nodded gravely, but didn't say anything. He got up and slowly walked over to take the leather seat facing her. His copper-threaded blond hair had gotten tousled from their race across London to view the destruction firsthand.

He raked the thick waves back from his brow and leaned forward, resting his elbows on his bent knees as he gave her time to get all of the words out. His oceanic blue eyes held her gaze, solemn in his sculpted, sun-bronzed face.

And while she was certain she must reek of smoke and death, his scent was fresh and clean, as crisp as a sea breeze. Its presence calmed her.

In this moment, with everything she once knew now blown to bits a thousand miles behind them, *he* calmed her.

More than she'd ever stoop to admit.

"I stayed late at headquarters most nights," she said. "Sometimes, if I finished one case earlier than expected, I'd start right away on another. Sometimes I worked all night."

Being a daywalker, a very rare thing among her kind, she didn't have to work at night like her Breed colleagues. But more often than not, she chose to. Why wouldn't she? It wasn't as if she had anyone waiting at home.

And she'd loved her work. It had been the one constant in her life, her purpose. The one thing she could call her own.

Until today.

"JUSTIS was all I had, Zael."

She practically cringed as the admission slipped past her lips. But she was too tired and empty to hold it back. And the weight of the terror and violence dealt on the hundred killed and the organization she'd pledged her life to was almost too much to bear.

Glancing away from him, she looked out of the oblong window at her side. In the distance, the sun was just beginning to crest the far horizon. She stared at it as if seeing it for the first time, all too cognizant of how fortunate she was to be alive to witness it. The realization raked at her, putting an acid burn in the back of her throat.

"If I hadn't been let go today, I'd have been there with the rest of them at headquarters."

"And you're feeling guilty that you weren't."

She swung her gaze back to him, astonished that he understood. "Many of those people left behind mates and children. They had lives waiting for them to return."

"Are you saying you don't?"

Oh, God. She'd gone too far down a path she had no intention of sharing with him.

Least of all him.

"JUSTIS was important to you, I get that. But it's not all you have. For one thing, you've got a very worried sister coming to meet us when we land in D.C."

Brynne couldn't deny the tender pang in her chest at the mention of Tavia. They'd only been able to exchange a few words when Zael had called in to the Order to report their location.

Tavia had been beside herself with concern—a notion that Brynne was still adjusting to. Although her connection to Tavia was strong, she and the other daywalking Breed female had not even known about each other until they were adults.

"Tavia and I are half-sisters," Brynne said, somewhat dismissively, hoping to close the door on this line of conversation before she allowed the Atlantean to crawl any further into her head.

"Did you have the same mother or the same father?"

Brynne stared at him. He didn't know the history she and Tavia shared?

The madman's laboratory. The breeding program that produced genetic anomalies like daywalkers and Breed females that had never been seen in the world before. The brutal experiments and abuse. The decades-deep web of betrayal that was used to keep the progeny of that breeding program under control until they could be utilized as weapons of war.

If Zael didn't know those pitiful facts about her, Brynne wasn't about to be the one to tell him.

Haunted by memories she'd kept locked up all of her life, she shook her head. "I'm tired. I don't want to talk anymore."

But there was another pitiful fact that she preferred would not come to life anytime soon. One that needed to be discussed, no matter how much she dreaded it.

"Speaking of Tavia and the rest of the Order, I would like to have your word that you won't mention what happened between us tonight."

Zael sat back in his seat, his gaze trained on her under the rise of his brows. "You mean the dancing?"

She glowered. "I'm talking about all of it. I'd like you to promise me you'll keep our indiscretion to yourself."

"*Our* indiscretion." Dark amusement lit his eyes. "If I recall correctly, I wasn't the one thrusting my tongue down someone's throat on a crowded dance floor then drunkenly suggesting we needed to tear each other's clothes off and get horizontal ASAP."

If she could have wilted into the leather seat, she would have gladly done so. Thank God she didn't go to bed with him. It was unbearable enough just to think she might have.

Cheeks flaming with outrage, she lifted her chin. "As you so accurately pointed out, I'd had too much whisky and it went to my head. I wasn't myself. I had no idea what I was saying and I sure as hell didn't mean any of it."

Zael grinned. "Don't get me wrong. I liked who you

were on that dance floor, Brynne. I hope I'm going to see that woman again, but preferably when she's sober."

She scoffed. "None of that would've happened if I'd been sober. Nor will it ever again."

"You sure about that?"

"Completely."

Although it hadn't been purely whisky doing the talking with Zael back in the bar. Or the kissing. Or...the rest of it.

She wanted to think so then. She desperately wanted to believe so now too.

She wanted to reassure herself that what happened with him had been an impulsive mistake. One that would not be repeated.

But she knew better. The one person she couldn't fool was herself.

And possibly Zael.

She could see that by the way he looked at her as the jet began its descent into D.C. air space. He held her unsettled gaze with unflinching, arrogantly assured intensity, as if he was recalling every second of their encounter the same way she was. As if he still felt the hard drum of desire in his veins too.

Brynne wanted to deny what she saw in him, what she felt.

But the truth sizzled in the air around them, and in those fathomless bright blue eyes that told her in irrefutable terms that what happened between them on that dance floor back in Cheapside was only a beginning, not an end.

CHAPTER 6

Brynne still wasn't speaking to him, even after they arrived at Order headquarters that morning. As soon as they'd touched down at the airport and were met by Tavia and her hulking warrior son, Aric—both of them daywalkers—Brynne had been swept into the military-grade black SUV amid tight hugs and anxious chatter with her sister.

As for Zael, he'd ridden shotgun up front with Aric, all too conscious of Brynne's disgust with him and the tension that only seemed to expand for every minute she strived to act like he didn't exist.

When they were brought into a private meeting room where Lucan Thorne and the rest of the Order's senior command had already assembled, she stubbornly kept her distance, taking a position as far away from him as she could get. Zael might have been tempted to continue goading her just for the pleasure of it, but the gravity of the situation facing everyone now demanded all of his attention.

Live feed from London filled the monitors that lined the back wall. On another wall, three more Breed warriors looked in on the meeting via video screens—one reporting in from Berlin, another from Rome, the other from Montreal. Zael had been briefly introduced to both of them in this same manner his first time to Order headquarters a few days ago.

He nodded to Andreas Reichen and Lazaro Archer, the European-based commanders, then to Nikolai, the formidable Siberian-born Breed male in charge of operations in Canada.

The mood in the room was thick with solemnity as the gathered members reviewed the carnage of last night and discussed their next tactical move against Opus Nostrum.

"Tell all of your teams to increase patrols immediately," Lucan growled from the head of the long conference table. "I want every recruit in combat gear tonight. We need an obvious Order presence in every major city starting at sundown."

Zael didn't miss the pause in conversation as he strode inside. He was still a stranger in their midst. The outsider they had no choice but to trust.

How it happened that he—a former warrior of the Atlantean queen's legion—had recently found himself in the position of advisor and ally to blood-drinking killers spawned from his people's greatest enemies, he had no idea.

Except the group of Breed males in the room with him were not killers. Not brutal animals like their race's Ancient fathers had been.

Not cowardly murderers like the skulking, anonymous members of Opus Nostrum.

The men of the Order were warriors, like Zael once was—before he defected from Selene's vengeful reign to walk a different path, far away from her Atlantean court.

As of a few days ago, the Order wanted him to return to the fray—fighting on their side this time. Against his own people, if that's what it came down to. He'd gone away thinking they asked too much. He still hadn't decided if he was ready to stand against his queen, but he couldn't deny that tonight Opus Nostrum had earned another enemy in him.

"It's a relief to see both of you are safe," Lucan said, extending his hand to Zael in greeting. He nodded to Brynne, who vigilantly kept her position near Tavia across the large room. "We're still collecting intel from our back channels and teams on the ground, but so far it looks like JUSTIS was the only target. They wanted to make a statement."

"And they did," Zael agreed. "But thugs like these thrive on making bold statements. That's how they build their empires. That's how they ensure the loyalty of their true believers."

On the video feed from Montreal, Nikolai uttered a curse. "Not to mention ensuring there's enough chaos and fear that a terrorized public will be ready to do anything to make it stop."

Sterling Chase dropped his fist on the conference table. "Not on our watch. Goddamn it, this shit with Opus has gone too far already. Multiple assassinations. The attempt to blow up the GNC peace summit a few weeks ago. Manufacturing and distributing Breed-killing UV technology, and narcotics to turn any law-abiding Breed into a blood-craving monster. Their list of criminal acts is as long as my fucking arm." The Boston commander's fury only gentled as he glanced at Tavia. "And then, a couple of nights ago, the bastards took our daughter."

"We got Carys back," Tavia said, holding his tormented gaze. "She and Rune are both safe and celebrating their blood bond. Thanks to everyone in this room. Especially Brynne."

Brynne's head snapped up at the mention. "Me?"

Tavia smiled. "If not for your quick thinking, we might not have realized Carys had been taken from Neville Fielding's party. The Order might've arrived too late to help her and Rune escape from Riordan and his men."

Brynne looked uncomfortable with the praise. Her eyes darted around the room—although, Zael noticed, still careful to avoid him—before she glanced down at the floor. "I was only doing my job."

"And you're damned good at it," Lucan said. "Your instincts about Fielding being dirty were spot-on. Without your hunch and your cooperation in getting us inside that party to search for intel, we'd be a lot further behind Opus than we are now."

Chase cleared his throat. "I'm sorry that cooperation was a problem for your colleagues at JUSTIS. Tavia mentioned earlier tonight that you'd been let go."

Brynne shrugged. "I suppose none of that matters anymore, right?" Her tone was crisp, but Zael heard the note of regret in her firm voice. "I would do it all over again, no hesitation. Even knowing what it would cost me. Like all of you, I also want Opus Nostrum stopped. Now more than ever, I want that. Whatever it takes."

Around the Order's war room, heads nodded in agreement.

Brynne looked over at Gideon. "I'm sorry I wasn't able to provide Fielding's computer hard drive or any of his data files for you. As soon as his body was discovered along with the poison he ingested, JUSTIS swept in to clear the house and seal it for investigation."

"It's all right." Gideon shook his head. "At least we have Riordan's files. Well, we *will* have them. Eventually."

"Still no luck breaking that encryption?" Lucan's question sounded incredulous. "You've been working on it for going on forty-eight hours. Hate to say it, but this must be some kind of record for you. And not something I want to hear right now."

"The encryption is…complicated. It's actually pretty fucking impressive."

"Also not something I want to hear," Lucan muttered darkly.

"Believe me, I'm as stunned as anyone that I haven't been able to get around it yet." Gideon raked a hand through his spiky blond hair. "I hacked Riordan's hard drive and passwords—that was cake. But aside from learning he had bad music taste and a fondness for farm animal porn that made me want to scrub my corneas with a razor blade, Riordan's hard drive was a bust."

Lucan frowned. "We're all but certain Opus members are in contact with one another electronically. Are you saying there's no trace of communication software or log files anywhere on that computer?"

"They're too careful for that. The process to delete directories and data was set to run every night like clockwork. I was able to kill it before it took off one last time. In Riordan's purge file, I found an ID fragment for a secured private network." Gideon blew out a deep sigh. "And that's where my problems began. There's a lock on the network—a very sophisticated program that acts as a booby trap on the whole thing. I nearly set it off today before I realized what I'd run into. Whoever programmed it knows their shit. We're talking pro skills and then some."

"Are you going to be able to break it?"

Zael hadn't known Lucan very long, but he doubted any man or woman in the room right now had ever heard the note of doubt that crept into the Order leader's deep voice.

Gideon was quiet for a long moment, and that silence said a lot. "I'll break it. I'm not going to rest until I do."

Lucan nodded grimly. "Good answer."

Then he turned his serious gaze on Zael. "I don't suppose I need to tell you that anything you hear in this room tonight is to be held in the strictest confidence."

Zael inclined his head. "Of course. You have my word."

Now that Lucan and the other warriors were looking at him, Zael felt the weight of their curiosity—even suspicion—come to rest on him.

"You never mentioned what you were doing in London last night, Zael. There on business of some kind?" Lucan studied him, his shrewd gray eyes assessing.

"No," Zael admitted. "I wasn't there on business."

"Pleasure, then?" The Order's leader was asking casually, but there was no mistaking that this was a test of trust. Lucan may not know for certain what sent Zael to the very city where Opus Nostrum had just done their worst, but he would damned sure know if Zael attempted to deceive him.

And if that happened, any alliance they'd forged would be weakened practically before it began.

"I didn't go to London for business or pleasure. I went there to see Brynne."

Across the room, her tense anticipation was a palpable current in the air. Zael glanced her way now, and instead of seeing her eyes divert or avoid him, she stared at him in resignation. In unspoken misery and contempt.

But Zael wasn't about to lie to his new friends. He needed their trust as much as they needed his.

"When Brynne and I met here last week, I thought there might've been some spark of interest. After hearing what happened with Riordan and the councilman who killed himself in the middle of a house party Brynne was attending, I decided to search her out and look in on her, make sure she was all right. See if I was right about her interest in me."

He didn't have to glance her way now to know that she was silently wishing for a sinkhole to open up and swallow him. Tavia, Chase, and several other Order members exchanged surprised looks before those intrigued gazes volleyed between Brynne and him.

"I was mistaken," he said.

Even if part of him knew better, he would give her this one courtesy in front of her sister and friends. Let Brynne call him an asshole for tormenting her when they were alone, but anything that happened between them was going to remain private if he had anything to say about it.

Still, just thinking about Brynne's lips on his was enough to ignite his arousal all over again. Even here, in a room full of lethal Breed warriors who'd likely want to string up any Atlantean who deigned to put his hands on one of their females.

Zael had wanted to do far more than that with Brynne last night, but he'd been serious about not letting her blame the alcohol—or him—for it later. Now all he had to show for his dubious display of honor was regret and a bad case of blue balls.

"By the time I realized I had overstepped with Brynne and was offering to see her home, all hell had broken loose in the city."

"Well, thank God you were together," Tavia interjected. "I'm glad my sister wasn't alone to face that kind of horror. I can't bear to think what might've happened if you'd been anywhere near the blast, Brynne."

"I was fortunate that I wasn't." Despite her fleeting look of acknowledgment that Zael hadn't betrayed her just now, Brynne still looked less than enthused to be associated with him. "Now, I'm just eager to put last night behind me and move forward. Which I plan to do just as soon as I get back home to London."

"Back home?" Tavia gave her an uneasy look. "I hope you don't mean that."

Zael curbed his knowing chuckle. What she meant was she couldn't wait to put a lot of miles between herself and him. If she was eager to run anywhere, it was away from him, more than back to a ravaged city where she'd admitted she had nothing waiting for her.

As of last night, even less.

He wondered now, as he had on the plane, just what it was that Brynne hadn't wanted to say about her past. He'd been surprised to see the hauntedness in her eyes.

He'd been furious to realize the shadows that darkened her pretty face hinted at wounds she couldn't bear to speak.

And he'd been stunned to feel a wave of protectiveness toward her that he had no right to feel.

Not for her.

Not for anyone.

If things got messy on an emotional level, he wasn't one to stick around. More than one person in his lifetime could attest to that.

"I'd feel better if you stayed close to us for a while," Tavia was saying now. She took Brynne's hand in hers. "I'm still getting used to the idea that I have a sister in my life. Do you really think I'm going to be okay with letting you go back into a dangerous situation alone?"

Brynne's lips parted with the beginnings of an argument, but Lucan spoke first.

"I've got to agree with Tavia on this. We have to assume Opus knows you're cooperating with the Order now, which means the odds of you ending up with a target on your back if you return to London are too damned high to risk."

"I'm a career law enforcement officer, Lucan. I'm a decorated investigator who's also been trained in combat and crisis negotiations."

"Good. Then if you don't want to accept the decision of a higher ranking official, you should be able to recognize when debating one will be futile."

She chose that moment to glance Zael's way, and he knew he hadn't been quick enough to hide his agreeing nod. Not that he wanted to see her unhappy, but he also didn't want to see her anywhere near the smoldering ruins of JUSTIS or the sadistic fucks who perpetrated the attack.

She would be safest with the Order, whether she wanted to believe that or not.

"They're right," Zael said. "You may not have been in the building when it blew last night, but that doesn't mean Opus knew you weren't there."

She crossed her arms over her breasts, clearly outraged by his interference. "Everything points to a well-planned attack. It took time for Opus to execute this. Much longer than the week or so that I've been working with the Order."

"Yes," he agreed. "But what's to say you didn't have a target on your back long before then? If not simply because you were part of JUSTIS, then for being kin to one of the Order's key commanders?"

"Jesus Christ." The curse came from Sterling Chase. The Boston commander's grave stare moved from Tavia to her sister. "We thought we were keeping your connection to each other confidential, but what if someone in Opus knows?"

Some of Brynne's outrage drained from her face as she considered the possibility.

"You're safe now," Zael told her. "That's the important thing."

She blinked and glanced away from him, refusing to look up again.

Since his presence wasn't helping the situation, he decided to make things easier for her—and for the people trying to reason with her.

"I'm sure there are many things the Order needs to discuss," he said, already taking a step toward the door. "If you have no further need of me now, I think it's time I take my leave."

Lucan cleared his throat. "Not so fast, Zael. Yes, there are things that need to be discussed—including recent developments concerning your people and their queen."

CHAPTER 7

A fter the Order drew Zael into a closed-door meeting in the conference room, Tavia brought Brynne to meet Lucan's Breedmate in the residence section of the sprawling D.C. estate.

"We've got an unusually full house at the moment," Gabrielle Thorne said as the regal, auburn-haired Breedmate led Tavia and Brynne down an elegant third-floor hallway in the Order's massive headquarters. "This wing doesn't get a lot of use these days. The entire third floor was reserved for visiting foreign dignitaries back when the old house was used as an embassy."

Old house? The place was palatial. Brynne had seen royal residences in England that were less impressive. Intricately tooled millwork lined the ivory walls of the passage and richly colored, thick Persian rugs covered the gleaming dark wood floors. Following her two companions toward the middle of the long corridor, Brynne couldn't help but admire the many carved busts and neoclassical sculptures that stood on polished pedestals along the way, or the antique photographs of significant landmarks and natural wonders that competed with paintings by master artists on the silk-covered walls.

Her stroll ended in front of the open doors of a sumptuous library that smelled wonderfully of aged leather book bindings and lemon-waxed, old wood. At another time, under different circumstances, she could see herself getting lost among all of those books for days on end.

"I'm sorry you're going to the trouble to make room for me. I imagine you've both got more important things to do, this week especially."

Gabrielle turned a genuinely warm smile on her. "It's no trouble at all. Even if you weren't Tavia's sister, after all you did for us the other night, you're part of the Order's family, Brynne."

Tavia nodded in agreement. "I know you'd rather be in your own place, but I hope you'll be comfortable here for now."

As she spoke, Gabrielle turned to open a door directly across from the library. The room inside was large, but cozy, with a small sitting area on one side and a four-poster bed on the other. The drapes on the tall window had been drawn to let in the morning light and the view of the manicured grounds below. On a bureau near the opened door, a vase of fresh-cut flowers perfumed the air.

"The room is lovely," Brynne said as she stepped inside. "Thank you both."

"Make yourself at home," Gabrielle told her. "That goes for the entire estate. And you're welcome to stay as long as you like."

"Or as long as my sister and the Order insist?"

Tavia exhaled a short sigh. "It's not meant to be a punishment, you know. We're only concerned for your well-being."

Brynne knew it wasn't. She waved her hand in dismissal. "It's all right. I understand. I even agree that London may not be the best choice for me right now. I guess you might say I'm a bit hard-headed, especially when it comes to being told what I can or cannot do."

Tavia and Gabrielle exchanged an amused look.

"I think you've definitely found your tribe," Gabrielle said around a laugh.

"What about Zael?" The question popped out of her mouth before she could even think to hold it back.

"What about him?" Tavia asked. A spark of curiosity lit her questioning gaze. "And why do I get the impression there is something more going on between you two than either of you is willing to say?"

"There's absolutely nothing going on between us."

Maybe her denial was too immediate, too insistent. It certainly didn't seem to convince her shrewd half-sibling if the look on Tavia's face was any indication.

Brynne shrugged. "You heard him yourself. Zael showed up in London last night with the mistaken idea that I would fall at his feet the way every other woman probably does."

No, she hadn't fallen at his feet. She'd pounced on him like a woman starved for sex. Which, technically speaking, she was. She was starving for a lot of things, but she'd been an idiot to let Zael glimpse even part of that weakness in her. Now, he'd likely never let her live it down.

What would he do if he knew anything about her

other secret shame? The dangerous one that lurked deep in her laboratory-mixed DNA. The one that she'd been hiding ever since she emerged from beneath the collar of her upbringing. Not even Tavia would look at her the same way if she knew. No one would, and rightly so.

Brynne tugged her thoughts away from her monstrous beginnings and back to the source of her more recent aggravation. "As far as the Atlantean is concerned, I have no interest in a romantic relationship or anything else."

"Mm-hmm," Tavia replied. "And is that why you've been trying so hard to ignore him since you arrived?"

God, had it been that noticeable?

Was it still?

She'd been trying to avoid looking at Zael today because every time her gaze landed on him all she could think about was the feel of his lips on hers. And when she recalled how hot and commanding his mouth had been—how good their bodies had felt, pressed close and moving sensually together on the dance floor—all she wanted was to feel that rush again.

Why couldn't she have done the smart thing last night and let that cute, clearly available and utterly harmless bartender take her home? Why couldn't she have said yes to any one of the other men—human or Breed—who'd either circled her at the bar or come right up to take their shot?

She knew the answer and unfortunately it all came back to Zael. She hadn't wanted any of those other men. She would have sworn she didn't want Zael either, but her body seemed to have other ideas.

No doubt about it, kissing him had been a colossal mistake.

One she couldn't take back and, unfortunately, would never forget.

It was going to be a lot harder to put him out of her mind so long as he was under the same roof with her. Even worse, if he was going to be closely involved with the Order for any length of time.

"Do either of you really think he's a wise choice of ally?"

"You don't?" Tavia asked. "If you have cause to think that, Brynne, we need to know."

She wanted to discount Zael outright, but the truth was, despite being a pain in her backside from the second she laid eyes on him, he did seem informed and engaged about the problems the Order was facing. He may be a charmless ass, but he seemed to be trustworthy.

Even where she was concerned, seeing how he hadn't made a fool of her tonight in front of everyone. Incredibly, after making her think she was fair game for his ridicule, he kept her secret to himself.

And maybe he wasn't *completely* without charm either. *Still...*

"He's Atlantean," she murmured, as if that should be cause enough to doubt him. To her mind, it was at least worth questioning. "What do we really know about him?"

Gabrielle glanced at Tavia, indecision in her soft brown eyes. "We know enough to assume Zael's alliance with the Order is worth any risk."

"Because of something to do with the Atlanteans' queen?" When both women looked at her in question, she added, "I realize I haven't been formally included in the conversation, but Lucan's comment to Zael downstairs didn't exactly sound reassuring."

That was putting it mildly. Brynne's instincts had gone on high alert at the ominous mention of the immortal race and their apparent ruler.

"Yes, because of her," Tavia said, after Gabrielle's permitting nod. "We learned we had an enemy in Selene a few weeks ago, when the Global Nations Council peace summit was compromised by Opus Nostrum—"

"Attacked," Gabrielle corrected. "They would've slaughtered every Breed dignitary in the place if their ultraviolet weapon had gone off before the Order was able to stop it."

"I remember," Brynne said. "There were hundreds of diplomats and world leaders at that gathering."

The news of the attempted assault had made panicked headlines around the world. As for the Order's heroic actions, it had done little to endear them to a population of humans who mostly despised the Breed as a whole, or to the Darkhavens who considered the warriors to be a volatile force among their kind with an over-reaching grasp on the law. Even JUSTIS was guilty of eyeing the Order with more suspicion than due respect.

"But what does Opus's attack on the GNC summit have to do with the Atlanteans or their queen?"

"The Opus member who masterminded the whole thing was Atlantean," Gabrielle explained.

"Reginald Crowe?" Brynne asked. She'd been shocked enough to learn one of the world's richest, most powerful business magnates was part of the deadly terror group. But this? "Are you saying Crowe was one of Zael's people?"

"No one knew," Tavia said. "Just before he was killed, he boasted to some of the warriors about how

Opus was only a game compared to what his queen was plotting. He said we should expect a war like we've never seen."

"My God." Brynne swallowed against the cold knot of dread in her throat. "As if dealing with Opus isn't bad enough, now there's this too?"

Gabrielle nodded. "We may have some advantages in our favor, though. We've been looking for ways to get ahead of Selene. Zael may be able to help us."

"He may be the only one," Tavia added. "But we're putting him in a hard place."

"Yes, but he's got reasons of his own to ally with the Order now," Gabrielle said. "Jordana, for one."

Tavia had told Brynne about the young woman during her visit to her sister in Boston recently. Jordana worked with Carys Chase at an art museum and had been recently mated to one of Sterling Chase's senior warriors. "What does Zael have to do with her?"

Instead of Tavia or Gabrielle answering the question, it was Carys who replied. She stood in the open doorway with another young woman. "What does Zael have to do with who?"

"Jordana," Tavia said, though whether in answer to her daughter or in greeting to the ethereal, willowy blonde who strode in with fiery Carys, Brynne wasn't quite sure.

Without pausing for greetings, Carys walked up to Brynne and pulled her into a fierce hug. "I'm so relieved that you're okay," she said, drawing back after a long moment. "When I heard what happened in London last night, I was so scared that you might've been injured— or worse."

Brynne smiled at the younger daywalker, equally

pleased to see her.

"I'm fine. And thankfully, so are you."

The two of them had a special bond even before their shared mission together at Fielding's house party. Brynne had been beside herself with fear and horror when she'd discovered Carys had been abducted right under her nose by one of Opus's most sadistic members.

"I wouldn't be here if not for you," Carys said. "The Order came just in the nick of time, all thanks to you."

"That's not quite the way I would explain it," Brynne demurred. "And from what your mother told me, you handled things rather impressively on your own. Maybe that talk we had about you joining the Order wasn't all that crazy, eh?"

Carys grinned, her pride beaming from her sharp blue gaze. "As much as I love working at the museum with Jordana here, I actually have been considering a career change."

Jordana snorted, shattering the illusion of the unearthly goddess. "You won't if Rune has anything to say about that."

"We're negotiating," Carys said with a waggle of her brows. "He knew what he was getting into when he blood bonded to me."

Her friend laughed and shook her head. "Hello," she said to Brynne. "It's a pleasure to meet you. I'm Jordana."

"We were just talking about you," Tavia said gently. "We were about to explain to Brynne that Zael knew your father."

"Oh." Her face lit up, but there was a trace of sadness in her eyes. "They were best friends. They served together as soldiers."

"In Selene's legion," Tavia added. "They both fled the realm years ago."

Brynne couldn't pretend the news didn't shock her. "He was a soldier?"

"One of the best," Jordana said. "After my father was killed recently in Boston, Zael kept me safe from the queen's guards who came to find me and bring back me to her. He protected me with his life."

Zael, the smooth-talking player, was not only a warrior of note to the Atlanteans but a savior to his fallen comrade's child as well? It wasn't easy to reconcile the two conflicting views of him, but Brynne's mind was struggling to process something else Jordana had said as well.

"I'm sorry about your father, Jordana. But… I'm not sure I follow. Why would the queen's guards be looking for you?"

Carys wrapped her arm around her friend. "Because Jordana is her granddaughter. Her sole heir."

"Oh, my." Brynne's mouth went slack. "Heir to the Atlantean queen. As in, the royal line?"

Tavia gave her a confirming nod. "We've been keeping Jordana's identity a secret for her own safety."

"My mother was Selene's only child," Jordana explained. "She and my father fell in love, even though it was forbidden. My father broke the law when he made her his mate."

"There is no law strong enough to forbid love," Gabrielle said.

"No, there isn't." Jordana smiled ruefully and shook her head. "After I was born, there were problems…consequences to be paid. Selene separated my parents. My mother grew despondent, then eventually, she took her own life. And so my father stole me away. He hid me with people he trusted on the outside, then he stepped out of my life to protect me and to give me freedoms I'd never have inside the realm. My grandmother put a price on his head. It took her guards twenty-five years to find him, but they did."

Brynne didn't know what to say. Torn between amazement and abhorrence for what she'd just heard, she stood mutely, aching for what Jordana—and her doomed parents—had gone through. "And Zael helped, you say?"

Jordana nodded. "When Selene's guards came to Boston and killed my father, Zael took me someplace safe. He even battled some of his former comrades to protect me. Without him, I wouldn't be standing here today."

Jordana's fondness for Zael was obvious. Given what he'd apparently done on the young woman's behalf, her affection was understandable. But Jordana seemed to be describing a different man than the one Zael presented to the outside world.

To Brynne as well.

This Zael was a courageous man. A noble one, the kind who would risk everything to protect the child of a dead friend from an enemy with cold, far-reaching power. Jordana had described a hero—not the first word that leaped to Brynne's mind when she thought of him.

She didn't know what to do with this new information.

She also didn't know what to do with the softening of her regard for the man she so desperately wanted to despise.

"Our lives would all be emptier if you weren't part

of them," Tavia said as she tenderly squeezed Jordana's hand.

"It's true," Carys agreed. "And we also wouldn't have the Atlantean crystal your father hid away from Selene all these years."

The odd reference pulled Brynne out of her unwanted musings about Zale and that troubling kiss they'd shared.

"What do you mean, a crystal? What are you talking about, Carys?"

"Ah, that is a whole other story," Tavia said. "We'll explain everything to you, Brynne, but let's do it over breakfast. You've had a very long night and I'm sure you must be starving."

CHAPTER 8

"**H**ave you thought any more about what I asked of you the last time you were here?"

Had he thought about it? Zael grunted at Lucan's question. "You asked me to consider betraying my people, Commander Thorne. I assure you, it's been foremost in my mind ever since."

The two of them had left the conference room to talk alone, and because Lucan had something to show Zael, he'd said. They strode the labyrinth of corridors that snaked past smaller meeting rooms, training facilities, and Gideon's high tech lair of computers and communications equipment where the eccentric Breed male was already deeply engrossed in his work on half a dozen touch-screen monitors filled with scrolling code.

"I haven't asked you to betray anyone, Zael. What I asked was for your trust. For your confidence as the Order attempts to learn all it can about your queen and her intentions."

"Selene hasn't been my queen for a very long time."

"You served her for centuries as one of her legion," Lucan reminded him.

"Yes. And more than a hundred years ago, I left the realm a fugitive. For as long as I'm alive, to Selene I'm merely one more defector with a price on his head." Just like his comrade, Cassianus, and the small number of other Atlanteans who'd escaped to begin again in a new place, without fear of a volatile ruler.

"But your loyalty is still intact?" There was weight in Lucan's question, and its implication.

Zael answered honestly. "I don't serve Selene, but I can't condemn her completely. She was good once, but she's a vengeful, powerful woman. Her heart iced over when Atlantis was destroyed by your Ancient ancestors."

"That's a damned long time to hold a grudge."

"She's immortal, Lucan. Her heart may never thaw. It went even colder after her only child was dead and her sole heir was stolen away."

"Along with the crystal Cass took at the same time," Lucan added.

"Yes, along with the crystal." Which was now in the Order's hands. Not that Zael had actually seen the treasure to verify that fact.

As crucial as their newfound alliance was, Lucan Thorne had been reluctant to let Zael anywhere near the crystal Jordana had received from her father and entrusted to the Order. For that, Zael had to respect the Breed male.

The crystal was one of five that the realm once possessed. They were each a source of immense power and versatile uses. Put into the wrong hands—the hands of an Atlantean whose motives were less honorable than

Zael's, for instance—and the outcome could be catastrophic.

Lucan paused in the corridor and faced him. "When we met here a few days ago, I asked if the Order could count on you as an ally."

Zael nodded. "And I told you that as long as I was confident we both wanted to achieve the same thing—lasting peace for all—that you would always have my trust and confidence."

"So you did." After a moment, Lucan motioned him forward.

Zael instantly recognized the huge chamber he was brought to. He'd been there on his first visit to Order headquarters just a few days ago, and he would never forget the vast archive room. Or the remarkable woman responsible for it.

"Hi, Zael."

"Jenna. Hello." He smiled as the lean, short-haired brunette set aside a journal she was recording and came over to greet him.

"Have you had a chance to see Dylan yet since you arrived?" Jenna asked. "She's come by here a couple of times already, hoping she might find you."

"I haven't seen her yet, no," Zael answered, feeling a pang of regret—and affection—at the mention of the other Breedmate. "I'll make sure that I do."

Lucan cleared his throat. "We'll all have plenty of time for reunions, but right now, I wanted Zael to understand where things are progressing with your visions, Jenna."

Even knowing her history and the astonishing cause of the Breed *dermaglyphs* that tracked all over Jenna's human skin, it was hard not to stare. But her outward appearance wasn't even half as interesting as the other thing that made Jenna unique.

After surviving a horrific attack by the last living Ancient—the savage fathers of the Breed race—Jenna was now gifted, or cursed, some might say, with the dreamlike memories of her attacker. The journals she'd been filling for the past two decades were a staggering chronicle of the Breed's history, as seen through the eyes of that now-dead predator.

She glanced at Lucan. "Did you tell him I've been seeing more details of the attack on Atlantis?"

"We were just getting to that," Lucan said. "I've decided it's time to show him."

Zael was about to ask for an explanation, but since he'd entered the room his temples had begun to fill with a persistent and distracting buzzing. His chest and limbs felt increasingly warm…as if a furnace had been turned on inside him.

"The crystal." He swung an incredulous look on Lucan. "It's here in this room."

He wasn't asking for confirmation. He didn't need to ask. Every cell in his body was responding to the close proximity of the otherworldly power source belonging to his people.

Lucan nodded to Jenna. "Show him."

She walked to a large safe that stood open on the other side of the chamber. Retrieving an object from within the sturdy vault, she returned carrying it in her hands. It was a small, unremarkable metal box with a broken seal.

Zael didn't have to look inside the titanium container to know it held the egg-sized, silvery crystal. Had the box been sealed, the metal's properties would have prevented any of his kind from feeling the crystal's power, even at close range. According to what Jordana had told him, that's how Cass kept this particular crystal hidden in the human world for so long.

But with the power source exposed to him now, Zael felt its heat and vibration as if it were a part of him. In many ways, the crystal was a part of him. He and all of his kind shared a unique connection to all five of the crystals that once belonged to Atlantis.

Jenna paused in front of Zael and Lucan, holding the box carefully in her palms. "The first time I touched this thing, it really kicked my butt."

Lucan grunted. "That's an understatement if I ever heard one. Her *glyphs* went crazy, rioting with color, and that crystal glowed as bright as the sun inside her hands."

Zael listened, marveling that she dared touch the crystal without knowing what it might do to her. But from what he'd seen of all the women who were part of the Order and their extended family, Jenna had a rare courage.

"The visions I saw after touching the crystal were the strongest I've ever had," Jenna explained. "Since then, I've been working a bit more with it, conditioning myself to hold on longer each time because it seems to make the memories stronger, more vivid in my mind. I've almost collected a full account now of the day Atlantis was destroyed."

Zael couldn't hide his amazement. "Remarkable work. I know it can't be easy, seeing the things you do when you look through the Ancient's eyes. The Order is fortunate to have you."

She laughed. "Do me a favor and tell that to my mate. Brock thinks I've lost my mind to be doing this."

"Because he loves you," Lucan said soberly. "He doesn't like seeing you suffer, even if it's only through hideous visions like the ones you've been chronicling. If you were Gabrielle, I'd rather smash this chunk of Atlantean rock to dust than let you anywhere near it."

Zael understood the sentiment, but what Lucan suggested was impossible. "The crystals can't be destroyed. Not through any means you or I might have."

He glanced down into the titanium box in Jenna's hands, awed to be seeing one of the five crystals up close. It drew him like a beacon, like the living source of power it truly was.

Beneath its glimmering, silvery surface, facets of sparkling light glowed deep in the crystal's core. The hum of cosmic power reached into him, waking his cells as it would any of his kind.

He heard Lucan's wary growl beside him as the energy within the crystal responded to Zael's nearness and began to pulse. And inside Zael's body, he felt the warmth of the crystal's power building in him too.

"The crystal," Jenna whispered, her eyes widening. "Something's happening to it."

"What the fuck is going on, Zael?"

"You'll understand best if I show you."

The answering look on the massive Breed male's face was anything but certain.

"Trust," Zael said. "Do I have yours?"

At Lucan's hesitant nod, Zael reached into the box and collected the crystal into his palms. "In close proximity of a crystal, an Atlantean's life force increases exponentially. As does our power."

To demonstrate, Zael pivoted toward the large safe across the room. Lifting one finger, he sent the hulking block of metal gliding across the marble floor as if it were nothing. He stopped it a split second before it crashed into the opposite wall.

Jenna gasped. "That safe weighs more than a ton."

"With this crystal," Zael said, "if I wanted to right now, I could break down the walls of this chamber with a sweep of my hand."

Lucan's stare was hard and flat with understanding.

Zael glanced at him solemnly. "Now imagine an entire Atlantean army with a crystal in its possession. They would be unstoppable."

"Why hasn't Selene unleashed this power on us already?" The Order's leader demanded. "Why not retaliate against the Ancients immediately after they destroyed Atlantis and drove her into exile?"

"Because to use a crystal for war, she would need to remove it from its other purpose."

"Which is?"

"Protection," Zael said. "The crystals have many uses. When there were five of them in realm, they provided energy for all our needs. If we required it, the crystals could've been used to power defensive weaponry as well, although that was never something our people hoped for. And, as you just witnessed, they can also enhance an Atlantean's own individual power."

"You said Selene uses them for protection," Lucan prompted.

"Yes. They're what kept Atlantis safe for thousands of years after my people arrived here. The crystals cloaked Atlantis beneath an impenetrable shield that concealed the island from the outside world. The shield kept the realm safe from any curious visitor or attack."

Jenna's brows rose. "You're talking about an actual

force field around Atlantis?"

"To simplify the concept, yes."

"And then Atlantis lost two of the crystals," she replied. "It weakened the shield."

Zael nodded. "Selene was betrayed by her consort—a human. He stole two of the crystals and gave them to your ancestors," he said, looking at Lucan. "For a population of Atlantis's size at that time, the three remaining crystals weren't enough to hold the shield in place."

Lucan studied the crystal that still glowed and pulsed in Zael's hands. "That's how the Ancients were able to launch their attack."

"And then they used them to power their bombs," Jenna added. "I've seen it in the Ancient's memories. They created a beam of light that ignited the explosion in the ocean off Atlantis's shore. Then the tsunami swept in and destroyed everything in its path."

Zael hadn't know the specifics of the Ancients' assault on the realm, but he had guessed at something like Jenna described.

Lucan's gaze came back to meet Zael's. "And you're certain Selene won't risk weakening her shield now to use her crystal against anyone?"

"She'd be a fool to try. And Selene is no fool."

"I sure as hell hope you're right."

So did Zael, although he kept that hope to himself.

Because if Selene's need for vengeance should eventually overrule her logic and reason, everyone on this planet would be doomed.

CHAPTER 9

B rynne returned to her suite next to the library, her mind spinning from all she had learned over breakfast with Tavia and the other women.

The investigator in her had been fascinated by the facts of Jordana's incredible origins. She'd listened raptly over a plate of crepes and fresh fruit as the pale blonde beauty had described the events surrounding her father's efforts to safeguard his infant daughter.

Not to mention the powerful crystal he'd taken from the Atlantean realm.

Cassianus had gone to extraordinary lengths to keep both of his treasures from falling back into Selene's hands.

Then there was Zael. From the way Jordana told the story, he had been ready to sacrifice anything for her safety too.

As professionally intrigued as Brynne had been about the details concerning the Atlanteans, their dangerous queen, and the powerful crystals at the center of so much bloodshed and strife, the woman in Brynne was equally fascinated by the deepening paradox that was Zael.

She couldn't help thinking that perhaps she'd judged him too hastily, and too harshly.

That had long been one of her many flaws when it came to dealing with anyone—and not something she found easy to change. After all, she'd found out a long time ago that life was a hell of a lot easier to survive when it was lived in basic black or white. Things were either right or wrong, good or bad.

The people around her were either on her side or against her.

Friend or enemy.

With Zael, her old methods didn't seem to hold up. Everything about the male shook the firm foundation she'd constructed for herself. He seemed to understand that too. Even worse, he seemed to enjoy knocking her off kilter, making her question herself. Making her squirm.

Lord knew he did *that* all too well.

She thought she'd had him pegged, but he kept proving her wrong. Now that she was forced to look at him in the flattering light of Jordana's praise and affection, Brynne didn't know what to think about Zael.

Stepping into the solace of her guest room, she hoped to find a few moments alone to rest and freshen up. She needed a shower and a change of clothes, the latter having been generously provided by Gabrielle. A light blouse and pressed linen slacks were folded neatly at the end of the bed. Brynne traced her fingers over the crisp fabric, moved by how readily everyone in the Order had welcomed her.

That didn't mean she wanted to stay.

It didn't mean she could. Not for long, anyway.

Not without letting them all see what was wrong with her.

Not without earning everyone's fear—and rightly so.

Because sooner or later, she would need to feed. Not on fancy breakfasts or other human food she was fortunate enough to enjoy in spite of her Breed genetics. Sooner—rather than later—she would need to nourish herself with blood.

An act that was as normal as breathing for any other member of the Breed was torment for her. Damned if she drank and damned if she didn't, Brynne had grown accustomed to stringing herself out as long as she could, if only to avoid the pain . . . the horror.

The shame.

She only hoped she could last until she was able to return to London and resume her life. What remained of it, that is.

Zael had accused her of being lonely and he was right.

He was right about so much where she was concerned, and it terrified her that he could see through her so easily when she'd worked all her life to shelter herself.

With her thoughts dimmed by the reality of her existence, Brynne drifted farther into her private suite. Sunlight streaming in through the parted drapes drew her across the soft Persian rug to the window where the estate's grounds spread out in an explosion of lush green and brightly colored blooms.

She had forgotten how breathtaking the back gardens were. Flowering bushes and elegant topiary trees complimented an intersecting maze of manicured hedges that meandered from one corner of the grounds to another. Off the back of the mansion, a broad terrace patio led out to flagstone walking paths that drew the eye from one tranquil corner of the grounds to the other.

And that's when she saw him.

Zael, standing in the center of the garden with his head tipped back, muscular arms spread wide open beneath the morning rays. This was almost exactly how she'd found him that other morning here at the Order's headquarters. The day they'd met for the first time.

As she had then, Brynne froze, utterly transfixed by the sight of him.

Bare-chested, his smooth skin and copper-shot, golden hair gilded by sunlight, Zael seemed to both absorb and reflect the sun's rays as he stood there, engrossed in his private ritual. Light radiated from the impressive outline of his body, gathering with brighter intensity in the open palms of his upturned hands.

He was unearthly...powerful.

Heart-stoppingly sexy.

She tried not to stare, but it was futile. Against her will, she felt those strong arms wrapped around her the way they had been on that dance floor. Warm, sheltering, so unexpectedly tender.

She could still taste his kiss. Catching her lip between her teeth and the tips of her emerging fangs, she groaned with the memory of his mouth on hers.

She wanted him.

And, maybe, she acknowledged ruefully, she had been wrong about him. After hearing what he'd done for his friend, Cass, and Jordana, Brynne struggled to hold on to her initial opinion of Zael.

In fact, she struggled to do much else right now besides gaze at him from her window and try to resist the urge to go out to the garden and join him. If for no other reason than to try to unlock their horns and see if they could move forward as something other than adversaries.

Not that they'd felt anything close to adversarial on that dance floor in London.

And not that the low thrum of her pulse had anything to do with making peace with him and moving on as if their kiss—and her embarrassing proposition—hadn't happened.

Brynne gnawed her lip in silent indecision as she watched him slowly lower his arms to his sides. She was about to collect her nerve and hurry down when Zael lowered his head, turning to face someone who approached him in the gardens.

Brynne's breath halted in her lungs. The woman was beautiful. Flame-red waves bounced as she walked, her beaming smile trained fully on Zael. She raised her hand in greeting to him.

He knew her. His answering smile conveyed recognition, affection. The way he opened his arms to her then enfolded her within them seemed to say that Zael felt something more than simple affection for this woman.

Brynne reflexively stepped back from the window, feeling awkward and intrusive.

Feeling stung.

She watched from within the shadows of her room as Zael and the woman finally released each other from their unrushed embrace, then began a leisurely walk together in the gardens.

Apparently, the Atlantean had no shortage of fawning admirers among the Order.

He certainly didn't need Brynne feeding his oversized ego any more than she already had.

With an unimpressed roll of her eyes, she pivoted away from the window. Although she'd come back to her room to relax, she knew if she stayed in there now she'd only be tempted back to the window eventually to look some more for Zael and his smitten female companion.

Instead, Brynne took her time showering, then slipped into her fresh clothes. She couldn't deny that she was still rankled by her reaction to Zael and the other woman, but the suds and warm water had washed away most of her indignation's edge.

She hoped the vast collection of books in the library next door would be enough to keep her mind distracted from any further thoughts of Zael for the rest of the day. With her damp hair falling in loose waves down her back, she padded out of her suite and into the adjacent room.

With any luck, Zael would not only be finished chatting up his pretty friend, but also be gone from Order headquarters long before Brynne had to leave her cozy third floor sanctuary.

Resolved to stay where she was until Tavia or someone else came to drag her out, Brynne perused the bookcases. Everything from contemporary novels and classics, to history and biographies, foreign language novels and poetry filled the beautiful old wood shelves. She browsed several different titles, flipping through the pages with preoccupied disinterest.

Wondering who Zael's companion was and trying

not to imagine how many other beautiful women the Atlantean probably had wrapped around his finger.

Not to mention other parts of his anatomy.

A female's laughter sounded somewhere near the far end of the hallway. The warm, happy sound snapped Brynne's head up from the tenth or twentieth book she'd taken from the shelf and replaced.

She didn't recognize the woman's pleasant voice.

But she did recognize Zael's. "I enjoyed our walk, Dylan. I hope we can find time to talk some more while I'm here."

A sharp, bitter emotion stabbed Brynne at the sincerity she heard in his tone.

"I never dreamed we'd have this chance to reconnect and spend time together like this," the woman said. "I can't tell you how much it means to me, Zael."

"To me as well."

Ugh, please. Brynne's unwilling jealousy morphed into alarm an instant later when she realized the pair was coming her way up the corridor.

Too late to make a smooth escape now, she was trapped where she stood. Or faced with the even less attractive option of attempting to sneak out to the passageway ahead of them and slip back into her suite. They were too close for that already, mere steps from the library's open door.

Instead, Brynne snatched the nearest novel off the shelf then hurried to take a seat in a high-backed wing chair, curled into it as if she'd been there for hours.

She made it barely in time to see Zael and the copper-tressed beauty pause right outside the library. He'd at least put his shirt back on since Brynne saw him outside, but the gauzy white linen was unbuttoned halfway down his bronzed chest, the sleeves rolled up to bare his tanned forearms and the leather thong that rode on his wrist.

"Here's your guest room," his companion announced as she opened the door directly across the hall. "If you need anything, you know where to find me."

At his smile and polite nod, she went up on her toes and kissed his cheek. She pivoted and started walking away, with Zael's bright blue eyes tender on her.

Brynne tore her gaze away, rooting her focus on the book she held open in front of her face. As much as she hoped—fervently prayed—he wouldn't notice her there, she knew she couldn't possibly be so fortunate.

"Brynne," he said, surprise in his deep voice. "I didn't realize you were in here."

Obviously. She glanced up from her book as if she was equally unaware of him. "Hmm? I'm sorry, I was reading and not paying any attention. What did you say?"

He smirked knowingly. Damn him. "I said, I didn't realize Dylan and I had an audience just now."

Dylan and him. He said it with a familiarity that grated more than she wanted to acknowledge.

"You had no such thing." To demonstrate, she held up her book. "I came in here to relax and read for a while. If you hadn't interrupted me just now, I might not have even noticed you were there."

Zael stepped inside, uninvited. "Engrossing stuff, is it?"

She started to reply, but the citrusy, ocean scent of him hit her senses like a drug and she couldn't find her voice. His skin radiated heat that made her cheeks flush and her own skin feel too warm and tight on her body.

He leaned over the side of her chair, until his face

was nearly level with hers. His arched brow and slow grin tugged her core, made her breath dry up in her lungs.

"Broody billionaires and red rooms of pain?" Zael chuckled. "I wouldn't have guessed that was your particular kink, but I have to admit I'm intrigued."

Brynne glanced at the cover and felt her face ignite. She set the book down on the side table next to the chair and folded her arms tightly across her chest. "I imagine all it takes to intrigue you is a warm pulse and a vagina."

He stared at her shamelessly. "It's definitely a good start."

"You're unbelievable." On a huff, she stood up and walked away from him.

"Hey. Wait," he said. He didn't let her get far before she suddenly found him standing right in front of her, blocking her path. He frowned. "It was a joke, Brynne. Don't tell me you're still upset with me because of the other night?"

"I'm not upset. I'm simply not interested."

"No? Then why are you acting like a jealous lov—" He drew back, a look of confusion on his face. "What do you think you saw between Dylan and me just now?"

"Nothing," she denied, then doubled down on the lie. "I could not possibly care less what's going on with you or any of the females you keep company with. I came in here to read and relax. Alone. So, if you'll excuse me, I'm going to find somewhere else to do that now."

She stepped around him, disgusted with herself for the bitter anger flooding her veins. She should be pleased he was directing his attention on another woman. She certainly had bigger things to worry about in her life than this male or anything he—

"Dylan is my daughter."

Brynne's feet stilled beneath her, two paces short of her escape. Slowly, she pivoted to face him again. "Your daughter?"

That explained the intimacy, the affection she saw in both of them. That explained Zael's obvious tenderness toward the woman.

Brynne had no experience with parental bonds, or the skills to recognize them. She'd never had anything close to that in her life. Her own parents were unwilling laboratory prisoners forced together as part of a sick breeding experiment. She'd never seen either one of them, and both were long dead now.

According to Brynne's research, the Breedmate who bore her had never escaped the lab. And while the Ancient who sired her and Tavia and all the rest of their dozens of half-sisters had eventually managed to break away from his captor some two decades ago, it was only to wreak havoc and cut a bloody swath across thousands of miles before being killed in a confrontation with the Order.

Brynne was little more than a genetic cocktail of monster and innocent—a fucked up mixture besides.

"I found out about Dylan when I came to meet with Lucan the first time," Zael explained, his deep voice level and sincere. "She's mated to one of the warriors, Rio. For more than twenty years she's been a part of the Order's family, but until last week I didn't even know she existed."

How stupid she felt now, how petty, for assuming the worst about him. Again. But why wouldn't she? Zael seemed to take great pleasure in provoking her and then gloating over her reaction.

But he wasn't needling her now. When he spoke, his

tone had been solemn, edged with something that sounded unmistakably like regret.

"I met Dylan's mother many years ago in Greece. I was passing through and she was on holiday from the States. She was also married. She wasn't happy, but that doesn't excuse the way I pursued her. We had a brief affair, then went our separate ways. I . . . never saw her again."

An affair with someone else's wife wasn't something he was proud of—that much was certain. But Zael wasn't telling her everything. Brynne's investigative training spotted the dodge around the full truth. She also thought she detected a note of shame behind those fathomless blue eyes—shame that went beyond what he felt about seducing a married woman.

But it didn't matter what he kept from her. Brynne hadn't been forthright with him about every shame in her life either. She wasn't about to start now.

Reminded of all the reasons she could never drop her guard with anyone, she steeled herself against the softening of her feelings for him.

"Congratulations on your reunion with your daughter. I'm sure it must be difficult keeping track of all the fruits of your affairs."

He stared at her, clearly taken aback. She couldn't blame him. It was a cheap shot, but she was desperate.

She turned to head back for the door, but this time Zael grabbed her by the wrist and yanked her back to him. His strength was a shock. As was the fury and confusion she saw smoldering in his narrowed glower.

"What are you doing, Brynne?" His low voice dropped to a fierce growl. "Why do you try so hard to push people away?"

She scowled, feeling her blood start to race. She didn't know if it was fear or fury causing her veins to light up. All she knew was that she was treading on dangerous ground with him now. Had been practically from the first moment they met. "Let go of me."

He didn't. Slowly, he shook his head. "Tell me why you fight so hard to be left alone. What are you so damned afraid of?"

"N-nothing."

"Not even me?"

Outrage surged inside her, but it was little match for the fire licking through her veins. She swallowed. "Zael, please…"

She hated how small and choked her denial sounded. His firm grasp on her arm and her gaze said he wasn't buying it anyway.

Panic beat inside her rib cage like a trapped bird. She knew she could break loose from his hold if she tried. She was no mere mortal either. She had to be equal to him in terms of preternatural strength despite his larger size and muscular bulk. And while she didn't actually think he would refuse to release her, she couldn't summon the will to test him.

"When was the last time you let a man hold you?" he demanded softly. "How long has it been since you let a man make love to you?"

"That's really none of your business."

"Wrong." His mouth curved, but that smile was anything but friendly. It was masculine and carnal, and it sent liquid heat curling through every fiber of her being. "You made it my business last night, Brynne. You kissed me like you needed it more than your next breath."

She scoffed. "I was intoxicated, remember?"

"You're not now, and I think you want it just as badly as you did last night. You want me. You want this, but you're too hard-headed or terrified to admit it."

"You're insane."

"Am I?"

Releasing her wrist to capture her face gently in his hands, he moved in close to her. Their bodies brushed against each other. His hard and demanding. Hers soft and yielding, melting under the heat of him.

Brynne parted her lips to say something—she didn't know exactly what—nor did she get the chance.

"Oh," a female voice blurted from behind them in the threshold. "Oh, shit! I'm so sorry."

Carys wheeled around, giving them her back as if she'd just walked in on them both standing there naked.

Brynne winced. Had she arrived a few moments later, who knew what Carys might have seen. Who knew how far Brynne might have been tempted to let Zael go.

Abruptly stepping out of his embrace, she smoothed the front of her blouse feeling awkward as hell. "It's all right, Carys. We were just…talking."

She tried to ignore Zael's disapproving growl as she walked to the open doorway and drew Carys back inside.

"Please forgive me for interrupting like this," the young Breed female said. Her discomfort went deeper than chagrin. There was something troubling about the set of her mouth. And her face seemed paler than normal, stricken. "My mother sent me to find you both. There's been another attack."

Brynne's stomach clenched. "In London?"

"No. Right here in D.C." Carys swallowed. "The Global Nations Council building has been attacked in broad daylight."

"Not another explosion," Zael said. "We would've heard it. This close to the government center, we would have felt it."

"No, nothing like that." Carys gravely shook her head. "Assassins opened fire inside the building a few minutes ago. Every high-ranking member on site today was killed."

CHAPTER 10

$\mathbb{C}$

Although there had been little question as to who had been responsible for the slaughter that took place in the Global Nations Council office, it was still a shock to see the brazen claim of responsibility by Opus Nostrum spread across the Internet and social media mere moments after the attack took place. Unsatisfied to simply issue a statement after the fact, Opus's boasting claims were accompanied by live bodycam video footage recorded by the perpetrators as the killings took place.

Lucan had already seen the footage once, but that didn't make his blood boil any less as he watched again with the Order and everyone else present in the D.C. compound.

Acting in unison, three men posted on the GNC building security detail had abruptly stepped out of rank and mowed down an entire office wing full of high-ranking council members and diplomats before turning their weapons on themselves. Every horrific second had been captured on video and streamed across the Web.

The victims of the attack were all humans, representatives from around the world. Many of the men and women were colleagues Lucan knew personally in his role as chairman of the GNC.

All of them executed in cold blood at the hands of Opus and their followers.

"First JUSTIS, now the GNC," Gabrielle said quietly from beside Lucan. There was fear in her voice, and in the blood bond that connected him to her. "Will the Order be next on Opus's hit list?"

Lucan gently stroked her worried face. "Make no mistake, both of these attacks have been strikes against the Order." He met the grim gazes of his fellow warriors. "Opus hasn't come for us directly, and they don't want to. They tried that at the GNC peace summit and failed, which cost them their leader when we killed Reginald Crowe."

Sterling Chase nodded in agreement. "Each time they've come up against us, we've shut them down, weakened their foundation."

"Opus doesn't need to risk taking us on in a true contest," Lucan said. "What they want is chaos. They want fear and mistrust between Breed and man."

"To what end?"

Lucan turned to see Brynne standing behind him alongside Zael. The former JUSTIS investigator's cheeks were flushed with color, though whether in reaction to the bloody attack playing on the monitors or from some other cause, he couldn't be sure.

"We've seen that Opus has both Breed and human members," she said. "How can they do this? Why unite with the purpose of killing innocent people from both of their races?"

"To profit off the strife," Zael murmured. "There are always fortunes to be made in war, regardless of which side you're on. Unfortunately, peace is a far less lucrative business."

The Atlantean was right. And unless the Order found a way to clamp a lid on the panic before it got any further out of hand, Opus might damned well succeed.

Lucan cursed as more video of screaming civilians and stampeding workers inside the GNC building filled the monitors. The attackers were dead, but the panic was still at a fever pitch.

"I'm heading out to the government center," he said, turning away from the images of carnage and terror.

Gabrielle anxiously caught his hand. "It's the middle of the day."

He didn't particularly relish the idea of a daylight tour of duty either, given that without proper equipment, his solar-averse Gen One Breed skin would start sizzling in under ten minutes. But it had to be done.

Opus attacked at a time of day that all but guaranteed little to no risk of Order interference. As the highest ranking official of the GNC and the leader of the Order besides, Lucan would be damned if he was going to sit back and wait for sundown before confronting the carnage and taking control of the situation.

"I'll prep the UV gear for both of us," Dante said, zero hesitation.

Chase and Tegan spoke up next, and soon the entire company of warriors—new and old—were volunteering for the patrol. It gave Lucan great pride to see the depth of commitment and courage in the faces that looked to him for leadership.

He only hoped he wouldn't let any of them down.

Lucan nodded to his team. "Dante and Chase, prep the gear. Tegan and I will get the weapons and the vehicle loaded up. Brock and Kade, you suit up too." He glanced to the other warriors. "I need the rest of you here. Hunter, you're in command. Even if we don't expect any direct hits from Opus, that doesn't mean I want to risk leaving our base short-handed."

The stoic warrior had once been a stone-cold killer in his own right. If Lucan trusted anyone to stand between danger and the people he cared about, he could find no better guardian than Hunter.

"What about the lead I dug up in Ireland?" Gideon asked.

Lucan raked a hand over his head. "Shit. I don't want to let it go cold, but we've got several fires to put out here."

"What lead?" Brynne asked.

Gideon explained. "Just before the situation went all to hell today, I managed to crack through the first layer of encryption on Opus's secured network. I followed a hunch down a rabbit hole and I found a name, one we haven't run across before."

"You mean an Opus member?"

"Possibly. It's also possible we just got a hit on the woman Crowe had been visiting frequently for the past few years."

Aric Chase snorted a laugh. "You mean the reputed mistress? If this woman is under thirty, brainless, and full of plastic, odds are pretty good Crowe was banging her."

"We don't have a physical description," Gideon said. "We also don't have work history, tax records, nada. All we've got is a name registered to an IP address, which I then ran down a bit more by hacking into several layers of the ISP's parent company records. A few more database taps, log file scrubs, and I got a hit on a location in Finglas, County Dublin."

Dante and Tess's son, Rafe, smirked. "Anyone with poor enough taste to be spending time with some Atlantean scumbag is suspect in my book." Rafe shot a glance at Zael. "No offense."

Zael arched a wry brow. "You're right. Crowe was a scumbag. What's the name of this woman?"

"Iona Lynch," Gideon replied. "Any ties to your people that you know of?"

"None that I'm aware of. Crowe may have been Atlantean, but he had been gone from the realm for a very long time. What he did and who he associated with in the time since is anyone's guess."

"I've never heard the name either," Brynne said. "If I could get access to my old JUSTIS records, I might be able to search—"

"Been there, done that." Gideon's smile was a little sheepish, but mostly smug. "I've had my hands up JUSTIS's skirts for a long time. Anything in their global databases or secured servers is ours as well. They don't have anything on this woman. No one does."

"Except us now," Rafe said. The warrior had his blonde mother's looks but his father's dark tenacity. "If this woman has anything to do with Crowe, she might be the only person we've got who can help us unmask the other members of Opus."

Dante nodded in agreement with his son. "And if Iona Lynch is part of Opus, then we need to get our hands on her and do it yesterday. We sure as fuck don't want another situation like what happened with that Irish lawyer, Hayden Ivers."

The men were right. And Lucan was still simmering over the Order's near miss with Ivers. They'd already had a team on the ground at the human's house, closing in on the bastard, when Ivers popped some poison then set his own house on fire to avoid capture.

Mathias Rowan looked Lucan's way. "Shall I put my London team on this?"

"No. You're spread thin enough, between the panic in the fallout of the JUSTIS attack and now this hit on the GNC. I need you and your team ensuring the security of the council members over there, Mathias."

The London commander gave a nod. "Nova and I can be ready to return anytime."

"Within the hour. We'll have the jet readied for you," Lucan said. He met the concerned faces of the rest of the Order. "We need to be vigilant in our other cities too. Commanders should head back to your bases as soon as possible and be ready for the worst."

"Worse than what's happened these past couple of days?" Aric Chase asked.

"Something can always be worse, son." Sterling Chase's grim reply echoed what Lucan and the other warriors surely were thinking.

Aric was new to the business of war, and although he was every bit as lethally skilled as any member of the Order, he was barely tested. He couldn't be expected to understand what Lucan and the other warriors had learned through centuries of bloodshed and death.

They had charged into too many battles with too many enemies to make the mistake of believing that any crisis was as bad as it could possibly get.

Something could always be, and often was, far worse than you expect.

All you could do was pray you beat the monster before it beat you.

"Rafe and Aric," Lucan said, his thoughts returning to the other problem they couldn't afford to ignore. "We do need a stealth team to track down this Lynch woman in Ireland and hold her for questioning. Can the two of you be ready to leave with Mathias and Nova tonight?"

The two warriors exchanged an eager look.

"Hell yeah," Rafe said. "Let's go get the bitch."

CHAPTER 11

A fter the warriors went off to carry out their orders from Lucan, Zael found himself pulled into a conversation with Dylan and Jenna. As much as he wanted to give both women his full attention, there was another female who was currently driving him to distraction.

It didn't help matters that she was gone.

Brynne left the room as soon as the meeting had ended. Left it as abruptly as if her hair was on fire, to be more precise. No explanation. Not even a glance in his direction before she slipped away and didn't return.

Was something wrong?

Where the hell was she?

Finally, he couldn't take not having those answers. With vaguely murmured excuses, he slipped out of the room and headed into the corridor at a determined pace. Maybe she was with Tavia and the other women. Then again, headstrong investigator Brynne might just as likely be in the technology center with Gideon, persuading him to brief her on all of the intel he was gathering on Opus.

"If you're looking for Brynne, she's not down here." Carys came out of another room up ahead in the corridor, accompanied by a dark-haired, hard-looking Breed male. The immense vampire held her hand possessively, yet tenderly, leaving no question that this was Rune, the cage-fighting nightmare she had recently taken as her mate.

"Did you see where she went?" Zael didn't even attempt to dodge the truth. It wouldn't have done much good with Carys anyway, considering what she'd walked in on a short while ago.

More accurately, what she had *almost* walked in on.

She pointed to the elevator that went to the residential areas upstairs.

"Thanks, Carys."

"Good luck," she called after him with a giggle as he all but sprinted in that direction.

Zael didn't bother waiting for the lift. Using the small bit of crystal on the thong at his wrist, he closed his eyes and pictured the third floor corridor. Light flashed behind his closed lids.

When he opened them a moment later, he was standing in front of the door to Brynne's suite. He knocked on the panel and waited.

And waited some more....

"Brynne?" He knocked harder now, his preternatural hearing picking up the sounds of quiet movement inside. He tried the knob and swore when he found it locked from inside. "Brynne, is everything okay? Open up."

"Go away, Zael."

His concern for her well-being lessened somewhat when he registered the note of annoyance in her voice.

"Open the door and tell me that. Talk to me."

"I don't want to talk you. I'm leaving. I'm going back to London."

Like hell she was. Zael gave the doorknob a light twist and the lock tumbled open.

Brynne gasped when she glanced up in midstride and saw him enter the room uninvited. Her look of outrage turned to fury as he stepped inside and closed the door behind him.

"How dare you! How did you—"

He held up his wrist, the one with the Atlantean bracelet on it. "Your kind isn't the only one with its special skills."

"What do you want, Zael?" She frowned, folding her arms militantly across her chest. "And just what the fuck do you think you're doing, barging into my private quarters like this?"

At the moment, the only thing he was doing was staring at her, slack-jawed and instantly aroused. She stood in front of him half-dressed in just her white button-down shirt she'd worn that night in London. Her long legs were bare, exposing the delicate swirls and flourishes of her Breed *dermaglyphs* that tracked down her slender thighs. The silky stems with those pretty, feminine *glyphs* seemed to go on forever.

Beneath the loose hem of her blouse, he caught a tantalizing glimpse of skimpy black panties and more creamy skin. God, she was beautiful. Exotic and strong and exquisitely female.

She was also visibly pissed off. At him?

"What's going on here, Brynne?"

She stood her ground, glowering at him. "Isn't it obvious? I'm getting dressed."

From where he was standing, it looked like she was getting undressed. And there were certain parts of his anatomy that approved of that idea very enthusiastically.

"You said you're leaving."

"Yes. I have to go back to London. That's where I belong." She turned away and began buttoning her shirt the rest of the way as she stalked to the bed. The pair of dark navy slacks she'd been wearing the other night lay folded there. Her shoes and purse were gathered nearby as well. "I mean to be on that plane with Mathias Rowan and the others later today."

Zael frowned at the announcement. "Don't you think we should talk?"

"About what?"

Was she serious? He didn't even know where to begin. "About this new Opus attack. About where you and I fit into the equation with the Order. We sure as hell need to talk about what's happening between us."

"Nothing's happening between us, Zael." Sharp words, delivered with a flare of amber in her dark green eyes as she threw a hard glance at him from over her shoulder. "As for the rest of it, you heard Lucan and the other warriors just now. You saw what's going on all around us. The whole world is going to hell right now."

"Yes," he agreed. "And it's going there regardless of what takes place between you and me."

She scoffed. "You'll say anything to get what you want, won't you? Is that how all the men of your kind operate? I suppose that explains all of the fatherless offspring you and the rest of your Atlantean brothers have left around the world."

Zael's jaw hardened at the jab. It wasn't completely without merit, but he also saw it for what it was. A defensive strike, meant to push him away.

She pivoted away from him again, as if she was finished with their conversation and finished with him. Maybe that ice-cold shoulder had been enough to shut out all of the other men who tried to get close to Brynne, but not him.

He'd seen the desire in her eyes when they had nearly kissed today. He'd felt her soften in his arms in that moment, not only resigned to the need that they both felt, but consumed by it with the same intensity that it owned him.

She flinched when he came up behind her and put his hands on her shoulders. She stiffened under his touch, but he could feel the heavy spike of her pulse, and the sudden, rapid rhythm of her breathing. "If you're so hell-bent on running away, at least be honest about it. You're running away from me."

"I'm sure you'd like to think so."

"No, Brynne. I don't want you to run away from me." He swore, low under his breath, and he turned her around to face him. Her mouth was set in a firm line, but her glittering eyes softened as he held her. "I should be glad that you want to run away from me, from this. I should want that as badly as you seem determined to go."

To his astonishment, she trembled as the seconds stretched out between them. Bold, defiant, hard-headed Brynne stared at him in silent trepidation. She licked her lips, and he glimpsed the sharp white points of her fangs.

"I told you earlier that I didn't want anything to do with you, Zael." Desperation crept into her voice. "Why can't you accept that? Why can't you just leave me alone?"

"Because every time I look at you, I see the same desire in your eyes that I feel burning me up inside."

He brought one hand up to stroke the softness of her cheek. Pinkness rose into her face as his thumb flicked across her parted lips. It made her look so fragile, almost innocent. The color spread downward, along the delicate column of her throat, then into the open collar of her shirt and across the pretty swells of her breasts.

Yes, Brynne Kirkland was hard-shelled and stubborn. Yes, she was a lethally powerful creature, born of a race his own had long feared and despised. But beneath her *dermaglyph*-covered skin, she was a woman. A woman who yearned for a man's touch.

His touch.

"Wanting you this way is the last thing I should be doing, Brynne. But I'm not going to stand here and lie to you by pretending there's nothing between us." He caught her face in his palms. "I'm not going to stand here and let you lie about that either."

"Zael—" She moaned the instant their mouths met. Her hands flattened against his shoulders, but it wasn't to push him away. As he took her deeper into his kiss, Brynne's fingers curled into the loose white linen of his shirt. She clung to him, her body telling him everything her words could not.

He growled low and possessive into her mouth as he pushed his tongue inside to meet hers. Her breath raced hot and heavy. The tips of her fangs grazed his lips as he claimed her hungrily, demanding her surrender. And she gave it to him.

Holy fuck, did she ever.

That kiss they'd been denied a short while ago only made the heat reignite all the hotter now.

Their mouths joined in undeniable need, Zael skimmed his hands over her arms, then traced his fingers along her sides. She shivered as he slid his palms under her blouse and onto the soft, bare skin of her torso.

The intricate lines of her *glyphs* throbbed beneath his fingertips, warm and pulsing. Unearthly and alive. Their pattern created a tempting, tactile roadmap across her belly and rib cage—one he craved to follow with his tongue.

He wanted to uncover and devour every sweet inch of her body.

But first, he wanted to hear her say the words.

"Now tell me there's nothing happening between us," he rasped against her kiss-swollen lips.

As he spoke, Zael reached around her and deftly unfastened her bra. The lacy cups slackened, freeing her naked breasts into his hands. She sighed deeply as he caressed her. Moaned sharply as he rolled the tight beads of her nipples between his fingers.

"Tell me you haven't been wanting this as much as I have, Brynne."

Her pleasured gasp tore out of her without resistance, but it wasn't good enough.

Pushing her shirt and bra out of the way, he bent his head and pulled one rosy nipple into his mouth. Each tug of his tongue and lips made the colors of her *dermaglyphs* intensify, their patterns churning and transforming in response to her rising desire. Brynne arched against him as he sucked and licked her. Her spine bowed, she plunged her fingers into his hair, her legs trembling beneath her.

The scent of her arousal filled his nostrils. Spicy and sweet. Ethereal and bold. Like earth and heaven combined.

Damn, she was lovely. Sexy as hell. Although he had bedded many women over his long lifetime, he had never been with a woman who was Breed. He never imagined he could want any woman the way he wanted Brynne.

The cynical part of him tried to dismiss this need he felt for Brynne as nothing more than sexual novelty, just his libido craving a new diversion. But if that had been the case, he never would have denied her back in London. Refusing her had been one of the hardest things he'd ever done. And he wasn't about to let her act as if he was alone in that torment.

"Tell me you want me, Brynne. Tell me what you said to me the other night on that dance floor. Now, when there's no whisky to hide behind. Nothing but you and me, and the truth between us."

He skated one hand down the length of her body, into the parted cleft of her thighs. The tiny scrap of black silk that covered her sex was soaked and so hot against Zael's fingertips he groaned with the need to touch her, to taste her…to brand himself on all of her senses.

He cupped his hand over her mound, one finger slipping beneath her panties to the silken heat of her naked folds. Her sex was slick and lush, her juices coating his fingertips as he caressed her swollen folds and the hardened bud of her clit.

"Tell me now," he said, "when you can't take it back later or tell me I'm insane for thinking you feel this need too."

She whimpered, a tremor shuddering through her as he stroked her wet satin flesh. He teased the tight entrance of her sex, stopping just shy of penetration, despite that her thighs clamped tight around his hand in unspoken demand.

He wanted to hear her admit the truth out loud, once and for all.

"Say it, Brynne. Tell me you haven't been wanting to feel me inside you from the moment we first saw each other right outside on that terrace last week."

She made an anguished sound and he glanced up to find her eyes blazing with fiery amber, her Breed pupils narrowed to thin slits. Her fangs gleamed from behind the plush line of her upper lip.

She was beautiful under normal circumstances, but like this, she was primal and otherworldly, so fiercely sexy that she defied any description.

Holding his gaze, Brynne licked her lips and the truth boiled out of her in a single word. *"Yes."*

CHAPTER 12

Everything he'd said was true.

She *was* trying to run away. From him, from what he made her feel.

From what he'd made her want.

After witnessing the latest attack by Opus Nostrum, a surge of panic had gripped her. She couldn't get out of that room fast enough. The world was on fire, under siege from so many new and deadly terrors. She had watched the fresh footage and felt swamped with shame that her biggest personal problem was an unwanted attraction to a male she shouldn't desire and who would probably only break her heart.

She ran because she realized that she needed to get her priorities straight—something she seemed unable to do whenever Zael was near.

It wasn't because she felt there was nothing between them.

It was because, sooner or later, she knew she'd be unable to deny him.

And now that her admission had left her lips, there could be no turning back.

She wanted him.

She had been trying to convince herself otherwise since that morning she saw him standing in the thin light of dawn—inhumanly handsome, gilded in sunshine like some strange, golden angel.

She had wanted him then.

She had wanted him the other night too.

"It wasn't the whisky," she murmured now, captivated by his hungry stare as he held her close, his fingers stroking her sex in exquisite torment. Her breath was shallow from desire, every nerve ending in her body lit up with need for this man. She shook her head, sending her loose sable waves shifting around her shoulders. "When I said I wanted to be with you last night in London…that I wanted you to take me home and to bed with you… Zael, it wasn't because I'd been drinking. It was the truth."

His low reply was less a word than a masculine growl of satisfaction.

Of triumph.

Taking her mouth in another searing kiss, he began unfastening the buttons of her shirt. When he tore his lips away from hers, his breath was sawing out of him, his blue eyes darkened with desire.

"Do you have any idea how hard it was to say no to you last night?" He grinned, but it was a hungered smile. "I wanted to bite these buttons loose with my teeth on that dance floor."

With that, he took off her blouse, then slid her undone bra off her arms as well. Brynne watched his gaze drink in the sight of her *glyphs*. Being something even purer than Gen One, her skin markings arced and twisted all over her torso and onto her limbs. Smaller flourishes danced along the undersides of her breasts and around her erect nipples.

Ordinarily, the *glyphs* were just a shade darker than her own pale skin, but with the intensity of her desire for Zael now, hers were awash in variegated hues of deep indigo, wine, and burnished gold. He traced some of them with his fingers, then bent his head to follow the looping line of one pattern with his tongue.

She hissed at the sensation of it. The warm, wet trail felt like fire on her skin. His touch inflamed her too. Caressing and stroking her breasts, he lifted his mouth to hers again and captured her bottom lip between his teeth. Brynne moaned, pleasure arrowing through her when she felt his tongue teasing the lethal points of her fangs.

It was a brazen thing to do—not only because she was Breed, but because he had no idea how sharp her hunger truly was.

She hadn't fed in nearly a week. That was skating a thin enough edge in her day to day life, but now, with sexual need coiling around her as well, she was treading dangerous ground.

Zael wasn't Breed, but he wasn't human either. Nathan and Jordana had already proven that a blood bond was possible between Breed and Atlantean. The last thing Brynne wanted was to shackle herself to anyone in a bond that could never be broken—and that went double for Zael.

Especially when seeing her feed would show him the hideous secret she kept.

She rocked back on a snarl, tearing her mouth away

from his.

Zael must have seen the misery in her eyes. He saw her torment, but he must have mistaken it as doubt. Doubt for what she wanted. Doubt for what she felt about him.

Frowning, he gave a rough shake of his head and took a step back from her.

"If you're going to say no, Brynne, do it now." His deep voice rasped, as raw and on edge as she felt. "Because if you let me take this any further with you—"

She didn't give him the chance to finish. Before he could think for another second that she wanted anything other than the pleasure he was giving her, Brynne closed the scant distance between them. Zael caught her in his arms, and their mouths crashed together in a kiss that obliterated all words and doubts and pretenses.

She wanted him so fiercely, she could hardly stand it. And she needed him inside her.

Her fingers speared into his silky hair, she backed toward the bed and brought him down onto the mattress with her. She was no seductress—far from it—but with Zael she felt powerful, sexy . . . more wanted than she ever had before in her life.

Wanted by an immortal male whose race had despised the forbears of hers for thousands of years.

She and Zael couldn't have been more different. He was born of light, and she was bred from a terrible darkness. But none of that mattered when Zael was caressing her naked breasts and kissing her as if he wouldn't ever get enough.

His desire for her didn't blaze from his irises the way hers did. His smooth, bronzed skin didn't churn with color-drenched *dermaglyphs* to betray the depth of his need for her. When his mouth suckled and licked at hers, she didn't feel the sharp abrasion of fangs.

But Zael was formidable in his need. His large, muscled body pressed her to the mattress beneath him. His fingers slid inside her panties as if he already owned every inch of her. His strokes were possessive, merciless. His thick moan rumbled against her mouth as he delved into her drenched cleft to roll the rough pad of his thumb over her aching clit in a teasing tempo that drove her wild.

Brynne arched her spine and ground her hips shamelessly, helplessly, against the wicked pleasure of his touch on her sensitive flesh. She couldn't bite back her strangled cry as heat began to coil and spiral through her core.

"You like that," Zael said. Not a question, but a confident statement of fact. "Tell me you don't want me to stop, Brynne."

"Don't stop." The words leaked out of her on panted breaths between kisses. It had been so long since she'd known a man's touch on her. And never with the same need for it that she felt for this man's touch. "Please, Zael... Don't stop."

He gritted a curse against her mouth and yanked her panties off in his fist. Cool air skated across her wet folds, only to be replaced by Zael's mouth a moment later when he slid down her body and buried his face between her parted thighs.

She had no words now. Only breathless gasps and raw, carnal sounds that should have embarrassed her but only amplified the intensity of her desire.

There was no more teasing in his touch, nor in his kiss.

With long strokes of his tongue and deftly moving fingers, he didn't ask for her surrender—he demanded it. God help her, but she had to admit here and now that this wanton part of her had been his all along.

Writhing and bucking, she clutched at the coverlet as Zael sucked her clit deeper into his mouth. Pleasure swamped every cell in her body, sending her senses reeling, higher and higher still. She shuddered as the first shockwave of release broke over her.

Brilliant and jagged, her climax tore through her like lightning. She couldn't stop it, couldn't hold back her sharp cry of Zael's name as she bowed up off the mattress with the intensity of her orgasm.

Her hands sought him out blindly, latching onto his hair when he refused to show her any mercy. His mouth and tongue moved over her quivering flesh with ruthless purpose, while his fingers invaded the molten and aching core of her body.

"You're beautiful," he murmured, glancing up and catching her watching him between her spread thighs. "I've never seen anything as lovely as you, Brynne."

His praise warmed her, even if she didn't believe him.

She knew how she must look to him. Her eyes burning hot as coals, pupils as thin as a cat's. Her *glyphs* were livid with color now, pulsing like living rivers of changeable, unearthly ink all over her skin. And with every breath that panted in and out of her, she knew there could be no hiding the long white points of her fangs. Fully extended now, they filled her mouth, sharp tips sinking into the flesh of her tongue.

"Beautiful," he said again, as if he knew she doubted him.

And maybe to prove it—to her or to himself, she wasn't sure—Zael rose from between her parted legs and slowly pulled off his clothing.

She had seen him half-dressed more than once, enough to be prepared for the naked splendor of his broad shoulders and the sculpted muscles of his chest and abdomen. But he still took her breath away as he stood before her next to the bed, his golden skin looking as smooth and soft as velvet over the sinewy ropes and lean planes of his body.

His cock stood long and erect, a thick spear of hard flesh. The sight of him so fully aroused made her blood thrum heavily in her veins. It made her mouth water for the taste of him.

To her, Zael always looked something slightly more than human. No mere mortal genetics could produce his heartbreakingly sculpted features and cerulean blue eyes, or the copper-threaded, golden mane that crowned his handsome face. Human men could spend their lifetimes at the gym and never emerge with the flawlessly honed muscles that wrapped every inch of Zael's powerful physique.

"You're the beautiful one." She couldn't hide her awe. "You look like a fallen angel. That's what I thought when I saw you that first morning."

"Is that so?" He smirked as he moved onto the bed with her. "I promise there was nothing angelic about the things I thought about you then. Or now."

Brynne's quiet laugh dissolved into a sigh as he levered himself over her, brushing the head of his heavy cock against the sensitive skin of her inner thigh. "Mmm," he groaned. "Definitely not now."

She bit her lower lip, every nerve ending tingling with

awareness as Zael stroked her wet clit with his fingers. She was still electric with desire for him, even though her orgasm had given her some relief. Her body undulated beneath his touch, aching for more.

"Tell me what you want, Brynne." His rough whisper nearly undid her. Yes, he was golden and beautiful, but he was also strong and commanding, formidably male. He nudged at the slick entrance of her body, his erection feeling immense and hot as fire-forged steel. "You want this?"

"I want *you*." She arched her hips in invitation… In surrender.

Zael claimed her in a slow, breath-stealing thrust that seemed to go on forever.

He was large and thick, stretching her as he seated himself to the hilt inside her. Brynne wrapped her legs around him, angling to accommodate more of him as he began to rock in and out of her.

Each stroke went deeper, every thrust held more ferocity, until the need and rhythm of their bodies was no longer either of theirs to control.

Brynne cried out as he pushed her to the limit—not only her body's, but the limit of her sanity. Bliss and need twined together in a coil that twisted tighter, hotter…beyond anything she knew before.

She came violently, scoring Zael's back with her fingernails as white-hot pleasure detonated inside her. And he kept moving, relentless in his tempo as he chased his own release now.

Brynne held on, her legs still wrapped around him, her hands gripping his shoulders as another hard orgasm began to build in the aftershocks of the one that still owned her. Behind her closed eyelids, her head thundered with the pound of blood rushing through her veins.

The drumming filled her ears, her mind—all of her senses.

It called to her…and when she dragged her lids open as Zael drove harder, deeper into her body, she realized that it wasn't her pulse beating like a hammer in her blood.

It was his.

Mere inches from her mouth, the thick line of his carotid throbbed.

Her mouth watered, saliva surging as her fangs ripped even farther out of her gums. Hunger clenched her in a tight fist as she watched Zael powering above her. So strong. So alive.

So dangerously tempting.

She couldn't pull her gaze away from his throat.

Nor from the pulsing beat of his blood, coursing so tantalizingly near her fangs.

The sound overwhelmed her, commanded all of her control.…

Hunger raked her, and she cursed herself for how long she'd denied her body the nourishment it demanded. She licked her lips, trying not to imagine what it would be like to sink into that potent vein and take her fill.

"Zael," she murmured, though whether in warning or apology, she wasn't sure.

But in that next moment, he spared her from deciding. His big body tensed as he drove deep one last time, then on a low shout, he reared back as his release overtook him.

Safely out of her reach, at least for now.

And as she reveled in the feel of him lost to his desire for her, there was a part of her that knew no matter how good they felt together, it wasn't meant to last.

It couldn't.

Nor could she wish for it to last—not longer than this moment, if she were being honest with herself. Not if she was ever brave enough to be honest with Zael.

Forcing her gaze away from him, Brynne stared at the window across the room where dusk was still hours away. The darkness inside of her was much closer, and it beckoned.

Soon she would have to answer her hunger's call, and face the monster clawing to get out.

CHAPTER 13

The smell of spilled blood was overwhelming.

Lucan's heightened Gen One senses had locked on to the coppery scent of human red cells as soon as he and his team of warriors had exited the Order's ultraviolet-shielded SUV at the front entrance of the GNC building.

Now, nearly an hour later, with the last ambulance having carried off the wounded and the dead, Lucan stood in the middle of a blood-soaked office in a state of barely restrained fury. Outside the building, sirens wailed. Inside, there was only silence.

And death.

Fifteen people killed in a hellish spray of gunfire, more than twice that number injured by three guards sworn to protect them.

"You know, I might be able to understand this better if these three assholes were new recruits," Chase said, his fangs extended in the midst of so much blood.

Lucan grunted. "They weren't new. They'd all been

on the security detail for years with highest clearance levels. Two of them were family men, for crissake."

When Dante glanced up, his fangs were bared too. "Which means no one can be trusted. Not when we have no idea how far Opus's reach extends."

"Or who's the one calling the shots," Tegan added gravely.

Lucan nodded, well aware that everything his comrades said was true. "Opus has had their pieces in place for a very long time, waiting for their chance to make a move. Now they're starting to play us like fucking pawns. They're setting us up for something big. I feel it in my bones."

And he could see from the sober expressions of his comrades that they also dreaded what might be coming next.

Heavy boot falls in the hallway drew the team's attention. Brock walked in, his UV helmet clipped to a tab on his weapons belt. He and Kade had been tasked with guarding access to the building after the dead and injured had been taken away.

The massive black warrior's mouth pressed flat as he paused in the open doorway. "We've got company outside. Whole damned fleet of press with cameras and satellite trucks."

Lucan cursed. "Haven't we already got enough footage of this slaughter circulating as it is? Keep the vultures away from the building. No one gets inside."

"Yeah, that's not the problem," Brock said. "The cameras and reporters aren't the only ones who just rolled up. The D.C. arm of JUSTIS is out there too. Looks like they're setting up for a press conference."

Lucan's outrage spiked. "Like hell they are."

Stalking out with the other warriors, he headed down to the glass-fronted lobby entrance of the GNC building at a hard, furious clip. Just as Brock had described, the scene on the steps outside was pandemonium. Scores of news crews and Internet entertainment site trucks lined the street in both directions. A growing sea of humans crowded on to the broad marble stairs, most with microphones or tablets in their hands. Everywhere Lucan looked, camera lenses and video screens were trained on the building's entrance like a thousand gaping eyes.

And at the focal point of the attention was a small company of JUSTIS officials and public relations types, all getting into position just outside the GNC's glass doors.

"Jesus Christ," Lucan muttered under his breath.

The press started shouting questions as soon as the JUSTIS officer in charge stepped up to the front of the crowd. A clamor of competing voices filtered through the glass where Lucan and his men stood.

"Have the three shooters been identified?"

"How long do you suspect the killers had been planning today's assault?"

"Was there anything in their backgrounds that might have been a red flag linking them to Opus Nostrum before today?"

"After the bombing in London and now this attack, is it reasonable to say that Opus Nostrum is targeting government and law enforcement?"

"Ladies and gentleman, a moment if you please." At the front of the gathered throng, the human JUSTIS official raised his hands in a gesture calling for calm.

It didn't work. The questions kept coming, voices

rising in demand.

"How much do we know about the assailants?"

"How can we be certain no other GNC security personnel have ties to Opus?"

"Can anyone assure the public that they are safe?"

Lucan ground his molars together. The people had a right to be anxious. Hell, they had a right to be terrified. And they also had a right to the truth.

As the JUSTIS official withdrew a prepared statement from the breast pocket of his suit, Lucan stepped out of the building. He saw the startled faces, heard the gasps of shock as he strode into the afternoon light with his head and face deliberately uncovered, his UV helmet tucked under his arm.

His name traveled the crowd of reporters in a buzz of wariness and surprise, a few uttering it with outright disdain. He didn't care if they liked him or the message he came to deliver. He'd never been interested in playing the role of diplomat, and he didn't intend to start now.

His fangs had not yet receded. He stared at the gaping crowd with amber-tinged vision and knew that his irises were still narrowed in reaction to the extended time he and his team had spent around the spilled blood of the victims.

He looked unmistakably Breed now, and he wanted every human gathered—and every camera's eye trained on him—to see that fact as he addressed them.

"You all have questions that need to be answered. You have fears—all of them justifiable—that you want someone to allay for you. You're looking for reassurances that what happened here today and in London two nights ago is not the portent of worse things still to come."

Murmurs of agreement rumbled through the crowd. Lucan looked at the uncertain faces and slowly shook his head.

"No one can make you those promises. Not me, not the Order. Not the allied heads of state represented by the Global Nations Council. And sure as hell not a bunch of JUSTIS stiffs reading off prepared remarks stamped and approved by some useless PR firm."

The group of suits he'd just upstaged started grumbling at his back. Lucan ignored them, just as he ignored the faint sting of his exposed skin as he stood beneath the sun's harsh rays and continued his message to the press and public who would see the day's coverage.

"These recent attacks and the one the Order thwarted at the GNC peace summit a few weeks ago have a single purpose. To instill fear and seed mistrust. Opus would like nothing better than to see us at war against each other."

One of the JUSTIS officials scoffed. "Our problems with Opus didn't start escalating until the Order got involved. Maybe these are retaliative strikes against you, not us."

Lucan turned to face the human male. "Yes, I have no doubt the attacks are meant to punish me and my warriors as well. Would you prefer the Order sat with our thumbs up our asses instead? Let Opus rip our world apart or watch all of us do it for them?"

The young man at least had the good sense to shrink back a bit under the withering blast of Lucan's anger and his amber-lit glare. The rest of the warriors had since come out to join Lucan in front of the building, solidarity in their presence and their uncovered faces as they met the apprehensive crowd and the bristling JUSTIS representatives.

"Opus wants us at war with each other," Lucan warned them all. "We've already been down that road once in our recent history. It's taken twenty years to come out of those dark days. We can't let anyone push us backward."

"No, we can't," replied the suit in charge of the PR brigade. "That's why JUSTIS will be replacing all security personnel in public and government facilities with our own officers, effective immediately."

Lucan barked out a curse as he rounded on the man. "Not if I have anything to say about that."

"I suppose you want to replace them with Order warriors instead?"

"You know, that's a damned good idea."

The official practically choked. "Try it and you'll have a battle on your hands, Thorne."

Lucan bared his teeth at the asshole, flashing more than a little fang. "I've got nothing but battles on my hands, so get in line. This press conference is over."

A glance at his comrades put the group of immense Breed warriors into motion behind him.

Securing their UV helmets on their heads, Lucan and his men stalked down the stairs, through the gathered press corps. En masse, the reporters hurried along after them, shouting more questions and leaving the befuddled group of JUSTIS public relations officials standing outside the building, forgotten and ignored.

CHAPTER 14

Zael had imagined sex with Brynne would be amazing, but damn… He hadn't been prepared. After a mind-blowing orgasm that practically turned him inside out, his appetite had only intensified rather than subsided.

Holding her against the front of his hard and ready body, he rocked his hips against the firm curves of her ass and moaned as his cock leaped with interest. There was no mistaking Brynne's lean, powerful body for a human's. There was a dangerously coiled strength about her that no Atlantean female could compete with either.

Brynne was utterly unique.

And a short time ago, when she was crying his name in the midst of her own shattering release, she had belonged only to him.

Zael didn't want to consider how deeply that thought pleased him. At the moment, all he wanted was to be inside her again.

"You feel so good, I want to keep you here all night,"

he murmured, nipping at the tender crook of her neck and shoulder.

Instead of sinking into his embrace the way he expected her to, Brynne tensed palpably. She moved out of his arms. Sliding to the edge of the bed, she swung her long legs off the mattress and sat up.

Zael frowned. "Where are you going?"

"I need a shower."

Without looking at him, she spoke to the empty space on the other side of the room, her body language as distant as her voice. When she got up off the bed, Zael followed.

Before she could make a hasty retreat into the adjacent bathroom, he reached out to grasp her hand. "What's going on?"

Given little choice, she slowly pivoted to face him. It was startling to see the crackle of fire still glowing in her eyes. Her fangs were arresting as well, larger than he'd ever seen them. The sharp white points glittered diamond-bright in the tense line of her mouth.

There was an odd, unspoken misery in her expression in the instant their gazes met, but she shuttered it from him with a slow blink and a downward glance.

"I need to clean up and get dressed. I'm sure I've missed Mathias and that flight back to London tonight, but I still intend to go home."

"Back to London?" Zael took her reply as the slap to the face she intended it to be. When she seemed adamant to avoid looking at him, he lifted her chin on the edge of his fingers. "What the hell just happened between us in that bed over there?"

Her eyes flicked up to meet his, her dark brows

drawn together. "What happened was a mistake, Zael. I don't expect you to understand."

"Then try me."

She stared at him for a long moment. In her tormented eyes he saw a thousand different emotions, but the only thing she seemed willing to give him right now was indifference. "I'm not saying the sex wasn't great. It was. But that's all it was, right?"

He didn't reply. If that's really what she thought, he'd be damned if he admitted to feeling anything more.

And Brynne wasn't finished. "I'll be the first to say that I'm not built for relationships. I never have been. And I think we both know that you aren't either."

"That's right," he replied tightly, although hearing her say it like that—like an indictment, a condemnation—gave him more shame than he'd ever managed to heap on himself personally.

She stepped out of his reach, folding her arms over her like a shield. "The sex was…more than great, Zael. But now that we've gotten it out of our systems, I hope we can be adults about this whole thing. I hope we can be friends and move on."

Damn. Was this how cold he came off to the women he seduced over the years?

No. He knew better than to give himself that much credit.

He never explained anything. His M.O. was to vanish when things got too real.

"Can we do that, Zael? Will you try to understand how I feel and not make things any more awkward than they already are?"

"Awkward," he muttered, then chuckled mirthlessly. "That's not the word I'd use, Brynne. The only word I'd use for what you're telling me right now is bullshit."

Her look said it all. He'd hit the mark, but the mutinous set of her lips showed no sign of softening.

"I thought I did a fairly decent job demonstrating to you that you don't have to run away from me," he told her, more gently than he felt himself capable for the disbelief and outrage coursing through him. "I thought I made it clear to you that I'm not going to hurt you."

Her soft laugh had a bitter edge to it. "I'm not afraid of you hurting me, Zael. Can't you just try to respect my feelings and stay away from me now?"

"That's really what you want?"

"Yes." She swallowed hard, and he could see how she fought to hold his gaze as she worked the lie to her tongue. "You and I—everything that's happened between us, Zael—it's been a mistake. Let's not make any more."

He listened in stony silence, weighing her words against what the hauntedness in her face was telling him, and what her body communicated to his when they were making love.

"All right, Brynne." He nodded slowly, then walked over to retrieve his clothing. He slipped his pants on, then pulled his linen tunic over his head. "You're right, I do have to respect your feelings. Even if I don't believe you for one damned second."

CHAPTER 15

"**R**edhead, blonde, or brunette?"

Rafe glanced over at Aric, who was riding shotgun in the Order-issued SUV Mathias Rowan had arranged for them to pick up in Dublin after they arrived from London.

For most of the drive to Finglas on their fetch assignment for the Order, they had been shooting the shit, something the two friends fell into easily enough whenever they were together.

Now that they were closing in on the address Gideon had given them for Iona Lynch's apartment, Aric had begun passing the time by speculating on the woman's various attributes. He'd already given his unsolicited guesses to a host of other topics where Crowe's potential mistress was concerned, so by comparison, hair color was about as innocuous a question as could be expected.

"Gotta go with blonde," Rafe said. "Crowe's definitely got a type, at least when it comes to his ex-wives."

"Can't argue that," Aric replied. "Then again, there's something to be said for variety, right? Miss Iona Lynch of Finglas, County Dublin, could be a saucy little redhead. Or maybe a smoking hot brunette with a fine ass and legs that go on forever."

Chuckling, Rafe shook his head. "You describing Crowe's taste in women, or your own?"

"I apply few conditions to my tastes in women." Aric's grin was shameless. "Why put limits on something you enjoy?"

"Spoken like a true manwhore."

Aric shrugged, unfazed. "You should try it sometime."

"You mean like the time you talked me into playing wingman for you with those twin strippers down in Southie? I spent half the night with their drunk friend's tongue in my ear."

"You say that like it's a bad thing."

"She was hopped up on liquor and narcotics," Rafe reminded him. "While you went off to have your fun with the twins, I was in a bathroom stall with Speedball Sally, sobering her up and healing her long-term drug addiction."

Like all of the Breed, Rafe had been born with a unique ability passed down from his Breedmate mother. In his case, he'd inherited Tess's healing touch. He could mend wounds, repair cellular disease or weakness, and, in one case recently—after a former warrior, Kellan Archer, had been mortally wounded by gunfire—Rafe and Tess together had even managed to reverse death.

"See? That's your problem, man. That gift of yours is a curse. You've got no shortage of female interest wherever we go—hell, even more than I do, and that's saying something."

"Jealous?" Rafe quipped.

"Hell, yeah. Women practically drop their panties at your feet, and yet you've got a look-but-don't-touch policy going on." Aric blew out a short breath. "I swear, you think you've got to save everyone. Climb down off the cross once in a while and have some fun."

Rafe couldn't deny there was some truth in his best friend's accusation. All right, a lot of truth. Maybe if he'd been gifted with Aric's ability to bend shadows, or their team captain Nathan's talent for sonokinesis, things would be different.

But Rafe felt an obligation with the ability he'd been given.

It wasn't as if he never got laid. He was male and he also had a warrior's blood in his Breed veins. He had all the female company he wanted; he just preferred to be selective—with his bed partners and his blood Hosts, both of which he drew exclusively from the human population.

He slanted a flat look at Aric. "You want to keep lecturing me for a while, or are you ready to get to work?"

He turned onto a quiet road leading away from the Finglas city center. Rows of small, nearly identical red-brick duplexes and townhomes lined one side of the lumpy asphalt. On the other side of the darkened residential road, an overgrown spread of grass that might have passed for a park at one time spanned several blocks.

"This is the street Gideon gave us?"

Rafe nodded. "This is it."

Aric's brows rose. "Not exactly the kind of posh

address I'd expect for one of Crowe's women. If she was sleeping with him, she should've demanded a raise."

"Maybe it's modest for a reason. If not for Gideon tracking her down, we probably never would've thought to look in a nondescript neighborhood like this for Crowe or anyone he associated with."

"Hide in plain sight," Aric said. "Crowe wouldn't be the first Atlantean to pull that stunt."

Rafe nodded, checking house numbers as the SUV rolled past one tiny cracker box after another on the narrow residential street. "Guess she's not hiding in plain sight anymore. Here we are."

Aric stared out the passenger side window at the tidy little apartment building that sat quiet and dark at the end of a short slab of cracked concrete. "Doesn't look like anyone's home."

Rafe peered closer and shook his head. "She's home. There's a light on in the back, first floor. Come on. Let's go say hello to Miss Lynch."

Killing the headlights and engine, Rafe stepped out of the vehicle. As soon as his boots hit the pavement, his senses went tight with alarm.

"Jesus Christ."

Aric swung a tense look at him. "You smell it too?"

Rafe nodded, his fangs prickling in his gums.

Blood.

Human blood. A fucking river of it, based on the way the stench was hitting his nose.

They rushed the house on silent feet, Rafe motioning Aric to round the place to the back while he took the front. Aric was gone in an instant, vanishing into the shadows.

Rafe touched the latch on the front door and found

it unlocked. No signs of forced entry, but there was no mistaking that something bad had occurred inside. He stepped in, nearly overpowered by the olfactory punch that slammed into him as he entered Iona Lynch's home.

The place was silent. As soundless as a tomb.

"Hello?" he called into the darkness, unsurprised to receive no reply.

He crept through the small foyer and past a neatly furnished little living room. Despite the stench of bloodshed filling his nose and making his irises burn with amber heat, he didn't see evidence of a struggle until he stepped toward the galley kitchen in the back of the house.

Then, the impact of what had taken place here—very recently, from the look of it—shook him to the bone. He drew up short, his boots halted in a pool of fresh blood.

Aric had just entered the kitchen from the back door now too, and his low curse echoed Rafe's thoughts. "Holy hell."

A young blonde woman lay crumpled and deadly still in the center of the blood-soaked kitchen tiles, a lethal gash at her throat. There was no question she was dead. She'd been cut so savagely, the wound had nearly decapitated her.

"Jesus Christ," Aric murmured woodenly. "Guess we weren't the only ones looking for Iona Lynch."

Rafe clamped his teeth and fangs together on a ripe curse as he strode through the slick lake of spilled blood to reach the woman. He was fucking up a crime scene, but if there was any chance he could revive her, he had to try. Not only because it was the right thing to do, but because Iona Lynch was the Order's best lead on Crowe and his Opus associates. They couldn't afford to lose her.

Kneeling down in the mess, he gingerly rolled her onto her back and touched the hideous wound at her throat. She had no pulse, no breath. Her skin was cool and waxy beneath his fingertips. There was nothing for him to work with, nothing for his ability to latch on to and draw toward healing.

"Shit." He glanced up at Aric and grimly shook his head. "I can't help her. She's too far gone by several minutes, at least. Goddamn it, we're too fucking late."

As he spoke, he heard the faintest shift of movement coming from somewhere nearby. It was muffled, but Rafe and Aric both stilled in recognition that someone else was there in the house with them.

Silently, stealthily, Rafe set Iona Lynch's lifeless body down on the tiles and rose to his feet.

The soft rustle came again, and he followed it to the closed door of a bathroom just off the kitchen. Then he heard a low, pained moan.

He opened the door and found another woman lying in a fetal position in the corner of the cramped room. Petite as an angel, the strawberry blonde was dressed in black yoga pants and a form-fitting pink tank top rent off her shoulder from an obvious altercation. Only semiconscious now, her body was coming awake slowly from the bloodied contusion on the side of her head.

Blood spatter on the white porcelain sink indicated someone had smashed the woman's head into the basin with enough brute force to knock her out.

Rafe stepped inside, and the woman's lids lifted. Hazel eyes widened as soon as she saw him. Then her mouth dropped open in a terrified scream.

"It's okay," he assured her, moving carefully as she bolted fully alert now and scrambled as far away from him as she could get.

"Don't touch me!" Panic and confusion filled her pretty face. "Stay away from us! Iona, run!"

"Shh." Rafe shook his head, hands out in front of him to show her he meant no harm. "It's okay now. You're safe."

She huddled deeper into the corner of the bathroom, her eyes as wild as a terrified animal's. As she moved, Rafe spotted a small red birthmark beneath the rip in the side of her tank top.

A Breedmate.

Rafe hunkered down to her level, speaking gently. "We're not going to hurt you. What's your name?"

She frowned, still wary, her breast still heaving with her labored breaths. She blinked slowly, glancing down at the floor. "Siobhan." A delicate name, spoken in a broken whisper that almost made it sound as if she'd said the word *chiffon*. She glanced up at him and tried again. "I'm Siobhan O'Shea."

He nodded soberly. "My name is Rafe. And this is my friend, Aric," he said, gesturing to the doorway where his comrade stood. "How do you know Iona Lynch, Siobhan?"

"She's my roommate. Where is she? What did those men want with her?" The Breedmate swallowed, her hand coming up to the bruising lump on her head. She winced at the light contact. "Is Iona... Is she okay?"

Rafe didn't answer. This young woman would see the grisly answer for herself soon enough. With Iona Lynch murdered, Rafe's mission priority had just switched from locating a potential lead on Opus to protecting a key witness who was also a Breedmate in potential danger now.

He glanced back at Aric. "We shouldn't stay here for long, and neither should Siobhan. Go call this in to headquarters, let them know what we found. Tell them we have an injured Breedmate on our hands who's in need of a safe haven."

CHAPTER 16

Brynne didn't leave for London. It had only been an excuse, anyway. A flimsy one that Zael had seen right through—just as he'd seen through the rest of her attempts to wound him and push him away.

After her stinging end to the incredible time she'd spent naked with him in her bed, she had soaked for nearly half an hour under a scalding shower before sequestering herself in her guest room for most of the afternoon, feeling cowardly and petty.

The urge to run back home to London—to anywhere else—was strong. She felt weak from hunger and raw from heightened emotion. Neither of those things made her fit to be around other people, least of all the ones who meant something to her.

Not if she cared for their safety.

Not if she didn't want to see horror and fear in the eyes of everyone who mattered to her.

Including Zael.

God, perhaps him most of all.

Her punishing shower and the hours of solitude afterward did little to assuage the bone-deep gnawing of her body's worsening hunger. It also hadn't lessened the disgust she felt for herself after the unfair way she'd treated the one man who had only shown her kindness and understanding since she met him.

Zael had a right to be angry with her after the cutting things she'd said.

Hell, he had a right to despise her now. Although if he did, it couldn't be with any greater intensity than she despised herself.

That feeling only worsened when she finally left the safety of her self-imposed exile in her suite to venture down to the living areas.

Zael was in the large kitchen with Dylan and Rio, the scarred Breed warrior who was her mate. Their easy conversation drifted out to the hall as Brynne descended the rear staircase to the main floor below.

Dammit. There was no escaping the inevitable now. To get anywhere else in the sprawling estate from where she stood, she first had to pass the kitchen.

Against her will, her gaze sought Zael out. There he was, lounging on one of the counter stools at the large center island, listening raptly to Dylan as she regaled him with a story about how she and Rio first met.

Zael's gaze was tender on his daughter, his smile so warm and affectionate, it made Brynne's chest squeeze.

Despite her most vigilant effort, just the sight of him made her breath catch and her pulse kick into a higher tempo.

It took concentrated effort to simply step past the broad, arched entryway of the kitchen without pausing to apologize to him and ask for his forgiveness. Nor did

LARA ADRIAN

she have the nerve to glance at him and see if he might be aware of her too.

She had to stay strong where he was concerned. Zael had been putting cracks in the veneer of her self-control from the first moment he turned those unearthly blue eyes on her. If today's slip in resolve was any indication, distance was the only way to avoid another mistake like the one she'd made by falling into bed with him.

If she wasn't careful, it might not be only her resolve that crumbled around Zael, but her heart as well.

Telling herself it was a relief that he didn't call out to her as she crisply walked by, Brynne headed for the foyer. She needed fresh air and space to think.

Even more demanding, she needed to feed.

Her hunger was the one thing she could control in her life, but even that was dangerously close to snapping. She'd held it off for too long, and now it clawed at her with sharp talons, a beast gnashing at its leash.

If she needed a reminder of why relationships were impossible for her, this damned sure was it.

She was halfway across the foyer and headed for the front door when Tavia's voice sounded from behind her.

"Brynne. There you are."

Given no choice, she pivoted to face her sister.

Tavia's fine brows drew together over her shrewd light green eyes. "Were you able to get some rest this afternoon?"

"Um, rest?"

Brynne felt her own frown crease her forehead, and at the same time a flush of heat threatened to fill her face.

Oh, God. She would be mortified if her indiscretion with Zael was now public knowledge at the Order.

"I went to look for you after the meeting earlier

today," Tavia said. "Carys told me you'd gone up to your room. She thought you might need some undisturbed sleep after all you've been through these past couple of days."

"Oh." Brynne nodded, relief flooding her. "Yes, I did. Rest, I mean. Thank you."

Tavia tilted her head. "Is everything okay? You don't seem very rested. In fact, you look piqued."

"I do?"

"Yes. You do." She stared too long, too closely. "Brynne, when was the last time you fed?"

Shit. "Oh, I don't know," she hedged, forcing a level of nonchalance into her voice. "It's been long enough, I suppose. I was actually just on my way out to take care of that now."

"Alone?" Tavia's hands went to her hips. "Things are too volatile out there, even in daylight hours. It's nearly dusk, Brynne. At least wait until you can bring one of the warriors with you."

"An Order escort to hold my hand while I feed?" Brynne hoped her dread didn't show in her expression. "Please, tell me you're joking."

Feeding had gotten perfectly civilized—and carefully regulated—since the Breed was outed to their human neighbors twenty years ago.

Where it used to be acceptable to tap any human's vein for a few fresh red cells as long as the blood Host wasn't harmed, now the business of feeding had become a polite, albeit paid, transaction between consenting parties.

That wasn't to say all members of the Breed adhered to the law. Some preferred the old ways for the sport of it.

Others, like Brynne, had reasons of their own to avoid the carefully monitored environments of the blood Host parlors and clubs that catered to the Breed and their various appetites.

Chief among those reasons, for her, being the fact that parlors prohibited mind-scrubs following a feeding.

The law was meant to protect human Hosts from being used without their consent—something Brynne never did, no matter how savage her hunger.

No, while she preferred to obtain her Hosts from less stringent environments, the humans she paid to nourish her walked away from the transaction with no memory as a courtesy to them.

And, if she were being honest, as an act of self-preservation for her as well.

Brynne couldn't use a Host in a monitored setting like a parlor. She certainly couldn't do it with one of the Order's warriors in tow.

"Even if I thought I needed an armed escort, Tavia, I doubt we'd find a reputable parlor that would even let me through the door in the company of one."

Her sister wasn't swayed. "You can go to the one in Georgetown that Carys used to visit when she came to D.C. before she was blood bonded with Rune. It's the best in the city, and not only will they let you through the door with an Order escort, Lucan and Gabrielle's son, Darion, keeps a VIP suite there that I'm sure you'll be welcome to use."

Brynne's hopes sank in the face of this helpful, and undeterred, offer. "I don't suppose you're going to let me refuse?"

Tavia's satisfied smile was answer enough. She looped her arm through Brynne's, steering her away from the front door while Brynne's hunger sank its talons deeper into the fraying fabric of her soul.

CHAPTER 17

Zael knew the instant Brynne had descended the stairs outside the mansion's kitchen.

He'd been enjoying a conversation with Dylan and Rio, glad for the time to get to know both of them a bit. But the moment Brynne's presence stirred the air, his attention went out the window and the only thing he could focus on was her.

He had waited for her to appear in the hallway outside the kitchen, even as he nodded and smiled at the right places while Dylan spoke.

If Brynne had so much as glanced his way even for a second, nothing would have stopped him from going to her right then and there. He would have taken her aside without a care for who saw them, and he would have demanded she be honest with him, instead of hiding behind the chilly, untouchable facade she seemed to put up so quickly whenever anyone got too close to her.

Especially him.

Not that he had any room to point the finger when

it came to honesty or honor. She had been right about him not being the type to stick around. He couldn't argue that, especially when Dylan was living proof of his life's most shameful failing.

If either woman knew the truth about his cowardice where Dylan's mother was concerned, they both might turn their backs on him. And rightly so.

But Brynne didn't seem to need any convincing to ignore him. She'd stepped past the kitchen entry without blinking or breaking her stride. He didn't even know if she was aware he was there.

Something told him she had been, and the fact that she sailed by without the slightest acknowledgment had burned him more than he cared to admit.

She had since disappeared with Tavia somewhere in the mansion. Zael couldn't deny that despite his agreement to give her space, there was a part of him that refused to bow to a lie.

She wanted him, just as he wanted her.

And yes, the sex was great. Hell, it was so incredible he was of the opinion they should be doing it again as soon as possible, not trying to pretend it was some kind of mistake both of them should regret.

But even more than that, something was happening between them that went beyond attraction. It went beyond the fact that they lived in two different worlds, from two races that had been enemies for longer than either of them had been alive.

This connection he and Brynne had shouldn't make sense and it damned sure wasn't anything he'd planned on, but it was real.

It was genuine and powerful, and it wasn't going away, no matter how much she wanted to convince both of them that it didn't exist.

That alone should have been enough to make him bolt. Great sex was one thing. He'd never been the kind to walk away from physical pleasure. But this was something else. And for some idiotic reason, instead of taking Brynne's rejection as the gift it should be, he felt compelled to get to the real reasons she was so determined to push him away.

And the longer he waited to get those answers from her, the more her silent treatment was going to drive him insane.

Making his excuses to Dylan and Rio, he slipped out of the kitchen and headed toward the Order's command center, the direction she'd gone with Tavia a short while ago.

Gideon practically slammed into him, coming out of a room with his head down and tapping madly on a tablet screen.

"Oh, shit. Sorry, man." The warrior glanced up distractedly. His spiky crown of blond hair was disheveled and intrigue lit his eyes behind the pale blue lenses of his glasses. "I'm working out a new protocol to see if I can find another way through Opus's server encryption. Got no time to waste, especially now that our best lead on Crowe turned out to be a dead end." He winced as he said it. "Bad choice of words."

Zael paused. "What do you mean?"

"The woman in Ireland," Gideon said. He tucked the tablet under his arm, his expression sobering. "Rafe and Aric called it in a few minutes ago. Crowe's mistress was murdered in her home right before our team arrived to drop a net on her. Opus apparently knew we were on to her. Sounds like they made quite a statement in killing her."

Zael didn't want to ask what constituted making a statement, but having seen some of the other violence Opus Nostrum's followers were capable of, he could easily imagine. "So, how were we able to confirm that this woman, Iona Lynch, was in fact Crowe's mistress?"

"We have a witness who's corroborated our hunch—Lynch's roommate. Her name's Siobhan O'Shea. She was in the house at the time of the attack earlier tonight. To make matters worse, the friend is a Breedmate."

"Jesus. Was she harmed?"

"Got knocked on the head pretty hard by the two men who killed her friend, but she obviously wasn't their main concern. She says Lynch knew the men. She let them in and things turned ugly pretty fast. When the roommate tried to intervene, they shoved her into the bathroom and knocked her out while they finished what they came to do."

Zael exhaled a low curse. "She's lucky they didn't finish her too."

"Extremely lucky," Gideon agreed.

"That's not to say this woman isn't still in danger," Zael considered. "From all I've heard and seen of Opus's tactics, they don't have a very good track record of leaving loose ends behind."

Gideon nodded grimly. "She'd be in Order protective custody even if she wasn't a Breedmate, but the fact that she is makes her safety a top priority. Not to mention we need her to tell us whatever she can about Crowe and Iona Lynch, and about the men who killed her."

Gideon's tablet chimed and he glanced at the screen.

"Damn. So much for that brilliant idea. Whoever put the locks on Opus's network is one shrewd son of a bitch. Looks like I've got more homework to do." He hooked his thumb in the direction of the corridor. "If you were on your way to see Lucan, that's where I'm heading now."

Zael hedged. "Ah, actually, I was looking to talk with Brynne. She went this way with Tavia a few minutes ago."

"Yes, she did." Although he was already tapping on his tablet, Gideon's brows rose with blatant interest over the rims of his glasses. "But you're too late. Brynne's gone now."

"Gone?" The newsflash hit Zael like a blow. "You don't mean back to London?"

"No. Gone to feed in Georgetown. Tavia sent one of the warriors out with her as an escort."

Zael wasn't happy to hear she'd left the safety of the command center, let alone that she'd done so with another male. If she needed someone to protect her, then damn it, she could have asked him to take her.

Of course, she'd probably rather swallow her own tongue than ask him for help.

He realized he must have been wearing his displeasure on his face, because Gideon froze for a moment, cocking his head at him. Then he chuckled.

"Well, I'll be damned." He reached out and cuffed Zael on the shoulder. "Don't worry, Atlantean. Happens to the best of us."

"What does?"

The warrior smirked. "You'll figure it out."

With that, he resumed his tapping, leaving Zael to stare after him as Gideon headed back down the corridor, once again thoroughly engrossed in his work.

CHAPTER 18

"You really don't have to wait for me to finish here," Brynne told the big dark-haired Gen One warrior who'd been tasked as her personal driver and bodyguard for the evening. "I feel ridiculous that Tavia insisted I be schlepped around like a child in need of supervision."

To make matters worse, her sister had assigned Jordana's warrior mate, Nathan, to the job. If Brynne had harbored even the slimmest hope of slipping her collar tonight in order to feed the way she needed to, she stood little chance of getting away from this warrior's watchful eye.

"It could take a while," she pointed out. "I'll have to register and sign the contract before they even admit me."

Nathan sat behind the wheel of the SUV as he parked at the curb, his expression unreadable. "Take whatever time you need."

He wasn't much of a talker, Brynne had gathered,

but she wasn't feeling particularly chatty herself. She'd been too busy calculating possible excuses for why she wasn't going in to the blood Host parlor, and trying to guess how much longer she would be able to stave off the worst of her hunger if she didn't get some relief tonight.

By the acid burn of her veins and the increasing throb of all her pulse points, she was perilously close to the edge already.

"You know, I'm a child of the labs too, Brynne."

She glanced at him, startled by the unsolicited confession. "Yes. Tavia had mentioned it to me at one time. You were part of the Hunter program."

"Assassins," he confirmed grimly.

Brynne knew the basics. The same Breed madman who tinkered with DNA to create Tavia and her and a rumored dozen or more Breed females like them had also bred a race of Gen One boys from the Ancient he kept imprisoned in the lab and a cage full of Breedmates abducted from their families and used like chattel for his experiments and twisted pleasures.

Hunters like Nathan had been raised by handlers, as Brynne and her half-sisters had been. But where Brynne and the other Breed females were shackled by lies and abuse and genetic-stunting chemical therapies, the Hunters were kept obedient by the use of even crueler tactics.

Nathan looked at her finally, and there was a bleakness in his eyes that touched her. Not because she pitied him, but because she admired how normal his life seemed now, with Jordana. With the Order. With his mother, Corinne, and Hunter, her Gen One mate who was also a product of Dragos's madness.

"No one who survived those damned labs did it unscathed," Nathan said.

Brynne nodded. "I know."

"Yeah, I know you do. But you look like you need someone to say it out loud for you now."

She stared at him in the dim light of the dashboard. Although he had no idea how deep her wounds had gone, or how hideous her reality was even years and miles away from the torture of the labs, his compassion moved her.

She swallowed on an arid throat. "Thank you, Nathan."

He gave a curt nod. "Go do what you have to do and take care of your needs. I'll wait for you here."

Certain she misheard him, or at least misunderstood his meaning, Brynne's breath caught.

Did he know she dreaded walking into that parlor?

Holy shit. Was he giving her permission to go feed on her own terms?

"Nathan, I—"

She didn't get the chance to say another word.

Without warning, something big fell from the roof of a nearby building and smashed onto a parked car about a block up the street. Metal crunched. Glass exploded. Alarm lights and sirens split the darkness.

People started screaming, pointing up at the roof of the nearby parking deck.

"What the fuck?" Nathan killed the engine. "Stay in the vehicle!"

He leaped out and vanished into the night before Brynne even realized he was moving.

She sucked in a gasp as she peered through the windshield.

Another body pitched to the street, plummeting down like a stuffed dummy freefalling off the parking garage rooftop. Except they weren't dummies. They were humans—brutalized, broken, their clothing shredded and blood-soaked.

Savaged.

Nausea swamped Brynne as she realized what she was seeing. "Oh, my God."

Something else descended to the street now. A Breed youth, his chin and the whole front of his body painted red from his crime. The young male dropped into a crouch next to his kill and howled like the animal he had become, his fangs enormous, his face feral with Bloodlust.

Holy shit.

The male was Rogue.

And he wasn't alone. Another descended to the rooftop of a parked van, wearing more evidence of the slaughter.

Brynne instinctively reached for her JUSTIS-issued firearm, but her fingers came away empty. Dammit. She'd lost her service weapon the same day she'd lost her job with the agency.

Panic swept the street as swiftly as a flash fire.

The humans who'd stopped to stare in dazed confusion now bolted blindly away from the scene. One after another, they streamed past Brynne in the SUV, shrieking as they raced for cover.

It was just what the pair of predators wanted.

They vaulted airborne, leaping over Brynne's vehicle and several others in one fluid bound. The fleeing humans in their sights didn't stand a chance.

But that didn't mean Brynne wasn't going to try to

save at least some of them.

She was Breed too—something even deadlier than that, thanks to the genetic cocktail that had spawned her. Whether armed with weapons or her bare hands, she was a nightmare neither of these two fucks would be expecting.

Jumping out of the SUV, she had her fists full of the first Rogue's shirt in a split second. She took him down to the asphalt. Her knee planted firmly in the center of his spine, the Bloodlusting male went wild, snarling and struggling in an effort to shake her off. Brynne seized the vampire's skull and gave it a sharp twist, snapping bone and tendons.

She released the dead Rogue, her eyes already piercing the night to track her next target.

There he was. While she'd paused to deal with his companion, the other Rogue had enough time to pluck one of the stragglers from the herd. Snatching a rangy human male under his arm, the vampire dodged into a side alley to enjoy his spoils.

"Shit."

Brynne was rounding the corner in a heartbeat, but she was already moments too late.

The Rogue had the human down on the pavement, his fangs sunk deep in the front of the man's throat, greedily taking his fill while his victim convulsed and sputtered wetly under the assault.

Brynne's bile rose at the sight.

"Get off him."

Her voice was an airless growl of sound, nothing like she'd heard before. It was her own hunger clawing at her, making her mouth feel desert dry and her vision burn hot with amber light. Twined with her battle rage, she was something beyond formidable now.

The Rogue grunted, swinging his head around to look for the source of the intrusion.

And although his mind was gone, his senses owned by the Bloodlust that made him Rogue, he apparently still had some small spark of sanity—enough to make his own glowing eyes go a bit wider in his skull as he registered what he was up against.

But the madness in him overruled everything else.

Still in his crouch, the Rogue let go of the dying human and swiveled on his bare heels, ready to face off with Brynne to defend his prey.

Brynne braced for the attack she knew was coming. On a roar, the feral vampire flew at her.

Instead of letting his greater weight and unhinged fury catapult her backward, she took hold of him and spun, using his forward momentum to pivot them together in midair. Then she shoved hard, slamming the Rogue into the wall of the brick building at his back.

The wall shook, old mortar crumbling with the impact. The Rogue was dazed from the crushing strike, but he wasn't down. He came at her again, another ferocious leap and crash that hurtled them both across the narrow alley to the wall on the other side.

She grunted in sharp pain as her back collided into the bricks. The Rogue dropped her, letting her sag to the ground. He rocked back on his heels as if to ready himself for the killing blow. As if he'd won.

Brynne's smile was not her own. It belonged to the beast inside her. The one whose power surged inside her now, more lethal than anything this lowly blood addict would ever know.

She rose like a wraith in front of the Rogue. He had

no chance to react, no chance to stop the violence that exploded out of her.

She lashed out, lightning-quick. Her fingers ripped through clothing, flesh, and bone. The Rogue roared as she opened his chest with slashing strikes of her hands, his agony only feeding her power.

His chest cavity shredded, the Rogue shrieked and convulsed on his feet. But that wasn't enough for the monster raging within her now.

Grabbing a fistful of the vampire's mangy hair, she bellowed with battle fury as she drove the vampire's head into the bricks at her back. The skull caved in with a sickening crunch.

She smashed it again and again, lost to an unearthly violence that seethed through her veins like poison. She didn't know what finally made her head clear enough to realize her opponent was dead.

But no, that wasn't right.

She did know.

The scent of fresh blood lifted her chin from the revolting carnage she'd wrought.

On the ground nearby, the human was shuddering in a growing pool of red. He was dying. Easily only moments from the grave already.

But his blood was still alive.

And it called to her.

It called to the beast who'd been pacing its cage for too long—since the last time she'd finally broken down and fed. She hungered now. So severely she could hardly stand the agony of it.

Brynne drifted over to the man. His gaping, sightless eyes probably didn't register the inhuman face looking down at him.

But Brynne saw what she looked like now.

In the scant light of the street, she saw her face reflected in the glossy surface of the dying man's blood.

It made her want to weep, that reflection of who—and what—she truly was.

Instead, she knelt down beside her dying blood Host…and she fed.

CHAPTER 19

Zael sensed the sudden shift of energy in the Order's headquarters even before he heard the heavy drum of boots on marble floors and the jangle of weapons. Following the sound down to the central artery of the command center, he found all of the warriors suited up and rolling out for patrols.

Or, rather, for battle.

"What's going on?"

Lucan cut him a stark glance. "Rogues. We've got upwards of a dozen of them on the loose right now."

Zael knew the derogatory term for a blood-addicted member of the Breed. In fact, there probably wasn't a person alive in the past twenty years—mortal and immortal alike—who hadn't at least heard of the violence and carnage Rogues had inflicted on the human population. But it had been a long time since they had posed any kind of threat, thanks in most part to the work of the Order.

It hardly seemed coincidental that this kind of

disaster was coming so quickly on the heels of two other shocking strikes against public confidence and security.

"You think Opus is behind this?"

"They haven't confirmed yet, but I don't think there's any question. This has Opus written all over it." Lucan practically spat the words.

"There have been isolated Rogue attacks in other locations recently," Tegan added. "Apparently, Opus got its hands on a chemical substance that makes bloodthirsty killers out of anyone who takes it."

"Fucking déjà vu all over again," Sterling Chase snarled as he fastened an arsenal of firearms around his hips.

"Yeah, it is," Dante agreed. "We grabbed a bunch of the shit and torched the rest when we took down Riordan, but there was already some of it in play."

"And now it's here in D.C.," Lucan said, his tone bleak. He motioned for the warriors to start rolling out. "Nathan took out three Rogues so far, but they're cutting a bloody path through Georgetown as we speak."

Zael's stomach clenched. "Ah, fuck." The alarm he'd felt upon entering the weapons room a moment ago now turned to ice-cold dread. "Brynne's in Georgetown."

Lucan gave him a curt nod as the commanders and other warriors began filing out to the corridor. "She's with Nathan. He left her in the vehicle while he went to check things out. If she stays put, she should be okay until we reach her."

"Where?" Despite the assurances, Zael's pulse kicked hard and didn't let up. "Tell me exactly where she is."

Darion Thorne was the first to speak. "Nathan was

taking her to a blood Host parlor. It's on Wisconsin Avenue, near M Street."

Zael knew the area. Not well, but enough for his needs right now. The Order and everything else pushed from his thoughts, he put an image of the intersection in his mind's eye. Then he glanced at the Atlantean emblem that dangled from the leather thong around his wrist.

The piece of silvery crystal responded to his psychic request with a brilliant flare of light.

It flashed brighter, enveloping him in its power— and then Zael was no longer picturing the Georgetown intersection in his mind, he was standing there in the flesh.

The street was ghostly in its stillness, only the bleating cry of a vehicle alarm piercing the night. Zael started walking. Up ahead of him, a brutalized body lay broken and covered in gore next to the smashed hood of a car. Blood streaked the asphalt, which was also littered with items the terrorized people had lost in their haste to vacate the area.

He saw the glossy, black bulk of the Order's SUV parked at the curb, just as Lucan had assured him it would be. But Zael's lungs constricted as he realized the vehicle was empty, the passenger door ajar.

He wheeled around in the middle of the street, his gaze searching for any signs of life.

"Brynne!"

There was no answer. Only the nagging drone of the alarm. He silenced it with a sharp mental command.

"Brynne! Where are you?"

His feet started moving on their own. It wasn't hard to tell which way the other people had gone. Personal effects, blood, even the savaged body of another victim lay in his path.

And then—a grim, but hopeful, sign.

A dead Breed male, his head twisted grotesquely as if by violent, monstrous strength.

One of Nathan's kills, perhaps. Zael didn't much care how the vampire met its end. One less Rogue was one less threat of danger to Brynne.

He shouted her name again, but still there was no answer.

Jogging now, he ran more than a block, then paused as he neared a narrow side alley. The sight—and smell—staggered him. He wasn't Breed, but even he was rocked back on his heels by the coppery stench of pooled blood on the pavement inside the alleyway.

He approached the foulness, his eyes rooted to the pair of bodies that lay in crumpled heaps on the ground.

Relief washed over him when he saw that neither of the dead was Brynne. One was a Breed male, his corpse savaged beyond description. The other was a human of slight build, whose bloodless pallor made his skin glow milky white in the thin moonlight.

The horror of what had plainly taken place in the alley sickened him. Although the Rogue's death had been brutal, the human had suffered horrifically as well. The front of his throat was torn away, no doubt by the Rogue. Another bite wound pierced his wrist—this one less violent, and certainly not the injury that killed him, but there was no mistaking the predation that had taken place.

Zael stared at the two large punctures, and something troubling nagged at his senses.

He wanted to call out to Brynne again, but the silence in the alley held his tongue.

He wasn't alone.

He took a step forward and the prickle in his veins became a throb.

"Brynne?" He said her name in little more than a whisper as he tilted his head back and looked up, following the wall of old red bricks that rose on both sides of the narrow street.

And there she was.

Huddled in the corner of a rickety black iron fire escape four stories up.

"Ah, fuck... Brynne."

The crystal at his wrist put him up there with her in that next instant. She flinched under the flash of pure white energy, drawing herself into a tight ball as far away from him as she could get. Her dark hair was a chaotic tangle that all but covered her face, many of the strands soaked and stiff with drying blood.

"It's all right," he said. "You're safe now."

The sound she made when he took a step forward and reached for her made the hair on the back of his neck rise in warning.

The growl that came out of her was anguished, pained...alien.

"Brynne, look at me. It's Zael. I'm not here to hurt you."

"Go. Away."

If he wasn't looking at her with his own eyes now, he never would have believed the twisted, gravely rasp belonged to her. She kept her head down, her arms wrapped around her updrawn knees. Her feet were bare, the skin on the tops of them covered with *dermaglyphs*. Deep colors surged and pulsed in furious, changeable hues on the backs of her hands too.

He looked closer, his gaze snagging on something peculiar about her fingers.

Her nails... They were black.

No, not fingernails, he realized now.

Talons.

Sharp as razors, the nails on the tips of her fingers gleamed as black as obsidian.

"Brynne," he murmured. "Let me see you. Let me help you."

"You can't." Anger lashed out at him with her reply. She gave a brief toss of her head, a moan leaking out of her. "Go away, Zael. Please."

"No. Not this time. You're not pushing me away when it's obvious you're in trouble and need help—"

"I said go away!"

Finally, her head came up. But it wasn't Brynne glowering at him now. Zael gaped at the molten amber light that poured out of her eyes. Thin pupils locked on him in rage—in staggering deadly intent. *Glyphs* surged all over her face now, drawing attention to the sharpened angles of her cheekbones and brow, and the enormous lengths of her fangs.

Not Breed, because not even the eldest Gen One transformed like this in the throes of hunger.

Brynne was something else. Something *other*.

Something Zael and his people hadn't seen up close for thousands of years.

The beautiful, tormented face staring back at him now in dangerous fury was the face of an Ancient.

CHAPTER 20

The Rogues were running through Georgetown like a pack of wild dogs.

Faces painted red with human blood, eyes blazing as bright as yellow coals in their feral faces, two more howling males bounded into the empty street where Lucan stood over the body of another he had just stopped a second ago with a titanium bullet to the head.

Like humans hopped up on heavy narcotics and adrenaline, Rogues didn't go down easy. It took brute strength or a hell of a lot of lead—sometimes a combination of both. Titanium helped. The metal was highly corrosive poison to the diseased blood system of a Rogue, as evidenced by the sizzling mess that was growing near Lucan's boots. The dead Rogue would be nothing but ash in a few minutes.

Lucan turned to deliver the same end to the pair of newcomers now closing in on him in the middle of the swanky Georgetown shopping district. He took the first one down with a single shot of titanium between the eyes—before realizing it was the last round left in his weapon.

Ah, fuck.

The second Rogue roared as his companion dropped into a puddle of melting flesh and bone. He charged at Lucan, head lowered and jaws snapping. Lucan drew his backup pistol and fired multiple times, but the lead rounds only pissed the Rogue off. The vampire vaulted at Lucan, leaving him no choice but to meet the threat up-close-and-personal.

They crashed together and tumbled onto the pavement.

Lucan scrambled to withdraw the titanium blade from its holster on his weapons belt as the Rogue's gnashing fangs came at his face and throat in blinding speed. Finally, he worked the knife free.

With the Rogue struggling for any advantage, he left himself open to attack. It was a fatal mistake. Lucan drove the titanium blade into the vampire's side. The resulting shriek was ear-splitting, purely animal. With the Rogue convulsing from the wound, Lucan shoved the body away from him and got up to his feet.

It wasn't until he was standing that he heard the sawing breath of another Rogue at his back.

He turned to face it, seeing the Rogue poised to spring at him. But instead of lunging, the vampire abruptly stilled, then dropped to the ground as dead weight.

Dante stood a few feet away, one of his curved titanium daggers planted solidly in the Rogue's spine.

Lucan gave him a nod. "Thanks."

The warrior arched a dark brow. "Just like old times, eh?" He strode over and retrieved his weapon, cleaning it on the disintegrating Rogue's jacket. "If this shit keeps up, Nikolai may have to go back to supplying us with titanium custom rounds from his command center in Montreal."

Lucan grunted at the reminder of the Siberian-born warrior with a penchant for weapons and explosives. "Things were different for us then. It's a hell of a lot easier to put a lid on isolated strikes by one or two enemies at a time. Opus is global. And they're making damned sure we feel the pressure from all sides."

As if the presence of Rogues in a major metropolitan city in the States wasn't troubling enough, before the Order had rolled out of headquarters tonight, they had gotten more bad news. Gideon had received word that all three European commanders were reporting a spike in Rogue activity in their regions as well.

"The hits keep coming," Dante remarked, a grim look in his eyes. "I hate to guess what Opus thinks they can do while they're keeping us busy playing Whack-a-Mole with Rogues and lone wolf attacks on government and law enforcement organizations."

Lucan didn't want to guess either, but they had to if they meant to stay ahead of them enough to take the brotherhood down. "Unless Gideon cracks that encryption on their communications network, we don't have many cards left to play."

"We've got the Breedmate in custody with Rafe and Aric," Dante pointed out. "If she can ID the men who killed Iona Lynch, we can start there and follow the trail back to Opus from that end."

He had a point. But the panicked recollections of a shaken and injured eyewitness were hardly the kind of odds Lucan preferred. Still, Siobhan O'Shea was a better lead than nothing at all. Which is why he'd given instructions for Rafe and Aric to keep her close for the time being.

The group was currently en route from Ireland to the command center in London. They needed to keep Iona Lynch's roommate safe, and that meant ensuring Opus didn't discover she was in Order hands.

And while Lucan hoped things wouldn't get bad enough to demand it, the Order also had another card to play against Opus if they had to.

The Atlantean crystal.

After witnessing its power with Zael and Jenna the other day, Lucan could not deny that he'd been thinking of little else. If two crystals had been used by the Ancients to destroy the entire realm of Atlantis, then nothing—and no one—would be able to stop the Order if they had another in their possession.

Zael had divulged when they met for the first time that a group of Atlanteans who fled the realm and formed their own hidden colony had taken a crystal with them. The Order had Zael's alliance, but Lucan dreaded that there might come a day—and soon—that they would also need his help in building a weapon capable of ending any war before it even had a chance to start.

As the thought churned in his mind, Chase emerged from out of the shadows of a side street and headed their way.

"Any sign of Brynne?" Lucan asked.

Chase shook his head. "Found the SUV where Nathan said it would be, but it's empty. Looks like she got out on her own and fled on foot. No sign of her anywhere, from what I could find."

Dante shrugged, smirking. "The way Zael poofed

out of headquarters at the mention of her, I have a feeling when we find him, we've located Brynne too. Also, where do I sign up to get one of those cool Atlantean transporter bracelets?"

Chase chuckled, but Lucan had a hard time feeling the humor. "Whatever is going on between Zael and Brynne, they picked a damned lousy time for it. We can't afford distractions like this at headquarters when everything is going to shit around us."

Dante quirked a brow. "Talk about old times. I recall you saying that to more than a few of us back in the day. No doubt you told yourself that same shit when it came to Gabrielle too."

Yeah, he did and he had. It was an argument he wouldn't win now, but that didn't mean he had to like it.

"Keep an eye out for both of them," he instructed the two warriors. As he spoke, his comm unit buzzed his ear with an incoming call from Tegan, who was commanding another of the patrol teams that had fanned out to cover more ground. "What've you got?"

"Six Rogues ashed between the park and the university," Tegan said. "We're all clear here. Rio and Kade are with Nathan near the government center and they've spotted another gang of Rogues over there."

Lucan swore under his breath. At this rate, it was going to be another long night.

"I'm with Chase and Dante. We're on our way there now."

CHAPTER 21

If she needed confirmation of how hideous she was now—a monster—she had it.

Zael went utterly still the instant his eyes locked on her transformation. He cursed something low under his breath, something in a language that she didn't understand.

"Brynne," he murmured. "My God..."

Her heart twisted at the stunned tone of his deep voice. She knew what he was seeing. She knew what she was—the flawed, imbalanced result of a DNA experiment that never should have happened.

An anomaly.

A mistake.

An abomination.

She slowly pulled herself up from her crouch in the corner of the old fire escape. Zael watched her move, caution in his stance and in his confused expression. The predator in her took great satisfaction in seeing a powerful being like Zael on guard as she rose to her feet.

It was that part of her that worried her, too, because once the monster took hold of her, not even she could fully rein it in.

"Stay away, Zael. I'm warning you."

"Tell me what happened. It's okay, Brynne. I only want to understand."

She scoffed, certain the softness that crept into his tone was based on pity or revulsion. The inhuman part of her preferred his wariness over this tender attempt to put her at ease.

She took a sideways step, following the railing of the fire escape.

"Are you hurt?" he asked gently. "Tell me what's wrong with you so I can try to help you."

She couldn't contain the miserable moan that leaked out of her at the sincerity of his plea.

He couldn't help her, and she couldn't stay near him. Not when she was like this.

Not ever again, now that he knew the ugly secret she could no longer hide from him.

"Brynne, please." His brows drew together over tender, determined eyes. "Are you injured? Did those Bloodlusting fucks... Did they do this to you somehow?"

A laugh burst out of her, caustic, coarse as gravel in her throat. "Those Rogues couldn't harm me if they tried. Can't you see that?"

She didn't want to throw his concern back in his face, but the predator in her was never stronger than in the grips of blood thirst or battle rage. Right now, Brynne was swamped by both. Fueled by hunger and adrenaline, she was a deadly creature.

As much as the woman in her yearned for Zael's

comfort—for his compassion—the part of her that was nearly pure Ancient saw only another obstacle in front of her. An enemy it recognized on a primal, instinctual level.

One that needed to be destroyed.

"Go away, Zael." Her stare bathed his handsome face in amber light. The care she saw in his expression, in the way he unflinchingly held her transformed gaze, tore at her heart the way nothing in her life ever had before. She snarled, forcing herself to look away from him. "I said, leave me the fuck alone."

"Sorry, sweetheart. That's not happening." He took a step toward her on the narrow ironwork platform. "You think I'm going to walk away and leave you here like this? Come on, Brynne. Let me help you."

He reached out to her. Brynne dodged him, catapulting herself off the fire escape in one fluid leap.

She landed in a crouch on the street below, ready to bolt on foot.

But Zael was there in that next instant. She barely registered his motion, yet there he stood, blocking her path in the alleyway. His scowl knit his brows. "Don't do this, damn it. Don't shut me out, Brynne."

His gentle tone made the beast in her bristle. "Get away from me, Atlantean."

He shook his head, obstinate. Immovable. So dangerously foolish. "This is why you've been pushing me away? Because you were afraid I'd see you like this?" He swore softly, his scowl deepening. "You don't have to be afraid of me, Brynne."

"Afraid of you?" The predator in her all but spat the words. "Never."

Her vitriol didn't seem to faze him at all. Zael held

her stare, even took another step toward her. "You're not alone. Don't you see that?"

"You're wrong. I *am* alone. It's you who can't see that." A hot breath gusted out of her, shaky, uneven. "I've been alone all my life. It's the only way I've survived."

He gently shook his head. "It doesn't have to be that way. Not anymore."

She eyed him warily as he closed more distance between them. Her senses filled with him, from the deliciously warm scent of his skin to the heat that radiated off his muscular body. Her head filled with the awareness of him as a man, as the one man she desired more than any before him.

"Let me in, Brynne. You can trust me."

She tossed her head in automatic response, torn between wanting to believe him and wanting him as far away from her as possible. Her vision locked on his throat as he moved in closer. The drum of his pulse echoed in her skull, in her temples, in her marrow. She stared, riveted to that hard ticking of his heartbeat, as she had been when they'd lain together, naked in her bed.

God help her, but the hunger with which she ached for him felt less about the monster and its cravings and more about the need to feel Zael inside her, comforting her with his body and his blood.

On a groan, she stepped around him. Or, rather, she tried to. Zael stopped her, his body planted in front of her, physically barring her from getting past.

"Dammit, Zael. Get out of my way and let me go."

He ignored all of her warnings. He ignored the unearthly rasp of her voice, which should have told him just how close she was to the edge.

And it was too late now, too much for her to bear.

Rage spiked through her, breaking loose from its thin leash. She shoved at him, but he was strong too. And he was fast. He grabbed her hands and held her still, restraining her.

She roared, no longer in control of her senses or her reactions.

The beast owned her now.

The monstrous power she could not contain exploded out of her and she knew only that she was lethal like this. She couldn't hold herself back—not even with Zael. A bellow shot out of her, anguished and unhinged fury setting her into motion.

She broke loose from his hold and flew at him on a banshee howl.

Zael raised his hands as if to fend her off. They were glowing, his fingers limned in pure white light. In the center of both palms, the symbol of a teardrop and crescent moon was illuminated with energy so pure it blinded her.

She couldn't fight it. Couldn't fight him.

Zael's power was too strong.

He touched her, and light instantly engulfed her vision. His light. It poured into her, obliterating her senses as it seeped into her mind and her limbs, and into every raging cell of her body.

~ ~ ~

Zael knelt on the pavement, holding Brynne in his arms. She was unconscious, unmoving, except for the slow rise and fall of her chest as she breathed.

He hated that he'd used his power on her—for

several reasons—but she'd given him little choice.

Brynne was formidable enough as a Breed female. What he saw in her just now was something far more lethal.

Ancient.

Or something damned close to it.

He didn't know how it was possible, but the proof had been right in front of his eyes.

If relations between the Breed and his people were tenuous, it was nothing compared to the visceral loathing that every Atlantean felt toward their otherworldly enemies who had spawned the Breed on Earth. That hatred was especially strong in Zael and his former comrades of Selene's royal legion, who had been on the front lines of every war with the Ancients.

Yet despite what he saw in Brynne just now, it wasn't hatred he felt for her.

Holy hell. Far from it.

Glancing down at her, he watched as the *dermaglyphs* that had been so livid and pronounced on her face and neck and limbs now began to subside. The *glyphs* on the backs of her hands had vanished, along with the black talons that had sprouted from the tips of her fingers in her transformation. She rested now, forced into a heavy calm.

The light had done that for her, just as he'd hoped it would.

He didn't know what she needed, but one thing was for damned sure—he had no intention of leaving her side. Nor would he let her endure her torment alone.

He needed to get her out of the city. He needed to see that she was safe.

They both needed to get somewhere secure, before

the recklessness of using his power brought even more problems down on them.

Although he could teleport using the crystal amulet at his wrist, he couldn't take her with him that way. Only Atlanteans could connect to the energy and use it to leap from one location to another.

Scooping her up, he rose to his feet and carried her out of the alley. The city was ghostly quiet, no sign of the warriors on this dark, empty stretch of asphalt.

Zael felt a jab of guilt for concealing Brynne and himself in the alley when Chase swept through earlier, searching for them. The Order was his ally, but if the warriors had a right to know about the secret Brynne was keeping, it would be on her terms and no one else's.

On the main street, the Order's SUV still sat vacant at the curb. Zael brought Brynne to the vehicle and carefully set her in the passenger seat. He couldn't resist reaching out to stroke her cheek. She stirred slightly under his touch, but her eyelids remained closed. Her face was slack and peaceful in her sleep, as sweet and innocent as a kitten.

Zael gazed at the dark-haired beauty who had come into his life so unexpectedly and turned it upside down. He couldn't deny the surge of possessiveness—the fierce protectiveness—that ran through him as he looked at her.

Brynne Kirkland was no helpless kitten in need of saving. She'd be the first to tell him that, more than likely with her fangs bared and claws unsheathed the instant she awoke from the drowse he'd put her under.

And given what he'd seen here tonight, he would do well to keep his distance.

Damn it, if he were smart, he'd leave Brynne and her

problems to the Order right here and now, and vanish back to the colony and his people where he belonged.

Except he couldn't stay away from this woman. Not since that first morning on the Order's terrace patio. And sure as hell not after seeing the anguish in her eyes as she faced off against him, looking like something out of an old nightmare.

She could fight him all she wanted. She could hate him for refusing to do what she begged of him and leave her alone.

It wouldn't change what he felt when he looked at her now.

She was his.

Zael closed the passenger door, then went around to hop into the driver's seat of the SUV. As soon as he hit the ignition, the dashboard comm unit illuminated with Gideon's face on the display.

"Zael," the warrior said, surprise in his expression. "Jesus, where've you been, man? I've got two patrol teams scouring the city looking for you. Any sign of Brynne?"

He nodded. "She's here with me."

"Glad to hear it. Is she hurt?"

"No." Zael glanced at her resting in the seat beside him. There was no trace of trouble in her features. Nothing left of the Ancient that lurked under her skin. "She's fine," Zael said. "I'm bringing her in now."

CHAPTER 22

Brynne startled awake from a nightmare more disturbing than any she'd had in a long time. Her breath raced, sawing raggedly past her parted lips. Her head throbbed. Worst of all, the back of her throat was raw and bitter with the coppery taste of blood.

She moaned, her eyelids peeling open a fractional crack in the tranquil semidarkness. Soft mattress under her. Tall ceiling framed by elegant crown molding above her.

Thank God.

She was resting in her guest suite at Order headquarters, not crouching in some dank alley in Georgetown with a dead Rogue at her feet and her fangs sunk deep into the wrist of a dying human.

Nor was she standing in front of Zael, blood-soaked and seething, exposed to him as the monster she truly was.

Please...not that.

And yet the images flew at her too vividly to be a

dream. Not even one of the hellish night terrors that had haunted her so frequently since her time in Dragos's labs could top the sensory torment that clung to her now.

She turned her head on the pillow and was sickened to catch the sharp metallic stench of dried blood in her hair. The ends of the long tresses were stiff and matted, reeking of death.

The blood was real, not imagined.

Not a dream.

"No!" She shot upright on the mattress in her bra and panties, pawing at her hair in abject horror and revulsion. "Oh, no... No!"

Warm hands came to rest on her shoulders. Calm permeated her panic, and she realized it was Zael's touch on her now, his deep voice at her ear as he came to sit beside her on the bed. "Shh, it's okay. You're safe, Brynne."

"No." She was shaking, her heart banging inside her rib cage. "It's not okay."

Breaking out of his light hold, she scrambled to the edge of the mattress. Her stomach roiled with disgust for what she'd done.

For what Zael must have seen.

She felt naked, exposed. Sick with herself for countless reasons, including the fact that he was looking at her with a sympathy and understanding that she didn't deserve.

"My clothes..."

"They were ruined," he said. "I took them off you so you'd be more comfortable."

Frowning, she glanced at the closed door that sealed her inside the room with him. She didn't remember returning. She didn't remember anything after the blinding explosion of light that had filled her head. "How did I…?"

"I brought you back from Georgetown with me," he answered as he rose to his feet beside her. "As for the rest, I told Tavia and everyone else that I found you in the alley unconscious. I told them I guessed you must've fainted after your struggle with a Rogue."

"Fainted." She scoffed quietly, gesturing to his hands. "I saw your palms glowing. You zapped me with them. You knocked me out."

He stared at her, a flicker of remorse in his eyes. There was still a combativeness inside her that flared at the thought of being overpowered by anyone—even if her behavior invited it. But it was difficult to hold on to her anger toward Zael, knowing she had left him little choice but to defend himself.

He could have done anything to her in that alley tonight after he'd subdued her with his light, even kill her. Instead he brought her back to the shelter of the command center. He'd sat with her while she slept. Now he stood here offering comfort when she wouldn't blame him if he wanted nothing to do with her ever again.

Instead of turning away from her in fear or abhorrence, he had looked after her. Protected her. And he still was.

"You lied to my sister and the Order for me."

He stepped toward her. "I thought you'd want to explain to them yourself. When you're ready."

"No. I'm never going to tell them. They'll never look at me the same way again."

The idea of allowing anyone else to know what she truly was sent a shudder through her. She had protected this secret all her life, keeping herself isolated, devoting herself to her work because it was the only thing she could hold on to. The only thing she had.

But now there was Zael.

She hated that he'd seen her as she had been in that alley.

As kind as he was treating her, she couldn't delude herself into thinking he would ever forget what she was. For his own safety and her peace of mind, she hoped he would finally stay away for good.

Yet he only drew nearer.

When she pushed some of the blood-stiffened strands of hair from her face, he gently caught her hand. Shook his head slowly as he threaded his fingers through hers.

"Come with me, Brynne."

He led her into the en suite bathroom, leaving her only long enough to turn on the water in the large shower.

"Let's get you cleaned up," he said, reaching around her to unfasten her bra.

She wanted to protest his careful treatment of her, but her need for comforting overrode all of her old defenses. She was miserable and distressed, and so very tired. Tired of the hiding. Tired of the loneliness.

Her bra fell away. Zael reached for her panties and slid them over her hips, down her thighs, then bent to help her step out of them completely. This wasn't about sex, and yet she could not keep her body from responding to every light touch of his fingers, from the clean, enticing scent of him as he stood close enough that she could feel the heat of his skin.

Her *dermaglyphs* began to darken with color as her

desire awakened. She had never been ashamed of the part of her that was Breed. But she was Ancient, too, and because of that she brought her hands up to cover herself as her markings deepened, their colors flickering over her skin.

"No," he murmured. "You don't hide from me anymore. Not after tonight."

She swallowed as he drew her hands away and placed them at her sides. "Zael…"

Without another word, he walked her toward the open door of the shower. She stepped in, grateful for the wet heat of the spray. At her back, she heard Zael moving, taking off his clothes too. He walked into the shower behind her, his presence making a new heat travel down her spine.

She sighed with bone-weary pleasure as he silently gathered her tangled hair behind her, then turned her to face him under the water. Red rivulets spiraled around their feet as the blood rinsed away and ran down the drain. Wordlessly, Zael reached for a bottle of shampoo and squirted some into his palm. He washed the rest of the foulness from her hair, his fingers combing through the tangles, then guided her forehead against his shoulder as he massaged the fragrant suds into her scalp and worked the knotted tension from her nape.

No one—not in all her life—had ever taken such care with her.

That Zael would do so now, after everything he saw in her tonight, humbled her in ways she could never express.

As if he understood the depth of her weariness and her gratitude, he lifted her chin and tenderly stroked her cheek. "Tilt your head back, love."

The endearment made the tender spot in her chest tighten even more. She did as he instructed, tipping her head under the spray to wash the shampoo from her hair. It was impossible not to notice how her naked breasts brushed the smooth muscles of his chest. Her nipples hardened as he ran his fingers through her wet hair, rinsing away the suds with one hand and holding her steady with the other palm splayed at the small of her back.

When her hair was clean, he soaped her body with equal care, taking his time, massaging every inch of her with slick, strong fingers and careful hands. Brynne wanted to weep for the gift he was giving her. Not only the physical comfort of his touch and attention, but the far bigger gift of his trust.

His unquestioning confidence.

She closed her eyes under the blissful sensation of his hands moving wetly on her body, stroking away all of her fatigue.

"I was twenty before I realized what I was."

Her voice sounded rusty, her words muffled under the hiss of the spray. When her lids lifted, she found Zael's bright blue gaze locked on her. He had set the soap back on its shelf and now sluiced warm water over her arms and down the wet planes of her torso.

"I never knew my parents." She laughed brittly at the term, frowning as she recalled the circumstances of her birth. "Does a lab experiment even have parents?"

Zael stilled now, studying her. Waiting for her to find the words.

"I was one of many...offspring that came out of a laboratory run by a madman named Dragos. He was trying to create an army, one bred to his exact specifications and needs." She shook her head. "He had the last living Ancient under his control in his lab. And he had Breedmates. Dozens of them, all held captive like animals in his breeding program's cages."

Zael's expelled curse was low, and utterly profane. "I know enough about the name Dragos to be thankful the bastard has been dead these past twenty years. But I didn't know this, Brynne."

She managed a faint shrug, even though her senses cringed at the recollection of all that Dragos had done. "His lab had been operating for decades before the Order killed him. He used the Ancient and the Breedmates to produce scores of homegrown assassins called Hunters. And because that program was so successful, Dragos began another one. But instead of breeding offspring through conventional means, he decided to start playing with DNA."

Zael said nothing, and for a long while the only sound was the quiet hiss of the shower.

"He tinkered and he refined, and eventually he produced the first Breed females. Many of the subjects didn't take. But a few—like Tavia and me and a small number of others—made it to adulthood."

Zael frowned. "So, then, are you saying that Tavia... That besides being a daywalker, she's...like you?"

"More monster than Breed? No." Brynne chuckled humorlessly, having heard the hope in his careful voice. "She doesn't know anything about what I am. As far as I know, I'm the only one whose DNA recipe got fucked up. Too much Ancient in my Petri dish and not enough humanity. I should've never made it out of the lab. I was a mistake. Dragos should've put me down. He seemed to enjoy trying, once he realized what he'd created. But it's not easy to kill a monster, even one that's only a child. Pain subsides. Wounds heal. He made a game out of it, trying to test my limits, seeing what I could withstand while he kept me drugged and restrained. The things he did to me..." She let the thought trail off, unwilling to revisit the worst of her imprisonment and abuse in the lab. "When I grew too old and too strong for his games, he put me in confinement and left me there."

Zael's growl sounded more than menacing, but his touch was achingly light on her face. "How long?"

She shrugged. "Years. I didn't find my way out until after the Order had killed him and the Minions guarding the lab died too."

"Minions he'd made," Zael guessed. "And when their maker died, so did they."

"Yes. Many of Dragos's prisoners escaped that day. I broke out of my cell and I ran. I just kept running. Eventually, I landed in London. I started a new life there."

"What about Tavia? Was she a prisoner with you?"

Brynne shook her head. "She told me she was sent to live with a Minion handler from the time she was a child. She was lied to, told nothing of what she was. Dragos ensured her Breed metabolism was suppressed with medications and her handler made her believe she needed the treatments because she was ill."

"Does she know what happened to you in the lab?"

"No." God, just the thought made her cringe with humiliation. "I let her think that I was in the same program she was. It seemed easier that way. Easier for me to keep living the lie I chose, not the one Dragos forced on me."

Zael studied her soberly. "Sooner or later, don't you

think you'll have to tell her the truth?"

"And watch her shrink away from me in fear for herself and everyone she cares about?" Brynne couldn't bite back the strangled sound of anguish that bubbled in the back of her throat. "She would hate me for lying to her all this time, Zael. But not before I see her pity for what Dragos made me. He would've done me a favor if he had just taken my head and finally ended me."

"Don't say that," Zael whispered fiercely. "Don't even think it."

"It's true. You saw for yourself tonight. I'm a monster, Zael." She astonished herself by how evenly she was able to say the words to him. Words she'd never spoken before. Not to anyone. Not ever. "Every time I feed, I lose a part of who I am. And if I don't feed, if I delay it because I can't stand what I become, then it's only worse when I finally do give in. If I feel threatened, or if I'm overcome with anger, it's the same thing. I can't control it."

"What if you took a mate? One from the Breed."

Her head snapped up at that. To hear him suggest it pricked at her, even if it was a reasonable question.

"Never," she said, appalled by the very idea. "How could I expect someone to share my life when I can't be certain I won't end up hurting them? Or worse?"

He ran his fingers down the side of her arm, his eyes searching hers. "Wouldn't a blood bond with a Breed male help you cope? I'm no expert on that, but I understand the bond strengthens both of the individuals it connects."

"And if it doesn't in my case? The blood bond didn't make the Ancients less monstrous. It didn't keep some of the worst of their kind from killing their mates." She

171

vehemently shook her head. "I tried to tell you, Zael. I'm alone for a reason. By my own choice."

His hand came up to cup her cheek. "You didn't hurt me tonight."

She gave him a wry look. "Only because you hit me with a dose of Atlantean electric shock treatment before I had the chance."

He didn't as much as smile at her attempt at levity. "I shouldn't have done it. Using my power like that was a risk I never should've taken." He stared at her, his expression serious. "And if I hurt you, Brynne—"

"You didn't." She pressed her hand to his cheek. "You didn't hurt me. You helped me."

His frown eased only a degree. "That's all I wanted. I could see you were hurting, and I had to help you through it if I could." He reached around her and cut off the water. "I wasn't going to leave your side."

She stared into his brilliant blue eyes, struck by his tender words and his patient care with her. How was he able to exasperate her with his overbearing cockiness and refusal to leave her alone, yet make her heart twist with yearning at the same time?

Now that the noise of the shower was silenced, she was achingly aware of the fast, heavy pound of her pulse. Standing so close to Zael, she heard his heartbeat too. She couldn't resist placing her hand against the bronze-skinned, corded strength of his chest.

He touched her, too, brushing his fingertips over one nipple, then the other, his caress light, undemanding. A rush of arousal streaked through her, and he responded with a low, approving growl in the back of his throat.

His cock had been erect since he'd entered the shower with her, but now it surged even harder in the narrow space between their naked bodies.

"I'm afraid, Zael." It was apparently a night for first admissions, because these were further words she had never said to anyone before in her life. "You scare me. You have from the very first day I saw you."

He lifted her chin, holding her gaze as he lowered his mouth to hers. His kiss seared her senses, despite its gentleness. It answered all of her fears, more than any words could.

She'd never had someone take care of her the way he had tonight. She didn't know she could enjoy someone's touch like this, or need someone's comfort so profoundly.

No, not just someone.

Just this man.

Only Zael.

And, yes, that scared her.

It terrified her, how deeply she was beginning to care for him.

He cupped her face in his broad hand and she turned into his palm, pressing her lips to the center of it, the spot that had been glowing earlier tonight. Her tongue darted out to taste him and he growled, low and deep and primal.

It was all the warning he gave her before he swept her off her feet and up into his arms.

With her hair dripping and their bodies still wet from the shower, he strode into the bedroom with her.

CHAPTER 23

Brynne was light in his arms, her face nestled against his chest as Zael carried her out to the bedroom. He held her close, hoping she couldn't feel the fury that was coursing through him after hearing what she had suffered at the hands of the man who made her.

He seethed over those other things she didn't say.

Abuse so heinous she didn't—or could not—put it into words. But it had been evident enough on her tormented face. Whatever had been done to her physically had left no traces on her body. Her advanced metabolism would have taken care of that. It was the other scars she carried inside that had obviously wounded her far worse.

Zael wanted to roar with his rage over what she had endured.

Never again. Not so long as he was alive to stop it would she ever know pain or mistreatment.

She would never have to be alone, locked in a prison of her own making because of fear for what she was.

It was a ridiculous promise for him to make even to himself—and all the more so when he knew his actions in the alley may have jeopardized everything. Using his power in the open as he had was tantamount to broadcasting his location to every Atlantean around the globe. His kind were all connected by the light within them. It was their strength as a people, but for fugitives like Zael, it was also a weakness that could have led his enemies right to him tonight.

But the need to help Brynne had eclipsed any risk to himself.

They had made it out of the city despite his carelessness, and she was safe.

So long as he drew breath, she would always be safe. He swore it with every fiber of his being as he brought her to the edge of the bed and carefully placed her there.

He thought she would lie back, but instead she came up on her knees in front of him as he stood at the edge of the bed. Unable to keep from touching her, from kissing her, he cupped the back of her neck beneath the tendrils of her damp hair and brought her mouth up to meet his.

She tasted even sweeter tonight, her vulnerability twining with the sexy strength that had attracted him to her from the start.

That she had trusted him with her past humbled him. It made the connection he felt toward her deepen, despite old habits that not so long ago would have urged him to get out while he could.

Too late for that and he knew it. He was in deep with this woman. And the baffling thing was, he couldn't think of anywhere else he wanted to be.

When he lifted his head from her lips, she was staring

up at him with searching eyes. Although fire simmered within her dark green irises, he saw hesitancy in her gaze.

"You still want me?" Her voice sounded so small and uncertain, it raked at him. "After everything you saw tonight? After everything I told you?"

His lips curved with the arching of his brow. "Isn't it obvious?"

He could hardly hide how much he wanted her. His arousal had been achingly evident from the moment he first stepped into the shower with her. It had taken all of his self-control to simply comfort and listen to her as he lathered her beautiful body and held her in his embrace. But she had needed his understanding in those moments more than anything else he had to give her.

Now, her smoldering gaze and awakening *glyphs* told him something different.

"Yes, I want you, Brynne." He kissed her again, reaching down to stroke her naked breasts. "Nothing you said tonight diminishes that."

She swallowed hard. "But you saw—"

"Yes, I saw. But when I look at you now, I see a woman who's been through hell and back and hasn't broken. What I see when I look at you is the woman I crave more than any other." He caressed her cheek, brushing his thumb over her parted lips, noting the bright glint of her emerging fangs. "I see *you*, Brynne. And, hell yes, I want you."

His name was a jagged sigh on her lips as he reached out and framed her lovely face in his palms. He drew her toward him for a deeper claiming of her mouth. Their tongues tangled, breaths mingling in hot gusts. Her hands roamed his body, tracing the droplets of water that still clung to him from the shower. Her fingernails raked over his skin, turning his already rigid cock to heat-forged steel.

Their mouths still joined in a fevered kiss, he reached down to caress her, too, hungry to feel her naked flesh in his hands. Her nipples were pebbled and hot as he rolled and tweaked them between his fingers. Her belly was firm and smooth like velvet under his palms as he skimmed lower, nudging her thighs apart when he reached the silkiness of her sex.

She moaned as he delved into the wet cleft of her body. She moved in soft undulations as he stroked her, his fingers slipping between her satiny folds. Her clit was ripe and swollen, a temptation he could not resist. She writhed as he teased and caressed her, her spine arching when he entered her with one finger, then another.

"Zael," she whispered breathlessly against his mouth as he thrust in and out, his thumb working her clit in a relentless rhythm. "Oh, God."

He didn't let up until she came. And when she shuddered and broke with her release, he swallowed her sharp cry with a possessive, claiming kiss.

He wanted to be inside her. His cock was more than eager, engorged and dripping with need for her.

But Brynne had other plans.

Still panting from her climax, she reached down to grasp his heavy shaft. Her fingers slid up and down his length, over the broad crown that was slick with his juices. He hissed with the pleasure of her touch, the firm and steady power of her strokes.

She moved in closer to him, taking one of his nipples into her mouth as she continued to torment him with her hands on him. And then she moved lower, her pink little tongue lapping at stray water droplets on his abdomen and hip before her mouth closed around the head of his cock.

Her lips held him firmly as her tongue flicked along the underside of his shaft with each deep stroke of her mouth. "Fuck, that feels good," he groaned, coiling her hair around his fist like a rope because he needed something to ground him as she licked and sucked every hard inch of him.

He moaned sharply at the light graze of her teeth and fangs against his flesh—not because it startled him, but because of how badly he wanted to know her bite. Anywhere. Everywhere. He just didn't want her to stop.

When she glanced up at him, her eyes glowed with hot amber sparks. She was beautiful, even like this. Hell, especially like this.

Fierce.

Carnal.

His.

He held her transformed gaze, needing her to see that he was still with her. Ready to take her as far as she wanted to go.

It stunned him how deeply he felt it.

From the flicker of understanding in her eyes, he saw that it stunned her too.

But while he wasn't uncertain, she drew back from him, averting her gaze. He refused to let her retreat. And he needed to be inside her.

Catching her shoulders in his hands, he eased her back onto the bed and followed her down, spreading her legs as he positioned himself between them. She closed her eyes as he settled atop her.

"No, Brynne." He stroked her cheek. "Look at me, love. See *me* now."

Her lids flicked open, the glow of her transformed eyes radiating otherworldly heat.

And desire.

Those amber coals surged brighter as he entered her with a slow, filling thrust. He refused to let her look away, holding her gaze as he rocked in and out of her, one arm propped beside her, his free hand stroking the elegant patterns and changeable colors of her *dermaglyphs*.

God, had he actually been idiot enough to suggest that she take another male as her mate? The idea of her bonding with someone else, in blood or affection, raked at him like daggers.

"You're mine," he growled as he drove into her. "Look at me and know it's true, Brynne."

A defeated sound slipped past her lips. But she held his gaze with a ferocity that shook him. She knew. Even if she wasn't prepared to say the words, she knew it in her heart.

She belonged to him.

Zael didn't know where they were heading together.

Their worlds had never seemed further apart than they had earlier tonight. Now, with their eyes locked on each other as they both tumbled into a staggering release, their lives had never seemed so impossibly entwined.

CHAPTER 24

It had taken several hours to clear the city and put down all of the Rogues. With dawn soon to break, Lucan and the patrol teams had returned to headquarters. He'd barely had a chance to clean his weapons and wash away the grit and filth of combat when Gideon excitedly summoned him down to the command center's tech lab.

Lucan entered the room filled with computer equipment. Monitors were mounted on nearly every square inch of wall space, all of them busy with scrolling data and images. "I hope you've got good news."

"I think we could be only minutes away from something," Gideon said, giving him a distracted glance over his shoulder as he continued typing on a keyboard with one hand, while the other swiped through data on a tablet.

Darion was in the room, too, seated in front of one of the large monitors. "He broke through a second layer of encryption. This machine is running a series of decryption key programs and looking for vulnerabilities in the network security."

Dare must have come straight from his post-patrol shower to the tech lab. His dark chestnut hair was still damp above the collar of his black T-shirt as he avidly studied Gideon's work.

Lucan's son had always been possessed of a curious mind in addition to his shrewd tactical skills and dauntless courage in the field. Gabrielle liked to say their son was a born leader, like his father. As much as Lucan was inclined to agree—and as much as the commander in him valued Dare as a warrior and comrade—he much preferred to see his son pursuing enemies in the virtual realm, as he was now with Gideon.

"How many layers of encryption are we looking at?" Lucan asked, glancing at Gideon.

"I've detected five, but I could be wrong."

"Meaning there could be less than that?"

Gideon's dubious look wasn't promising. "I told you, man, whoever's working Opus's communications knows their shit. And then some. Brick wall after dead end after quicksand trap. But we're getting there. All I need is one little piece of luck with this decryption key sequence, and I'll have—"

As Gideon spoke, the monitor in front of him went dark.

Then another one went black.

"What the fuck?" Gideon vaulted to his feet and hurried to a different computer.

One by one, every screen in the room blinked from buzzing activity to full-stop, nothing.

"It's not the power," Darion said, gesturing to the lights that hadn't so much as flickered.

"The entire command center is on private underground generators," Gideon murmured distractedly. "We can run for a full year without power. He tried another workstation without success, swearing harshly.

Lucan scowled. "Then what the hell is going on?"

"I don't know. *Fuck.*" Gideon raked both hands through his spiky blond hair, disheveling it. "This shouldn't be happening. It's completely impossible, and yet it's as if something has interrupted our…"

His words trailed off as each monitor abruptly came back online.

Not with Gideon's data or program feeds filling the screens.

But the face of a woman.

An incredibly beautiful woman with long, platinum hair and eyes the color of Arctic ice. Those frigid eyes stared out of a heart-shaped face with high, sharp cheekbones and pale, milky skin that glowed with the luminescence of a pearl. Her beauty was too menacing to be called angelic. Too ageless and unearthly to be confined to any description at all.

There was no need for introductions.

This woman could be none other than the Atlanteans' queen.

"Holy shit," Gideon whispered.

Darion's response was a low hiss. "Selene."

Both Breed males moved in to flank Lucan in front of the largest of the monitors.

Selene's gaze traveled deliberately over each of them before settling on Lucan.

"Lucan Thorne," she said, her voice clear and unrushed. The voice of a being accustomed to reigning over all others. The voice of a disapproving goddess. "This conversation is long overdue."

"Not to mention unexpected." He didn't as much as blink as he spoke. "Of course, the way things have been going lately, I shouldn't be surprised that you'd choose to make your appearance now."

Her brows arched, as if their troubles amused her. "Don't tell me the mighty Order is being pushed to their limits by a gang of violent opportunists?"

"Do we have you to thank for that?"

"Me?"

He grunted at her noncommittal reply. "Someone's calling the shots for Opus Nostrum. Is it you?"

She smiled now, a cold smile full of disdain. "Don't be absurd. Opus is nothing to me. Their trivial efforts are nothing compared to what I am capable of on my own."

Darion exhaled a sharp breath. "That's what Reginald Crowe said about you too. Right after he tried to detonate a UV bomb in the middle of a Breed peace summit. He lost his head to the Order for that."

Selene's narrowed glower slid to Dare. "When the time comes to wipe out your kind, Darion Thorne, I won't need someone like Reginald Crowe to do it. Or Opus Nostrum."

Lucan's blood spiked to hear the Atlantean queen speak his son's name. As leader of the Order, to hear her confirm what Crowe had asserted—that Selene was plotting war against the Breed—only added more fury to the fire that flared in him.

"What do you want, Selene?"

"To start with, the traitor, Ekizael. He is one of my subjects and I will see him stand trial for his defection."

Lucan kept his expression neutral. "Why do you expect that I can help with that?"

"Don't make the mistake of thinking I'm a fool," she replied, her smile cold. "Zael is in your city. Unless I miss my guess, he has allied with you against me."

"If he has, you've certainly given him ample reason," Lucan parried back. "You had his comrade, Cass, struck down in the street like an animal by your guards. Then you sent more guards after Zael when he tried to protect Cass's daughter from being captured by you."

Selene's rage flashed across her ethereal features. "Jordana is *my* daughter's child. My last living kin. But then I'm sure the Order is aware of that too."

"Yes. There's a lot we've heard about you, Selene. Not a very flattering picture."

Her chin rose imperiously. "You know nothing of me or my people. Tell me, Lucan Thorne, what do you truly know of yours?"

Reflections of all the violence and bloodshed his otherworldly forebears had delivered during their time on this planet filled his head. They'd been a terror worse than anything that had been seen before or since. And although the Ancients had been ruthless in their dealings with mankind and even with their own sons among the Breed, it could not compare to the decimation they visited on Atlantis.

"I know my race's fathers attacked you without provocation," Lucan said soberly. "I know they killed thousands of innocent people among your population and drove you into exile."

"They annihilated us," she corrected sharply. "But that was then. It only served to make us stronger. It made me stronger."

Although her fury obviously still boiled, her tone was too brittle to be simply anger. Lucan had not forgotten that Selene was betrayed by someone she once loved, and that the betrayal was the spark that lit her destruction. She was still nursing old wounds. Wounds that had festered, making her dangerous, a viper cornered and coiled, ready to strike.

"Your own people seem to think the attack all those centuries ago made you unstable," Lucan pointed out. "There are many who think it made you dangerous, unfit to rule."

She barked out a caustic laugh. "Did Zael tell you that? Or was it Cassianus? Be careful what you believe when you listen to men with flimsy honor."

Lucan had learned enough about the honor of both Atlantean males to trust what he'd been told. If Selene had been a good and just queen once, as Lucan understood to be true, that benevolent ruler bore no resemblance to the scorned Valkyrie in front of him now.

"Cass believed it enough to take Jordana away from you," he reminded her. "And that's not all he took when he fled your realm."

The decision to play his strongest card now produced the effect he'd hoped for. Selene was visibly taken aback at the news. Her eyes widened in surprise, in accusation. "You have the crystal. Cass gave it to you?"

"Does it matter how we obtained it?"

She smiled, but it was a tight expression. "You have no idea what to do with that kind of power. It is beyond your limited capability or your unsophisticated, Earth-bound technology."

Lucan shrugged. "We know that two crystals can be used as a weapon, as the Ancients used against Atlantis. We know you have only one in your possession. The one currently protecting you and your realm."

"How clever you must think you are," she replied, acid in her chilly tone.

Darion scoffed. "Call it whatever you want. Just know that you're never going to have another crystal. You'll never be trusted with that kind of power."

"I suppose you think the Order can stand in my way?" she countered, zeroing all of her outrage on Dare again. "The Breed is hardly more than mortal, as far as I'm concerned. You are practically human, and just as offensive to me."

Dare smirked, too bold for his own good. "Are you forgetting, Selene? There's Atlantean in our blood too."

"Only the foulest blood from our most faithless," she shot back. "I could erase you all from the face of the Earth. Don't think I'm not tempted to do it right now."

"But you can't," Dare said, speaking despite Lucan's low growl of warning that he tread carefully with this volatile new opponent. "The biggest fool is the one who thinks that he—or she—has no weaknesses."

Selene's glower should have withered Darion, but he didn't as much as flinch. Lucan agreed with everything his son said, but there was no mistaking that the young warrior was making a very dangerous and personal enemy here today.

The Atlantean queen's eyes flashed as she glared at Darion. "You wish to test me? Do it at your own peril. I warn you, you do not want to stand against me."

Lucan moved closer to the monitor. "There's not a man or woman among the Order who will bow to you either. I promise you that."

She smiled as if he had just invited her out for tea. "I don't intend to make the Order bow, Lucan. I mean to make you break. And that is my promise to you." Her gaze slid to Darion. "To all of you."

The monitors abruptly went black.

Selene was gone.

As if no interruption had occurred, all of Gideon's machines came back online, programs churning data as they had been before, screens filled with scrolling code and images.

Gideon ran a hand over his scalp. "Holy. Fucking. Hell."

Lucan cursed roundly, his pulse hammering in his temples and behind his sternum.

"How the fuck did she do that?" Darion demanded. "What the hell happened that she would choose to confront us now?"

"It's my fault." Zael's deep voice was contrite, coming from where he now stood in the open entryway of the tech lab. "I opened the door. I led her to you tonight."

CHAPTER 25

Zael could not have been more stunned than when he approached the command center's tech lab just in time to see Selene deliver her threat to the Order before vanishing off the monitors.

Although it had been hard to leave Brynne sleeping naked and peaceful in her guest room upstairs, he had been interested to meet with the warriors and discuss the outcome of the night's patrols.

Now, as he stepped inside the tech lab, the three warriors in the room all stared at him expectantly.

"What do you mean this is your fault, Zael?" Lucan's brow was deeply furrowed, his tone guarded. "How did you open the door to Selene? What the fuck is going on here?"

"Tonight, in Georgetown," he explained, sober with remorse. "After I left here to look for Brynne, I found her in an alleyway. She'd been in an…altercation with a Rogue." He kept his disclosure purposely vague, still mindful of Brynne's trust and confidence in him. "I used my powers—the light in my palms—to calm her, to help her. An Atlantean's light is a powerful thing. None of us can discharge it without the rest of our kind feeling the ripple of energy. I'm sorry. I understood the risk, and I made the choice anyway."

Gideon studied him. "Are you saying Selene triangulated your location based on that?"

Zael nodded. "She knows I'm here."

"No shit, she knows you're here," Darion interjected. "She just demanded we turn you over to her to stand trial as a traitor."

Fuck. He'd had a bounty on his head for too long to register any kind of surprise at that news, but he never meant to pull the Order into his problems.

Zael swore under his breath. "Now that she knows I'm in D.C., don't think she'll hesitate to send her guards to try to collect me. They could be on their way even as we speak."

"Then they'll have a fight on their hands," Lucan said. "We're damned well not going to surrender you to Selene. As commander of the Order, my first priority is the protection of this location and everyone inside it. That includes you now, Zael."

The conviction in Lucan's statement moved him, but Zael shook his head. "I appreciate that, but I would never ask it of you."

"You didn't. I'm offering," Lucan said. "You're a friend to the Order. We protect our own."

Zael smiled. He had his own warrior's code, even if his blade and shield had once been bloodied in Selene's name. He inclined his head at Lucan. "Because I feel likewise about the Order, I cannot stay. It will be better for everyone here—safer for all—if I go."

All three warriors standing before him appeared ready to argue his decision, but instead of them answering, it was Brynne's voice he heard behind him.

"Go where?"

He turned to face her. She stood there, looking drowsy and adorable in her untucked button-down and black pants that hugged her long legs. Her dark hair was a mass of bed-tossed waves that made his pulse kick with the urge to have her beneath him again.

Zael couldn't couch his pleasure at seeing her, nor did he care if the rush of affection he felt was on display in his gaze for everyone in the room.

"To the colony," he murmured in answer to her question, regret in each syllable. "I should go as soon as possible."

The expression on her lovely face was one of confusion. And more than a trace of hurt. "You're leaving."

There was accusation in the words. A look of resignation creeping into her dark green eyes.

"Selene knows Zael is here," Lucan informed her.

"How?" Brynne's troubled gaze never left Zael. "What's going on?"

"When I used my light in that alley earlier tonight, it broadcast my location to the realm." He held out his hands, palms open to her. The light was absent now, but she still stared at him in dawning misery.

"Oh, my God. She found you because of me?"

He firmly shook his head. "My actions, Brynne. My decision."

"She knows Zael is in D.C., and she knows he's allied with the Order," Lucan added. "She just overtook our computer systems to inform us that she expects us to turn him over to her."

Brynne sucked in a shallow breath. "She'll kill you."

"Most certainly," Zael agreed. But then, that had been the risk from the moment he first crossed the barrier that shielded the realm from the outside world.

It had been easier to accept that fact in the past, easier to disregard it. The thought of death took on new meaning when his heart still beat with the memory of Brynne tangled naked with him in his arms.

He wanted to draw her into his embrace and reassure her that if they separated now, it wouldn't be forever. But he wasn't certain he could make that promise to her. Not out loud. Selene drawing a line in the sand with the Order had changed everything.

Until the threat of war with her had been neutralized, so long as he was within Selene's reach, Zael was a hazard to anyone close to him. Selene's grudges knew no limits. Neither did her wrath.

"Selene can make all the demands she wants," Lucan said. "She's going to find out that the only thing she'll get by pushing us into a corner is war."

Darion made a derisive sound. "She'd better prepare herself for disappointment. I'd like nothing better than to deliver her defeat personally."

Zael wanted to warn the tenacious Breed male that Selene was not an opponent who would go down easy. Before he was too eager to charge into battle against her, Darion Thorne would do well to remember that it had taken the combined efforts of several Ancients to bring Selene down the first time, and only because they were aided by sabotage, betrayal, and stolen otherworld technology.

But that was a conversation for another time.

Right now, all of Zael's attention was rooted on Brynne. He watched her absorb all of this unpleasant news in silence. "I can't stay now," he told her gently. "I've already stayed too long."

She didn't reply. The tenderness they had shared a short while ago was still there in her eyes as she looked at him, but Zael also saw the beginnings of mistrust. Her dark lashes shuttered her gaze, as if she were already starting to withdraw from him.

"I have to go, Brynne."

"Yes. Of course, you do." She nodded crisply, refusing to meet his gaze. "I understand."

No, he didn't think she did. He knew her too well now to mistake her emotional retreat. He was far too familiar with her attempts to push against anything, or anyone, that might be able to hurt her. He felt that resistance from her now.

More than anything, he wanted to close the distance and offer her a proper explanation—at the very least, make her understand that his leaving didn't diminish anything they'd shared. It didn't lessen what he felt for her. If anything, it was only driving home to him just how much she meant to him.

In the corridor outside the tech lab came the commotion of approaching people. In moments, the room was filled with a cacophony of voices as most of the warriors and many of the Order's women crowded into the room to hear what had happened.

After Lucan relayed his conversation with Selene, the Order's leader turned to Zael. "Now more than ever we need to take steps to ensure that Selene does not amass any more power than she already possesses."

Zael nodded. "We are in complete agreement on

that."

"And the colony?" Lucan prompted.

"What about them?"

"They also have one of the crystals. I will need their promise that if the time should come that Selene escalates this thing into war, the colony will pledge their crystal to us."

Zael slowly shook his head. "That won't happen, Lucan. As I told you, the colony's crystal is their shield from the world outside—the same way Selene's remaining one protects what's left of the Atlantean realm. Without it in place, the colony—like Selene—is vulnerable to breach and attack. They will never give it up. For their own security, they can't."

"Then I will need their agreement that they will never surrender it to Selene either."

"That much I can assure you," Zael said.

Lucan didn't look convinced. "I hope you'll understand when I say that I need more than that to make me comfortable that the colony can be relied upon in this. I need *their* word, Zael, not just yours."

"The colony wants peace as much as anyone. I have to believe the elders can be persuaded to give your their commitment that the crystal will never be given up to Selene."

"Excellent," Lucan announced. "I hope you're right. We can make arrangements to leave for the colony as soon as you're ready."

"We?" Zael nearly choked at the suggestion, but it was obvious from the warrior's determined expression that he had every expectation of making the trip with him. "Er, that's not... Lucan, that will not be possible."

A black brow arched in challenge. "I wasn't asking,

Zael."

"I realize that. However, the colony does not permit outsiders. They never have. Most certainly not a member of the Order, and least of all the Order's formidable Gen One leader." Zael cleared his throat. "I'm afraid your reputation precedes you, Lucan."

"They will have to make an exception."

"They won't. And if I try to bring you—or any Breed warrior—through the veil, the sentries on watch will have no choice but to kill us both."

Lucan grunted. "They'll die trying."

"With all due respect, my friend, you're only proving the point." Zael held the hard gray stare, knowing if the tables were turned, he'd likely be pressing the Order just as insistently. "The colony has survived this long because they're hidden, protected by the crystal. I am the only one they allow to travel in and out, and that's by special arrangement with the council elders. I won't break that trust by bringing a warrior to their doorstep." Zael shook his head. "I'm afraid I cannot accommodate you on this, Lucan, but I will do my best to present the Order's case to the elders."

"And if you are unable to convince the colony to ally with the Order? Granted, diplomacy has never been my strong suit, but I'd feel a hell of a lot more comfortable sending someone in to plead the case for us alongside you. Someone who can speak for the Order and represent the Breed as well."

"Perhaps I should be the one to go with Zael," Jordana suggested from where she stood with her mate, Nathan. "I'm part of both the Atlantean world and the Order's now. Let me speak for both."

"Not without me at your side," Nathan said, his tone

dark and protective. "No fucking way am I letting you near that place or any other Atlantean stronghold unless I can be there too. It was only a couple of weeks ago that Selene did her damnedest to take you from me. Never again."

"Nathan is right," Zael agreed. "And as an Atlantean, you would not be permitted to leave the colony if you did pass through the veil, Jordana. They would hold you for your own protection and theirs."

"Then what about Brynne?" Tavia's question drew the attention of everyone, though no one looked less enthused than Brynne herself.

Eyes widened in surprise, she glanced from the intrigued faces of the Order and their mates, to Zael. He could read the reluctance in her gaze.

She frowned at her sister. "Tavia, I... I don't think that's a good idea. I don't imagine Zael would think so either."

No, he didn't, and for many reasons. Not the least of which being that, like Nathan with Jordana, he wanted to keep Brynne as far away from the front lines of the coming battle with Selene as possible too. She would be safest here with the Order. Even if leaving her behind was the last thing he wanted to do.

But Tavia didn't give him or Brynne the chance to argue.

"Why not you, Brynne? Bringing a warrior from the Order is out of the question, but why not a diplomat who can also demonstrate to the colony that the Breed can be trusted as an ally if and when the time should come? Especially one that Zael can personally vouch for?"

As much as he wanted to reject the idea outright, he

had to admit there was some merit in it. He could say all he wanted to attempt to convince his people to look at the Breed as something other than an enemy, but nothing would be so persuasive as meeting one of their kind and seeing that they had similar goals and desires for the world they inhabited.

Zael considered for longer than he should have. It was a bad idea, and he knew it. But as reluctant as he was to drag Brynne into the fray with him, the even less palatable option was leaving without her.

"All right," he relented, catching Brynne's reticent gaze. "But we don't have much time. If you agree, then we can—and should—depart immediately."

CHAPTER 26

From the moment Tavia suggested it, Brynne had her doubts about acting as the Order's liaison with the Atlantean colony.

Those doubts hadn't left her, even after she and Zael had departed on the Order's jet out of D.C., headed for Athens, Greece, where a private car had picked them up and taken them to a small Mediterranean port and a fully equipped sailing yacht that waited at the dock for their arrival.

Zael hadn't told anyone precisely where the colony was located. That was a secret he intended to keep, even from her. And since he couldn't teleport with a non-Atlantean accompanying him, they had to travel there by more mundane means.

Although mundane was hardly how she would describe the billowing white sails and the endless, impossibly blue water that surrounded them on every side of the boat as it cut through the waves with Zael standing at the helm.

For what seemed like endless hours, they had sailed straight into the open sea. By Brynne's estimation, at the clip they were going, they should have been able to spot the shoreline of the African continent any minute now.

Should have…but didn't.

She ventured out from beneath the shade of the bimini where she sat near Zael and peered at the horizon ahead of them.

No land in sight.

Nothing but turquoise water as far as she could see. And a thick, fluffy cloud bank that clung to the horizon. One they seemed to have been chasing for a good part of the day.

Finding no landmarks to gauge their progress, she ducked back under the canopy, glad for the shelter from the sun's rays. Even though she was a daywalker, the idea of lingering in open sunlight for long periods of time went against her nature.

She glanced at Zael, who was looking far too enticing as he stood behind the ship's wheel in his white tunic and linen pants. When they'd arrived on the sailboat, Brynne had found similar clothing in her size pressed and waiting for her. She toyed idly with the string that laced the front of her top.

"We must be getting close…to somewhere?"

The trace of a smile edged Zael's sensual mouth. "We are."

"You don't need a map or anything to stay on course?"

"There's no map that will take us where we need to go." He slid a wry glance at her, blue eyes the same brilliant hue as the sea now glimmering with droll humor. "You'll just have to trust me not to lead you astray."

She met his look with an arch of her brows. "Seems to me you've been trying to lead me astray from the first moment we met. I'm surprised you didn't blindfold me as soon as we landed in Athens."

He grunted, his gaze heating. "An interesting option. I wish I'd thought of that."

She laughed, even as her veins throbbed in answer to his playful suggestion. It was good to see some of his tension ease. Since they'd left to begin this journey, he'd been uncharacteristically quiet—more contemplative than she'd ever seen him. No doubt his thoughts were distant, his worries more onerous than she could ever comprehend.

Compounded by the fact that he was saddled with unwanted company on this journey, which might mean neither one of them would be welcome at their mysterious destination.

"I shouldn't be here, Zael."

She had seen his reaction when Tavia first suggested the idea. He hadn't like it any more than Brynne had. If not for being pressured by his alliance with Lucan and the Order, she had no doubt that Zael would have returned to his people alone. Possibly for good.

Instead, he was taking an enormous risk with the bond he had to his own kind by bringing a member of their enemy's race into their midst. Especially after he'd personally witnessed her at her monstrous worst.

"It's my fault any of this is happening in the first place," she added. "If you hadn't used your power to help me, Selene never would've known where you were."

His brows drew together. "None of this is your fault.

I knew what I was doing. I'd do again, if it meant the difference between my safety and yours. As for Selene, she put a target on my back a long time ago. If I let fear of that fact dictate how I choose to live, I may as well lie down and let her finish me now."

Brynne couldn't help but admire his courage. She liked to think that she was brave too—a survivor—but her fears had colored every aspect of her life. Fear had kept her isolated and shut off from the people around her. Fear had kept her alone...lonely.

Until Zael.

"Thank you," she murmured, emotion swelling in her breast as she looked at him, this man who had drawn her out of the shadows of her existence and into the light.

His light.

She swallowed against the affection that clogged her throat as she held his unwavering gaze. "Thank you for helping me, Zael. And I don't mean just last night in that alley."

His mouth curved as he reached out to her and brought her under the shelter of his strong arm. He kissed the top of her head, his heartbeat thundering against her ear as she rested her cheek against him.

He held there for a long while, one arm on the wheel of the sailboat, the other wrapped comfortingly around her shoulders. Brynne couldn't deny her contentment, the perfect moments of bliss, as they stood together at the helm while the boat rocked over the waves, still chasing that frothy white mass of clouds near the horizon.

But for all of his warmth with her, there was an undercurrent of tension in the sinew of his body.

Something troubled him. She felt it even before he spoke.

"When we get to the colony, Brynne, it will be better if no one knows that we're involved." When she drew back to look at him, she found his expression grave with warning. "They will not understand."

"You mean they won't approve."

He acknowledged with a slight nod. "Bringing you in as an envoy of the Order is asking much of them to begin with. If they think I'm motivated by my feelings for you, they may be less apt to hear us out."

"Of course," she answered, nodding as if she didn't feel the pang of hurt inside. Perhaps she needed the reminder that he was only bringing her to his people in an official capacity, and nothing more. Better she understand that now, before her heart flitted off any further into fantasies of what it would be like to feel this man at her side for always, not just a few pleasurable hours.

She and Zael came from different worlds; she knew that. Selene's personally delivered threat had driven that point home with stark clarity.

But hearing him remind her that she didn't belong with his people—that she shouldn't expect them to accept her, and particularly not if she arrived there on the arm of one of their own—made all of the contentment she'd felt moments ago dry up and scatter on the warm breeze that blew in off the water.

She used the excuse of a rolling wave to extricate herself from his loose embrace. "How long has it been since you were at the colony?"

He gave a vague shrug. "A handful of years. But time is measured differently by my people. Years pass as days after you've lived for many centuries. Or longer."

"How long for you?"

"My age? I was there when Atlantis fell." Some of his wry humor returned to his deep voice now. "Suffice it to say I stopped counting the centuries a long time ago."

"So old," she said, returning his grin. "You don't seem a day over a thousand."

He gave her a sensual smirk that sent a lick of heat through her veins. "Don't tempt me, or I might change course just so I can make you eat those words."

She nearly begged him to make good on that threat. But as they spoke, she noticed how the sunshine that had followed them the entirety of their sail had started to become lost amid the curtain of thickening mist they were passing through now.

No, not quite a mist, Brynne realized.

It was the bank of clouds that had seemed perpetually floating just beyond the bow of the boat. They had finally reached it. Sailed directly into the heart of it, in fact.

And now that she was paying attention, she saw that the waves had begun to gentle beneath them. Instead of slicing through the water, the boat had slowed to nearly a stall.

Zael let go of the wheel and stepped out of the cockpit. Brynne followed warily, mesmerized by the stillness of the sea as it lapped gently against the hull. The cloud that enveloped them was cool against her face as she walked carefully to where Zael now stood at the bow of the boat.

"What's happening?"

He didn't answer. He glanced at her, no trace of

levity or flirtation in his eyes anymore.

Only sober purpose.

Raising his hand—the one bearing the silvery Atlantean amulet at his wrist—Zael closed his eyes and went very still for a moment. As he did, the small crystal on the leather thong on his wrist began to glow.

The foggy mist hanging in the air began to swirl and dissipate before Brynne's face.

When it cleared, she found herself looking at a gleaming, sun-spangled island paradise.

A pristine stretch of pearly white beach ribboned the perimeter of the land, which was resplendent with soaring, lush green hillsides dotted with flowering bushes, vineyards, and citrus orchards. Staggered rows of snow-white stucco cottages with sunbaked, terra cotta tile roofs overlooked the water as they followed the land's incline and flanked the narrow passages of meandering footpaths and cobbled streets.

It was breathtaking.

Magical.

The most beautiful place she'd ever seen.

When she tore her gaze away to look at Zael, she found him studying her unabashed awe.

"Welcome to the colony, Brynne."

CHAPTER 27

"Zael," Brynne murmured warily, nodding toward the highest hill. "Up there."

"Yes. I see them."

He'd spotted the four Atlantean sentries the instant the sailboat had cleared the mist. He'd felt their energy even before he and Brynne approached the colony's veil—as his fellow Atlanteans had most surely felt his. The three males and one female stood on the promontory of the hillside scouting the water, observing as the sailboat entered the protected domain.

Beside him, Brynne drew in a sharp breath. "Zael, their palms."

Light glowed from the scouts' hands, the combined power holding the boat suspended in the water. Because they knew him—two of the sentries having served with him in Selene's legion before the fall of the realm—his vessel was merely stopped on the water, not immediately driven back... Or worse.

"It's all right," he told Brynne. "They don't mean us

harm. Not unless they decide we pose an immediate threat."

He lifted his hand to them, his own palm glowing dimly in greeting. Inside the protective veil provided by the colony's crystal, Atlanteans could use their light freely, without the threat of betraying themselves to anyone on the outside.

As he held his hand up to the lookouts, the sea started to churn and bubble between the boat and the beach. Brynne gripped the railing, a look of astonishment on her face as a platform of smooth stone rose up from the surface of the water to meet them, forming a temporary dock that led to the shore.

"That's amazing," she gasped, her eyes filled with wonderment.

Zael dimmed his light and gestured for her to follow him. "Here we go. Let me do the talking when we reach the shore."

She nodded and stepped in behind him as they disembarked and headed across the wet stones toward the beach. The four sentries materialized on the sand, forming a physical barrier at the end of the path.

"They aren't carrying weapons," Brynne remarked quietly. "That must be a good sign, right?"

Zael didn't reply. He kept his gaze trained straight ahead, knowing all too well that his comrades wouldn't need weapons to disable Brynne and him if they felt they posed a threat.

Hard stares greeted Zael as he strode up onto the beach with Brynne at his side.

One of the two former legion soldiers gaped at him in outrage. "What the fuck is this?"

"Elyon." Zael acknowledged the sentry with a nod.

"I'm here to see the council of elders."

"Bringing an outsider with you?" The sentry scoffed. His brows shot up, his blue gaze incredulous under the crown of his golden curls. "Have you lost your mind, Zael?"

The other of his former comrades, a craggy-faced, dark-haired behemoth named Vaenor, stared at Brynne. "What's the meaning of this, Zael? Does this human understand you may have just sealed her death warrant by bringing her through the veil?"

Zael didn't correct the error, nor did Brynne. She stood silent, didn't as much as flinch under the harsh glower that used to make seasoned Atlantean soldiers quiver in their boots, nor the grimly issued warning.

Pride swelled in Zael's chest, along with a dark, vibrating current of protectiveness that made him fully ready to take down all four of these guards if any one of them dared an untoward move against her. For all of the many reasons he should have been reluctant to bring Brynne to the colony, this was the one that settled upon him most heavily now.

He would destroy anyone who sought to harm her, even his own people.

Even if it meant losing his place with the only home he still had.

After a long moment, Vaenor's scowl slid to Zael. "I knew sooner or later you'd wear out your welcome here. This move is ballsy, even for you, *captain*."

The male leaned heavily on Zael's old title, his disapproval more than evident in his tone.

Indara, the sole female of the group, nodded as Vaenor spoke. "He's right, Zael. The elders will have no choice but to banish you."

"If they don't order us to take both of your heads first," added Rasaphael, the fourth member of the guard detail.

A booming, deep voice rose above the others. "That decision will be the elders' and no one else's."

Zael knew the Atlantean who had materialized on the beach behind the sentries. Nethilos, one of six individuals who comprised the council of the elders, now strode up to confront Zael.

The tall male's shoulder-length, walnut-brown hair was brushed back from his dark olive face, making his golden-brown eyes seem even more arresting than usual. His brows furrowed as he glanced from Brynne to Zael.

"We've known each other too long for games, so I'll assume this breach of colony law is with good reason."

"It is," Zael said, inclining his head in deference to the elder who was also a long-respected friend. "I'm here on a matter that concerns everyone within and outside the veil."

Nethilos considered him in a prolonged, measured silence. "Do you come here with a pure heart and good intent?"

It was a vow Zael was asked to make each time he returned to the colony from outside. And one he gave freely now. "Yes, my friend."

"And you?" Nethilos demanded of Brynne.

She glanced anxiously at Zael, then answered when he acknowledged with a subtle nod. "Yes. You have my word."

"Then that is good enough for me," Nethilos announced. "Whether it will be good enough for the rest of the council remains to be seen."

The elder glanced grimly at Zael, a silent command

to follow him as he waved off the sentries and began walking back up the beach. Zael and Brynne fell in alongside him, heading for the cobbled street across the sand.

Nethilos strode in silence for a long while, leading them up one of the island's twisting paths that would eventually bring them to the heart of the colony's settlement.

He cast a sidelong look at Zael. "Despite the...unusual circumstances, Diandra will be pleased to know you're here. As will Neriah. They both spoke of you for weeks after your last visit."

Although Brynne said nothing, Zael felt her unease at the mention of the two colony females. "If I'm so fortunate," he told the elder, "I shall look forward to some of your mate's fine cooking and your daughter's lively music."

Nethilos grunted, and while Zael had been careful not to glance Brynne's way as he indirectly explained who the women were, he figured he'd be a fool to expect the unspoken exchange to go unnoticed by his wise old friend.

They had known each other for ages, although Nethilos had been a teacher during his tenure in the realm and Zael a soldier. Following the ruin of Atlantis and the defections that followed, Nethilos had helped to establish the colony. He was the first elder to agree to give asylum to Zael and the other legion warriors who had fled Selene's rule. Over the centuries, their friendship and mutual trust had remained strong.

But Nethilos was only one of six elders on the council. There were five others they would need to win over, more than one of whom would find great satisfaction in holding Zael's fate in their hands.

Not to mention Brynne's.

As the three of them continued to walk the cobbled road, a few curious heads popped out of open cottage windows and doorways to peer at the newcomers. Zael knew almost everyone in the population of a few hundred Atlantean exiles. He was always a bit of a curiosity on those rare times he returned to the island, but it wasn't him drawing the most attention now.

"We've never had a human on the island," Nethilos remarked discreetly, glancing at Brynne. "Then again, I don't imagine we do now either."

Zael uttered a quiet curse as he paused to face the elder. "Brynne is Breed."

Nethilos's brows arched over widened eyes. "Daywalker?"

She gave him a slight nod.

"Remarkable. And utterly reckless on your part, Zael."

"I brought Brynne out of necessity," he hastened to explain. "She's here as an emissary for her people. And for the Order."

"The Order?" Nethilos's expression went from surprise to darkening suspicion. "This is no breach of colony law, Zael. What you've done is something much more dangerous."

"Yes," he agreed. "And I never would've risked it without damned good cause. We need to discuss an alliance between the Order and the colony. The elders need to understand the Order's position and the goals they share with the colony."

"Our shared goals? What could we possibly have in common with Lucan Thorne and his warriors?"

"Selene," Zael stated grimly. "She's threatening war with the outside world, and the Order specifically."

"And that's our concern, why?"

Brynne spoke up now. "Because for her to start a war with the Breed—for her to be certain she will win—she needs to have a second crystal."

"The Order has one," Zael confessed to his friend. "Cassianus left it hidden where only Jordana would find it."

Nethilos scrubbed a hand over his firm jaw. "The rumors were true. The bastard really did steal one."

Zael gave a sober nod. "Good for all of us, or Selene would already have everything she needs to be unstoppable."

"And the other crystal is here in the colony," Brynne added.

"I know I don't need to convince you that neither of our crystals can end up in Selene's hands," Zael said.

"The colony will never surrender our crystal. It would be the beginning of our end if we lose the only thing that's kept us safe all this time."

Zael agreed completely. "Don't think Selene hasn't thought of that every day since you and I and all of the others escaped the realm. She's growing restless...reckless. I saw it myself, Nethilos."

His friend's scowl deepened. "What do you mean you saw it?"

"Before Brynne and I left to come here, Selene had intercepted communications at the Order's headquarters to issue a personal threat to them, and to me." Zael held the elder's wary gaze. "Losing Jordana to the Order may have been the final blow. You and I both know how deep her fury runs—and her vengeance. She's been licking her wounds for a very long time, but now I fear she's ready to fight."

Nethilos stared, absorbing the weight of what he was hearing. "Come then, both of you. I will summon the other elders to the council chamber at once."

CHAPTER 28

If the Atlantean elder, Nethilos, had seemed less than eager to entertain the notion of working with the Order, it was nothing compared to the resistance Brynne and Zael received from the five other members of the council. The fact that Brynne was Breed hadn't helped.

After the initial apprehension over having one of their enemy's kind standing in front of them was soothed, the three women and two men who sat with Zael's friend on a dais at the front of the immense chamber had listened silently as Brynne and Zael laid out the case for an alliance to protect the two crystals and ensure that neither of the power sources found their way back into Selene's possession.

They had questions, of course. And understandable reservations. Brynne and Zael had fielded them as best they could, working together to allay concerns and persuade the council to the Order's side.

Standing with Zael as his diplomatic partner felt oddly natural in this otherwise very *unnatural* setting.

More than once they had finished each other's sentences or offered answers to a question at the same time. They were an effortless team, and it took all of her focus to keep from smiling at him or beaming with pride as he tackled the elders' questions with a diplomatic aplomb she hadn't realized he possessed. Zael was a tangle of contradictions, each one more fascinating—and attractive—than the last.

"I can assure the council that the Order will act as our friend in all ways," he told the elders now. "I have spent time among the warriors and with Lucan Thorne personally. They are not always gentle in their methods, but they are just."

Nethilos steepled his fingers and leaned forward in his seat. "And you can assure this council that under no circumstances will we be exchanging one volatile ruler for another?"

"I am prepared to promise it on my life," Zael replied.

"As am I," Brynne added, feeling Zael's fingers subtly brush hers as the elders looked at each other and murmured among themselves.

Although Brynne's JUSTIS training in diplomacy and negotiations served her well in the talks with the council today, she never would have imagined she'd end up using those skills here, standing beside Zael under the scrutiny of five high-ranking members of his kind. And try as she might to be professional, it was nearly impossible to keep from staring at the unearthly, ageless beauty of the assembled elders.

Nethilos was the tallest and most distinguished with his rich, olive skin and intelligent, contemplative golden-brown eyes. The two other males, Haroth and Baramael, were also imposing figures on the dais.

Haroth, a handsome black male with dark brown skin and sage-green eyes, looked as much a warrior as a diplomat with his muscled body and ebony hair shaved close on the sides and rising into a short mohawk.

Baramael's dual-colored eyes were what set him apart—one pure blue, the other as gold as a coin. Beneath his jet-black crown of silky, spiked hair, his stare was unsettling, utterly unreadable.

As for the women, the three of them were beyond beautiful too. They had also been the most resistant of the council, firing one question after another. Blonde-haired Nathiri's silvery gray eyes were as gentle as her interrogation was shrewd. Fortunately, she'd seemed satisfied with the answers she received, as did soft-spoken Anaphiel, a female with creamy, mocha-colored skin and a coil of delicate black braids seated on her head like a crown.

Anaphiel's fathomless, sapphire-blue eyes had been a comfort during most of the meeting—as they were now, when the last of the council elders, Tamisia, pinned Brynne with a challenging stare from her seat on the dais.

"You say the Order will only ask us to consider sharing our crystal with them under the worst of circumstances."

The gorgeous Atlantean female had long, platinum blonde hair with a single streak of bright gold running down the left side. Her sky-blue gaze had slid between Brynne and Zael for the duration of the meeting, her slender form perched at the edge of her chair like a viper waiting to strike.

Brynne hadn't missed the oddly combative posture, but she hadn't let it intimidate her either. Nor would she now.

"That's right," she answered solemnly. "The Order is fully aware that the colony depends on its crystal for many things, including protection. They will never ask it of you unless they feel the crystal is in jeopardy, or if they deem it necessary to combine the power of two in order to prevent a war—or, in the worst case, stop one."

"Hmm." Tamisia's mouth pursed. "And if we agree to this alliance, then one day find ourselves asking the Order to surrender their crystal to us for these same reasons, how will they answer?"

"The Order is prepared to never let it come to that," Brynne assured her, confident in that fact. "The Order will ensure the colony's protection from all enemies and will assist with anything the colony should require to maintain its autonomy."

"Anything except the crystal." Tamisia's smile was smug. She swung her flat stare to Zael. "This is no alliance. It is a one-sided proposal from a race that's been out to wipe us from the planet since the moment they arrived on it."

"Do not confuse the Breed with their Ancient ancestors," Zael interjected sternly. "The Breed has shared this planet with us for well over a thousand years. They've never been a threat to us or the humans they've lived alongside all this time."

She grunted, clearly unconvinced. "Tell that to the scores of humans who were slaughtered in a single night two decades ago."

Brynne shook her head, outrage flaring in her. "That was an attack instigated by an animal named Dragos. He unleashed hundreds of blood-addicted Rogues to retaliate against the Order and create a worldwide panic.

No one among the Breed wanted that to happen, least of all Lucan and the warriors."

Tamisia ignored her, never taking her eyes off Zael. "Why did you really bring this female here?"

His answering look was darker than Brynne had ever seen in him before. "Because I trust her. And I trust the Order—as should all of you."

The elder lifted her chin, her gaze icing over, as dismissive as her tone. "You ask too much, Ekizael."

"Damn it, Sia." Zael's sharp utterance sent her brows high on her forehead. "This is about peace. It's about the future of this colony."

"Is it?" she replied airlessly. "I wonder."

Brynne's chest tightened at the unexpected familiarity that crackled between Zael and the woman. Animosity flared in Tamisia's tight expression in the long moment that she held Zael's hard stare. And from beside her, Brynne felt an angry heat radiating off his tense body.

"This will suffice for now," Nethilos announced. "We have enough information to consider and make our decision. We'll convene again in tomorrow at daybreak."

He rose, and four of the elders did too. Tamisia was last, defiant as she lifted fluidly from her seat and then glided off the dais in smooth, long-legged strides.

"Come on," Zael said, placing his palm against the small of Brynne's back to show her out of the chamber.

All the breath leaked out of her lungs on a relieved sigh as soon as they exited to the open courtyard outside. "What was that about?"

Zael shook his head. "Nothing important. Tamisia will come around, I'm sure. Nethilos is on our side. As is Anaphiel, and possibly even Baramael."

"How could you possibly tell that?" She couldn't hide her surprise, recalling the dark-haired Atlantean's indecipherable bicolored gaze.

"Didn't you see his smile?"

She laughed. "I most certainly did not."

Zael was obviously trying to lighten the mood, set her at ease. For the most part, it was working. Although how they would get through the rest of the day and night without knowing the elders' decision, she had no idea.

"Zael!"

A light, female voice called to him from across the sun-filled courtyard.

Brynne swiveled her head in the direction that the excited shriek and giggle had come from and spotted a pretty young woman running toward them. Or, rather, toward Zael.

Coltish and cheerful, the Atlantean female beamed at him with unabashed glee, the spiral curls of her burnished copper hair dancing around her shoulders as she raced to greet him.

"I was so excited to hear you were back on the island!" she gushed, throwing her arms around him.

Maybe it shouldn't shock Brynne to learn that the charming, golden male who evidently had no shortage of women outside the colony should also have his fair share of admirers within it too.

That didn't mean she had to like it.

As if he just recalled Brynne was standing there, Zael extricated himself from the female's arms. "Neriah, this is Brynne Kirkland."

Recalling the name now, she smiled at Nethilos's daughter. "How nice to meet you, Neriah."

This close, she realized the young woman was likely

no more than a teen. Eyes of a similar golden-brown shade as her father's studied Brynne in avid interest.

"Brynne is my...colleague from the outside," Zael said.

He glanced at Brynne as he spoke, his gaze reminding her of their agreement to maintain a platonic facade in front of his people. After the uncomfortable way the meeting with the elders had ended—with Tamisia in particular—Brynne couldn't fault him for wanting to maintain an air of professionalism while they were there.

"Are you really a daywalker?"

Brynne smiled at the girl. "I really am."

"And you really drink blood?"

Zael cleared his throat. "Neriah."

"Sorry." She grimaced and gave an apologetic shrug. "Maybe we can talk more later?"

"I'd like that," Brynne replied.

As they spoke, she noticed Zael's head was turned toward the council chamber, to where Tamisia was now standing. Her arms were folded over her chest, her expression coldly assessing.

If there had been room for doubt before, when the Atlantean female had been staring daggers at Brynne and doing her best to undermine the discussion of an alliance, there was no denying it now. Tamisia's problem with her was jealousy.

The jealousy of a lover.

"I'll be right back," Zael murmured. "Brynne, will you be all right?"

"Of course." Her answer was a lot more confident than she felt in that moment. "I'll be fine. Go do what you have to do."

"I'm going to take Brynne to the guest cottage," Neriah announced helpfully.

He nodded. "I'll catch up with you as soon as I can."

Brynne stood there, refusing to watch as he strode back to meet Tamisia. She didn't want to see the other woman's smug reaction, nor wonder what Zael might be saying to soothe her ruffled feathers.

Unfortunately, not even her pride was strong enough to deny her foolish heart.

She turned her head to look for Zael, but he and Tamisia were already gone.

CHAPTER 29

Zael hated abandoning Brynne so abruptly, but he could tell from the look on Tamisia's face that the female had something on her mind. Something more than just the seething jealousy she had made no effort to conceal as she watched him with Brynne in the courtyard.

And while Brynne had given him permission to go, without as much as a backward glance as he approached the other woman, he didn't believe for a moment that she wasn't at least a little suspicious about his relationship with the Atlantean female.

With good reason.

Tamisia's chilly stare warmed considerably as he approached. "I didn't mean to lure you away from your companion."

"Of course, you did." Zael side-stepped her attempt to kiss his cheek in greeting, earning him a frown. "What do you want, Sia?"

She lifted a slender shoulder, although her

expression was anything but nonchalant. "It's been so long since I saw you last. I hoped we might have a chance to talk for a while...privately."

Ever the confident one, she pivoted and began walking toward the halls of the council chamber. Zael's jaw clenched with a hundred shades of misgivings, but he fell in behind her. She led him into an empty library and closed the door. He stayed put only a couple of paces inside the room while she dropped elegantly onto a silk-covered sofa beneath a sparkling stained-glass window.

"She's pretty," Tamisia remarked idly. "For one of her kind, that is."

Zael grunted, not about to play this game with her. "I doubt you brought me here to discuss the attributes of other women, Sia. I seem to recall that was always your least favorite subject. What's on your mind?"

"You mean, besides you?" Long lashes framed the knowingly coy gaze she fixed on him. "I've missed you, Zael. Each time you leave the island, it seems you're gone longer and longer."

She spoke in that sultry voice that used to have some power to sway him. Not anymore. And to hear her plying it on him now only made him suspicious of her motivations. Tamisia was a shrewd woman who went after what she wanted. So, what did she want from him now?

He leaned against the library wall, studying the beautiful blonde elder who was so accustomed to wrapping any male around her dainty finger. "Somehow, I doubt you've been waiting here, pining for me, Tamisia. We were only together a few times. You're hardly the type to waste away."

Her pout faded into a sly smile. "You know me too well, Ekizael. No, I haven't been pining. Elyon has been seeing to that lately."

"Elyon?" Zael balked at the mention of his former legion comrade who served as a sentry for the colony. "Now, there's an odd match. The rebel of the elder council and one of the most idealistic of Selene's old guard."

"It's nothing," Tamisia said with a dismissive flick of her hand. "It's a dalliance. One I have no intention of continuing."

Zael chuckled. "Does poor Elyon know that?"

She eyed him haughtily. "You of all people have no room to judge me. You never stay with anyone."

No, he didn't. Until recently, he'd never given much thought to his nomadic way of life. Nor the women who came and left his bed, creating barely a ripple of regret for their loss.

And then he met Brynne.

It was impossible to think of going back to his old ways—the endless wandering or the rest of it—now that she had entered his world.

But it was even worse than that.

Now that Brynne Kirkland was in his life, Zael couldn't imagine what a day without her would look like.

To say nothing of his nights.

"When do you expect you'll return to the outside again?" Tamisia asked, breaking into his thoughts.

Zael shrugged. "As soon as the council delivers their decision, or soon after. Why?"

Although she shook her head as if she meant nothing by it, there was a note of hesitancy in her stare. A plea— one she didn't seem certain how to put into words.

"What's wrong?"

She swallowed. "Do you think... Do you think it might be possible for me to go with you?"

Well, he sure as hell hadn't been expecting that. He was taken aback and couldn't hide it.

Tamisia was a high-ranking, well-respected member of the colony. An elder responsible for helping to shape the laws and direction of the entire community. He never would have dreamed she'd be willing to give all of that up.

"Go with me?"

"Not as your woman, if that's your concern," she quickly added. "Although if you wanted to try, you might be able to convince me to change my mind on that."

"I don't," he told her gently. "And what you're asking of me... You must know that if you leave, there's no coming back."

A strange hauntedness crossed her face, but it was there and gone in an instant. "I know it means if I go. It will be for good."

Zael was the only one in the colony to be granted access to come and go as he pleased, and only because Nethilos trusted him as he would one of his own kin. Tamisia was asking him to throw that away. Incredibly, she seemed willing to throw away everything she had built for herself in the colony too.

"Why would you want to leave? The colony is who you are. You've never seemed restless here in all the time I've known you."

"I have my reasons for wanting out, for wanting a new life. As I'm sure you had yours."

"Have you mentioned this to the other elders?"

"No. They wouldn't understand." She gave him a sad

smile. "I hoped that you might."

He raked a hand over his scalp. "I can't take you out of here—you know that, right? Not without the council being aware first. Not without their permission. If I do, we'll both be banished."

It was hard to ignore the small voice in the back of his conscience that wondered if being barred from his people might not be the worst thing that could happen to him.

After all, a life with Brynne might wait for him on the outside. He didn't know what that kind of life would look like, but part of him hoped for it—wanted it with a desperation that staggered him.

But the thought of turning his back forever on the part of him that was Atlantean wasn't something he could consider lightly.

"I can't take you with me, Sia. Not without the colony's blessing." He cursed under his breath, considering everything that was currently at stake. "And I sure as hell won't do it while I'm here trying to win the council's trust for an alliance with the Order."

"I'm sorry," she blurted, looking edgy and uncomfortable now. "Forgive me. You're right. And I shouldn't have asked it of you, Zael. Please, don't tell anyone I did."

She got up from the sofa. Before he could say another word, she vanished from the room in a brilliant flash of Atlantean light.

"Shit." Zael stood there for a moment, processing everything she'd said.

It hardly made sense. Not to mention the fact that he'd never seen the strong female look so unsteady. He didn't know what her true reasons were for wanting to separate from the colony, nor did he expect Tamisia to tell him.

Especially not now.

He could only hope his refusal to help her didn't jeopardize everything at stake for the alliance.

CHAPTER 30

Brynne stood at the water's edge on a secluded stretch of beach, watching the crystalline blue waves lap at her bare feet. Neriah had shown her to the small white stucco cottage that would be her quarters while she and Zael were on the island. According to her, Zael had his own cottage farther up on one of the hillsides, the home he kept for those rare visits he made to the colony.

Was that where he'd gone to now? She refused to think he might have gone there with beautiful Tamisia, even though the sting of his abandonment still burned in her breast.

That wounded part of her wanted to reject the idea that she had any stake on him. Zael had lived a long life before he came swaggering into hers. She couldn't expect him to pretend he hadn't, or that the people he'd met along the way didn't still mean something to him.

They did mean something to him. She saw that today. For some reason, she had been deluding herself into thinking Zael was as alone and isolated as she was—that they had that in common somehow. Today she saw that despite all of his wandering, he had a home.

Here, with the colony.

She'd never had anything like that. She didn't know how to be part of a community, a culture, a family. She had never quite fit—not anywhere. She'd never felt she belonged, not to anyplace or anyone.

Except when she was lying in Zael's arms.

"This view has never looked better."

The sound of his deep voice startled her. She spun around to find him strolling down onto the sand, his white linen tunic riffling in the breeze, his eyes as bright and brilliant as the water she'd been admiring a moment ago.

"I trust Neriah got you settled with everything you need."

Everything I need except you, she thought, her pulse quickening at the sight of him.

She nodded. "I'll be fine. You didn't need to check on me."

His brow furrowed as he approached. "I'm sorry for leaving you the way I did. I was concerned Tamisia might use her jealousy against the alliance if I left her standing there ignored."

"Of course, I understand. We have to do what's best for the alliance. After all, that's the only reason you brought me here."

"Is that really what you believe?" He reached out, brushing the backs of his fingers against her shoulder.

She deliberately side-stepped a pace, dodging his touch. "Careful. What if someone sees? Remember our arrangement."

He glanced around at the palm trees and flowering bushes that hemmed the cottage in from three sides. "It's all right. No one's here to see us."

Which was apparently the only reason he felt comfortable showing up.

"Did you and *Sia* have a nice talk?" Her spite was petulant and childish, but she couldn't rein back the hurt.

Zael's frown gave way to surprise, then an aggravating smirk. "You're jealous."

She had to bite her tongue to keep from confirming or denying it.

"You think I want her?" Zael moved closer. "You think I could ever want her when I have you?"

Sunlight haloed him, glinting off his copper-shot, golden waves. His handsome face always took her breath away, but especially now, with his sculpted lips curved in a sensual smile and those oceanic blue eyes darkening as his gaze penetrated hers.

He radiated a magnetic heat that permeated straight to her core, making her pulse hammer and her sex clench with desire. He smelled amazing, too, as exotic and lush as the island that surrounded them. The citrusy, clean scent of him was as intoxicating as the breeze rolling off the frothing surf at her back.

"My beautiful, headstrong Brynne," he said, cupping her face in his palm. "Do you honestly think there is any other woman I want to be with more than you—here on this island or anywhere else?"

She tried to hold on to her anger, but it was difficult with Zael filling her vision, dominating her senses. His hand slid around to the back of her neck, warm and strong against her skin.

"Since you don't seem to know that, let me tell you.

There isn't."

"Was there ever?" she whispered, needing to know. "I mean, with Tamisia."

"No. Not with her. We've been together a few times, but it was never something that would've lasted."

He shook his head, but there was a hauntedness in his gaze. A flicker of shame she struggled to understand.

"Not with Tamisia," Brynne guessed. "But there was someone once. From the colony?"

"No. She was human."

Brynne swallowed at the unexpected admission. But then maybe it wasn't so unexpected. "Dylan's mother?"

"I should've told you about her before," he murmured. "You deserved to know what happened. Why I have a daughter I never knew existed until only a few weeks ago."

She recalled the few details he had given her about the woman. "You told me you met her while she was on holiday in Greece."

He nodded. "Mykonos."

"You also told me she was married. Unhappily, you said."

"Yes, she was."

Brynne tried to guess at the cause of his guilt. "Did she go back to her husband?"

"She did."

His wooden tone conveyed more depth of emotion than if he'd shouted the words. He had loved this woman, and he had lost her. "I'm sorry."

He expelled a sharp breath. "Don't feel sorry for me. I don't deserve it. I'm the one who pushed her back to him. Because of my cowardice."

Brynne touched his rigid jaw. Although it hurt to see

that he'd once loved this woman a great deal, it pained her even more to see the torment in his eyes.

She had given him numerous opportunities to explain what had happened, especially on those times when she'd suggested he was an irresponsible libertine with a possible slew of fatherless daughters around the world.

And yet, he'd preferred that she believe that, rather than share the truth about the woman who'd borne his child.

Brynne drew him down onto the sand with her. They sat together for a long moment, just looking at the waves in silence.

"What was her name?" She prompted him gently, giving him somewhere to start again.

"Sharon." He stared out at the water. "She was a sweet girl, the most open-hearted woman I'd ever met. Once we ran into each other on that beach in Mykonos, I pursued her relentlessly. Finally, she gave in. It wasn't until we slept together—when I had the chance to lay my hands on her mortal skin—that I realized she was very ill."

Brynne glanced at him, confused. "What was wrong with her?"

"Cancer. It was everywhere, small enough to escape detection for many years, yet already terminal. There was no mistaking it."

"You could feel all of that with your hands?"

He nodded soberly.

"And you didn't tell her?" Brynne's heart climbed into her throat. "Oh, Zael…"

"I didn't tell her because there was nothing that could be done. The cancer would kill her, even if it was treated. There wasn't going to be a miracle."

"But you kept the truth from her."

"Yes. Because I didn't want to see her spirit crushed. I didn't want to be the one to crush it." He tipped his head back, silent for a long moment. When he looked at Brynne now, she saw the full depth of his self-hatred. "I didn't want to be with her, knowing I was holding that secret. So I left. I didn't tell her I was going. I didn't tell her anything. I just…left."

Brynne didn't say anything. She knew he didn't want sympathy, but she felt it for him anyway. It had been many years since he met Dylan's mother, but he still carried the pain. And the guilt.

"You want to know the ironic thing?"

She gave him a wobbly nod, still trying to process everything she'd heard so far.

"In the end, it wasn't the cancer that killed Sharon. Dylan told me that just a few days ago." He turned a stark look on Brynne. "It was Dragos who killed her."

"How?"

"Sharon was dying from the disease, but during that same time Dylan and her warrior mate, Rio, were just getting to know each other. It's a long story, but Sharon became entangled in some of Dragos's schemes and when he attempted to use her to get close enough to hurt Dylan, Sharon sacrificed herself to save her daughter. My daughter."

"Oh, my God." Brynne blew out a heavy sigh, her heart breaking for Zael and for Dylan. And for the special woman who had meant a great deal to both of them. "I'm so sorry."

"Now you know," he said, his deep voice solemn, yet still burdened. "I'm not a good man, Brynne. I've taken my pleasure wherever I've wanted, with little thought for the consequences. What I've never taken well is responsibility. I've never been steady or reliable. I've never been committed to anything but myself. You need to know that. You needed to know it a lot sooner than now."

"No, Zael. You're wrong." She combed her fingers through his hair as he stared out at the horizon, her eyes tender on the tormented, beautiful face of the man she had somehow come to care for so deeply. "That's not what I see in you at all. It's not what I saw here at the colony today. It's not what I saw in you with the Order." She put her fingers beneath his chin to bring his troubled gaze to hers. "It's not what I see when you're with me."

He cupped her face in his palm, his thumb lightly stroking her lips. "After Sharon, I never allowed myself to feel that deeply again. I didn't let myself feel love because I never wanted to feel pain or loss. But with you... Everything changed when I saw you, Brynne."

She wanted to believe him, but there was a part of her that was still afraid. Still certain the day would come when he rejected what she really was inside—or when he would regret that he hadn't rejected her.

"I've been alone all my life, Zael. It's where I feel safe." She turned her face into the cradle of his palm. "But you were right when you said I was lonely. I never realized how empty my life was. I didn't realize it could be any different. But now..."

"Now, what?"

She took a breath, needing to say the words before she let herself fall any deeper. "I'm afraid that I'll wake up one day and my life will be empty again. I'm afraid of what I am—what Dragos made me—and I'm afraid of what I may still become."

"None of that scares me." Zael's touch was tender as he reached out to trace the faint pattern of a *glyph* that was awakening on her chest. When he glanced to her eyes, his gaze was resolute. "We'll get through it together. My light helped you through the worst of it once; it can do it again."

She laughed sadly. "For how long, Zael?"

"As long as you want me."

"What if that's forever?"

The question fell from her lips before she could stop it.

He didn't say anything for a moment, and she closed her eyes, praying the beach beneath her would open up and drag her down.

But then Zael's lips were brushing against hers. She melted into him on a moan, her fangs tingling in her gums. His tongue teased the seam of her mouth, then slipped inside on her hushed sigh.

He moved over her, pressing her down onto the sand as his hungered kiss devoured all of her doubts and fears.

CHAPTER 31

He didn't want to let go of her.

She felt too good, her soft body moving beneath him on the sand, holding him close as their mouths joined in a desperate tangling of lips and tongues and panting, fevered breaths. Although this stretch of the beach was secluded, kissing her like this was going to get out of hand quickly.

Hell, who was he kidding?

What he shared with Brynne had been out of his control from the start. He meant it when he said it didn't matter that she was Breed or something darker. He craved her, cared for her. Felt more deeply for her than he ever had for another person in his life.

Holy fuck.

As the understanding settled on him, he drew back on a low growl and stared down into her beautiful, transformed face.

He was in love with her.

He wasn't going to deny it anymore. Not to himself,

at least. He couldn't. Not the way his chest throbbed simply to be near her, to be touching her. To know that she was his.

After how she had looked at him here today—after all of the tender things she'd said—there was a part of him that believed she might love him too.

Forever, she'd said.

His heart had answered without hesitation.

Yes. Forever.

But the words stayed jammed in his throat. They were still there now, along with all of the promises he couldn't make her until he was certain the target Selene had put on his back wouldn't someday land on Brynne's as well.

And the idea that his people and hers might one day be at war if Selene had anything to say about it?

That was a prospect he refused to consider, especially when Brynne was wrapped around him so deliciously, her hands tunneling into his hair to drag him down for another searing kiss.

He gave her what she demanded, then broke away on a hungered growl. "Give me your hand, love. I'm taking you to bed."

Her eyes flashing with amber light, she smiled and placed her fingers in his palm. Zael hauled her up from the sand with him, unable to resist another kiss as he dragged her up against his rigid length. Her hand found his erection, but it was only a wicked tease before she danced out of his embrace and started jogging back toward the cottage.

Zael met her inside, flashing there in less than an instant.

She yelped as he caught her, caging her in his arms.

"Cheat!"

"Never," he swore solemnly, then lowered his head to kiss her again.

He didn't need to feel the scrape of her fangs across his tongue or feel the heat of her amber irises radiating from behind her closed lids to know that she wanted him inside her as badly as he needed to be there. The sweet scent of her arousal jacked his pulse into a fevered tempo that made his cock surge heavy and rigid against her hip.

She arched into him as his mouth licked a trail from below her ear to the sensual curve of her neck and shoulder. He nipped at her tender skin, spurred on by her raspy cries of pleasure as his lips and tongue savored her heated response.

They undressed each other quickly, their need too urgent for patience.

Zael backed her toward the bed, his mouth still roaming her soft, naked skin and supple lips. She was panting and pliant in his arms, her curves crushed against the hard slabs of his body as he guided her over to the mattress and eased her down beneath him.

She spread her legs to receive him, her sex glistening and ready for him, so pink and pretty and perfect. He sank between her thighs on a low groan, wanting to savor every sensation yet knowing he was too far gone to be gentle.

His cock nestled into the hot, wet cleft of her body. His groan was ragged, his curse reverent, as he pushed inside and felt her tight walls stretch to accommodate his size. Brynne sighed as he drove deep, all the way to the hilt. Her spine arched up to meet his thrust, her small cry of pleasure gusting against his ear as he dropped his head and began a firm and steady rhythm.

Her ecstasy was a drug to him as he rocked in and out of her. He watched it play across her features, which were now fully, gloriously Breed. Amber light swallowed all the green of her irises as she stared up at him, her pupils narrow slivers amid all of that smoldering fire. With each blissful moan, every escalating sigh, the tips of her fangs surged longer, diamond-sharp and deadly, erotic as hell.

Bracing himself on one elbow while he rolled his hips into hers, he reached out to caress her transformed face. Only his touch was gentle, his need too urgent as he watched her cheeks flush with rising color and her mouth dropped open on a sigh of imminent release.

"Oh," she moaned thickly, clutching him as a hard shudder washed over her. "Zael... Oh, God... I can't hold it back."

"That's good," he murmured, almost beyond the capability of words as the sheath of her sex began to tighten and contract around his cock. "Oh, yeah. That's it, love. Let it go. Never hold back with me."

He bent his head and kissed her, drawing her plump lower lip between his teeth for a moment before burying his face into the tender crook of her neck and shoulder. Caging her between his forearms, he thrust deeper, faster, giving her what she needed to push her over the edge. Her long legs came around him as he rode her, her crossed ankles clamped down on his ass like a vise, holding him close, her arching body demanding as much as he had to give.

And he wanted to give her everything.

Not just now, like this, but in every way.

He wanted to hear her tell him that she could never have this with another male. That she was his, as he knew with a soul-shaking certainty that he belonged to her.

Forever.

The thought became a vow as her firelit gaze locked on his and she surrendered to the tremendous force of her climax. Her cry boiled out of her, throaty and wild. Sharp fingernails scored his back, searing lashes that made him roar with satisfaction as she broke apart beneath him in wave after wave of powerful release.

His own orgasm was rolling up hard on him too. But before he gave himself over to it, he wanted to witness Brynne coming again.

Hell, he would never have his fill of that beautiful sight.

Not even if they had as long as forever to be together.

He grasped her hands and started to drag them above her head so he could send her off the cliff of another climax, but she evidently had other plans.

On a sexy, animalistic snarl, she flipped him onto his back. Her long sable waves tossed around her shoulders as she straddled him, their bodies still intimately joined. His cock heartily approved of the change in position, and so did he.

Brynne sat atop him, her body on full display as her hips rocked and undulated, her wet core grinding against him as she took him impossibly deeper with each merciless slide of her body over his. The arcing twists and spirals of her *dermaglyphs* were flushed with deep colors, playing across her smooth skin like a living work of art. He reached up to touch the lacy patterns that adorned her breasts and belly, his gaze and fingers worshipping every extraordinary inch of her.

"So lovely," he murmured, sliding his hands down to her hips as she settled into her own fevered tempo. "I may never let you out of this bed."

Her answer was a low, pleasured moan. A sensual shudder slid through her body. Her breath turned ragged, a sexy panting that made his arousal coil tighter at the base of his spine. Fuck. He was trying to keep a leash on his orgasm, but she wasn't making it easy for him.

Arching as she pistoned on his shaft, her breasts jutted out, nipples as dark and plump as little berries. He reached up to touch them, rolling the pebbled peaks under his palms and fingers, reveling in the frantic little sounds she made as her climax started to overwhelm her.

"Zael..." His name was little more than a gasp as she bowed sharply and lost herself to her release.

She closed her eyes, tipping her head back on another shivery cry. Her sex gripped him like a sleek, velvet glove. Each tremor that shook her sent vibrations rippling along his shaft.

He kept moving beneath her, taking control of their tempo in order to prolong her pleasure. And his own.

He growled with satisfaction as she came again. But the sudden explosion of hot, liquid heat on his cock was more than he could handle. Snarling with the ferocious need that owned him now, he pumped into her one last time and his orgasm boiled out of him in a scalding rush.

She collapsed atop him, a warm and pleasant weight on his chest as his body shuddered with aftershocks. He was still hard inside her, even after the staggering blast of his release.

Her fingers lightly caressed his bare chest, tracing the contours of his muscles. He sucked in a slow breath when he felt her lips press warm and wet at the base of his throat. His cock twitched reflexively, along with every nerve ending in his body.

He wanted to feel more than her kiss at his throat.

Holy fuck, he wanted it with a certainty he could not deny.

Brynne went utterly still now.

He knew she must sense the change in his body. Hell, she had to be able to hear the sudden throb of his pulse, hammering in anticipation—in need of what only she could give him.

She reared back, silent. Barely breathing.

Her hot amber gaze was filled with deep affection as she stared down at him. But he saw anguish there, too. And when her eyes drifted away from his face and down to the exposed column of his throat, he saw a longing in her that rattled him to the core.

She wanted this too.

She wanted him, in the same irrevocable way that he wanted her.

As a mate.

Bound together by blood.

When she would have retreated even further, Zael slowly shook his head. He reached up, sliding his palm to the back of her neck. Her pulse was racing, throbbing as heavily as his.

"Don't run away from me now, Brynne. Come back here where you belong."

She didn't resist him as he pulled her to him and swallowed her broken moan with his kiss. Her fingers delved into his hair, clutching at him as their mouths came together in a heated, hungry joining.

The slight abrasion of her fangs against his tongue

sent a current of white-hot need licking through every fiber of his being. He dragged her deeper, thrusting into her mouth as his cock began to thrust inside her sex.

She moved with him in an increasingly urgent rhythm, until they both were lost to the frenzy of their desire for each other.

And the deeper need that refused to be denied.

Brynne tore away from his kiss, breathless and panting, her eyes shining more fiercely than stars. Behind her parted lips, her fangs gleamed.

He smoothed his hands over her beautiful, transformed face. "You're mine, Brynne. My blood already knows it. So does my heart."

He tugged her down to him, and this time when their kiss ended, instead of pulling back, Brynne lowered her head to the side of his throat. Her tongue brushed like silk across his carotid.

Zael growled in response, his pulse hammering in permission and demand.

She answered with a pretty moan that vibrated straight into his marrow.

And then she closed her mouth over his vein and sank her fangs into his flesh.

CHAPTER 32

B rynne moaned as the first taste of Zael's blood rushed into her mouth.

Quicksilver and exotic, it was nothing like the pungent copper red cells of the humans she had fed from all her life. But then, she should have known Zael's blood would be a powerful, intoxicating force. Like the male himself, his blood dominated her senses, owning her from the very first taste.

Each sip she took from his vein streaked into her system like liquid fire, awakening her every nerve, fiber and cell. She couldn't get enough. Drinking from him made her feel as though she'd been dying of thirst for centuries and was only just coming to life for the first time.

He had done this for her—awakened her, brought her to life. Dragged her out of the shadows and into a brilliant, irresistible new light.

He'd done all of that for her from the moment they met.

Now this.

His blood would live inside her forever. That bond was unbreakable. It settled on her so profoundly, she wanted to weep with the power of it. Wherever either of them went now, together or apart, she would always feel him. She would know his joy and sadness and every pain.

But in a troubled corner of her conscience, she also knew that if the day should come that he looked at her in all her monstrous worst and felt regret for this moment—for having brought her into his life, she would feel that too.

Right now, all she felt was his love.

Her heart overflowing, she licked her tongue over the punctures her fangs had made, sealing the wound. Zael's arms were warm and strong around her as she lifted her head to look at him. He held her in a sober, unblinking stare. His blue eyes had never seemed so dark or so solemn.

For a moment—one terrible, brief moment—she worried that she would see doubt in his handsome face. Or worse, the beginnings of the revulsion she dreaded might one day come.

But the bond told her something different. So did Zael, as he tightened his hold on her and flipped her beneath him on the bed.

His mouth came down on hers in a kiss so primal and raw, it nearly unraveled her on the spot. He was wild with passion now, and she felt every measure of it in the bond that now linked her to him.

"Oh God, Zael." Her voice was little more than a broken, panting sigh.

It was all she could manage. She had neither breath nor voice as he spread her out and began a fevered exploration of her body with his lips and wicked tongue.

Her pleasure exploded now that it was combined with his. The blood connection to him multiplied her ecstasy, and the power of her desire twined with his was almost too much to bear. She arced off the mattress as his mouth latched on to her clit. Hot and wet and relentless, his tongue licked and sucked and teased her swollen bud. When his finger slid inside her sheath and began to thrust in time with his mouth's torment, she spiraled toward a pleasure she could not contain.

Her orgasm crashed over her like a tidal wave. It swept her high and left her shattered, totally at his mercy.

And he gave her none.

She was still soaring, every nerve ending electrified and vibrating with bliss, as he prowled up the length of her body, then entered her on a low snarl of possession. He drove deep, deeper than she thought possible. Her head tipped back on a gasp, her hands fisting in the sheets as he rolled his hips, hard and fast and claiming.

"Look at me, love." His rough command brought her searing gaze back to him. "Watch me take you. Know that you're mine. Tell me you feel it."

"Yes, I'm yours. I feel it, Zael." She stared up into his eyes, swamped with pleasure and emotion. And so much love. It filled her with a growing, powerful light. His light, inside of her now. "Oh God, Zael. I feel...*everything*."

"Show me." His gaze burned with intensity as he pushed her higher, ever higher. "Let me feel it too, Brynne. Let me taste it, right now."

She frowned, uncertain she understood. Afraid to hope.

But the truth was there in his eyes. It was in the

emotional connection she had to him now—the one he was asking her to complete with him. He wanted this. He wanted her bond.

Would he want it when she was at her worst?

The question scraped at her coldly. Yes, he had seen her in the throes of blood thirst. He knew what she became then.

But to feel it in his own blood? To know the savagery that filled her when she was less Breed than monster?

Bonding him to her meant bonding him to everything she was, including the part of her that was Ancient. How could he ever look at her with desire—or with any kind of affection—if she let him take that hideous part of her into his own soul?

The fear that he would regret it made her veins freeze up.

The very thought that he might one day look at her in revulsion or loathing was too much for her to bear. Especially now, when he was holding her so lovingly, making her wish for things she could never have.

"Zael, no." Extricating herself from his embrace, she pushed away from him and scrambled to the edge of the bed.

"What's wrong?"

The concern in his deep voice made her wince in misery. When his hand came to rest gently on her shoulder, she flinched. Stood up abruptly and moved out of his reach.

"I'm sorry," she whispered. "I can't do this. Neither should you. Please... You should go."

"Go?" So much confusion in that one word.

He got up from the bed and walked toward her. His face was drawn with bewilderment, and with tender affection. Seeing his care for her now only reinforced the dread that if she let things go any further with him, that love would turn to disgust.

"I can't do this, Zael. Drinking from you was a mistake."

"It sure as hell didn't feel like a mistake to me," he shot back, anger overtaking his disbelief. "It felt right. And I know you felt it too."

She shook her head. "I can't do this, Zael. Not here. Not now. We shouldn't even risk being together until after the alliance is decided. You said that yourself."

"Fuck the alliance." His reply exploded out of him, his voice clipped and harsh. "This is about you and me, Brynne. Nothing else matters to me."

"Not even the colony?"

She knew it did. And if he tried to deny it, she could see that he knew she'd call him on the lie. She had only been on the island for a few hours and she could plainly see that for all of his wandering, this place and its people had been his only semblance of home. His infrequent returns and brief stays hadn't diminished the fact that for most of his immortal life, the people here had been the closest thing to family he'd ever had.

He would never truly turn his back on them, and she would never belong here.

No matter the outcome of the alliance they had been entrusted to make happen.

"I shouldn't have taken your blood, Zael. It was selfish. The most selfish thing I've ever done. I can't let you make it worse by shackling yourself to me too."

"Are you joking?"

His anger and confusion had now hardened into pain. She felt it vibrate in her veins as he stepped closer to her. She retreated deeper into the shadows of the small room.

"Zael, please... I want you to go."

"Brynne." He reached out to her.

"Go!" It was the beast that lived inside her that shouted the command at him.

She felt her nails harden into black talons as her misery morphed into desperate fury. Her skin prickled with the eruption of her alien *dermaglyphs*, the tangled patterns rising to the surface to cover most of her body.

Zael stood motionless, his handsome face unreadable. But she could feel his reaction in his blood. It wasn't fear or anger. It was pity.

She steeled herself to the hurt. "Please. Just go."

She turned away as he slowly retrieved his clothes and put them on, knowing if she watched him start to walk away from her, she might be tempted to call him back.

He didn't make her suffer the waiting for long.

The room lit up with a sudden blast of light.

Then he was gone.

CHAPTER 33

Brynne didn't sleep at all that night.

Her own misery would have been enough to keep her lying awake until the soft light of dawn began to fill the small cottage, but she also knew Zael's restlessness through her bond to him.

He was as unhappy as she was. But he was angry too. He was confused and hurt.

Because of her.

Because she was too weak to admit what she wanted—him, as her forever mate—and too scared to believe he could ever look past the abomination that she was.

He had gotten an irrefutable reminder of that in the moments before he'd left her.

Self-directed rage had brought her monster out in all of its hissing, lethal worst. He'd seen it, and he had felt sorry for her. She'd felt his pity. The sting of it still burned like acid in her throat…and in her heart.

Maybe he finally understood just how impossible any

kind of future would be for them. Maybe seeing her like that again was just what he'd needed to admit that she was right. They were from two different worlds, and although she'd never had much to call her own and even less to return to now, he had everything waiting for him here at the colony.

The last thing she wanted to do was jeopardize that for him by shackling him to her through a blood bond.

Even if pushing him away had felt as though it were killing her inside.

She couldn't deny that a shameful part of her had hoped he might return to the cottage and demand another chance to convince her.

Nor could she pretend that she wasn't disappointed when the knock came on her door that morning and she found Neriah waiting there, instead of Zael.

"Hi, Brynne." The girl smiled cheerfully in greeting. "The council is going to be meeting soon. Zael's on his way there now. He asked me to come and fetch you, if you're ready?"

"Oh." He was already there. Already adjusting to the distance she'd insisted upon. She schooled her expression into one of pure professionalism, even though an ache was tearing open inside her. "Of course, I'm ready. Let's go."

She barely registered Neriah's bubbly chatter as they walked up the cobbled street to the council chamber building. Her steps felt heavy, her heart pounding rapidly in anticipation of seeing Zael again after the terrible way she'd ended things with him.

He waited inside alone, facing the vacant dais. His stance was rigid and somber, his tall, muscular frame clothed in a fresh white linen tunic and pants, his burnished mane of golden hair still damp and curling at the ends from a recent shower.

Every cell in Brynne's body lit up at the sight of him, her senses evidently unaware of just how stupid she'd been in pushing him away. He wasn't hers now—after yesterday, maybe not ever again—but her body didn't seem to recognize that.

Nor did her blood.

Her veins throbbed as she watched him go utterly still when he realized she was there. She felt the spike in his heart rate, too, as he pivoted slowly to watch her as Neriah took a seat near the back of the chamber and Brynne approached him at the dais.

"The council's delayed," he informed her, his tone level, even though his gaze was heavy with all the words he wouldn't say. "I'm told they should be here soon."

"Do you think something's wrong?"

He shrugged. "It probably took some extra time for all of the elders to reach an agreement."

As they waited a few minutes in awkward, uncomfortable silence, she couldn't keep from recalling Tamisia's hard stare in the courtyard, or the skepticism she had expressed toward the prospect of the alliance.

That concern only deepened as the council of elders appeared from an adjacent room and began to file into the chamber to take their seats. None of the six revealed anything in their expressions, but Tamisia would not even look at Zael or Brynne.

Nethilos called the meeting to order.

"I apologize for the delay," he announced. "The council has been discussing your proposal for the past couple of hours. I'm sure you realize there is much at stake in this decision."

Zael nodded soberly. "I do, my friend. Brynne and I both realize that."

Nethilos's brow drew together. "This council had been prepared to give you our agreement today. However, we received new information just moments ago. Troubling information that we cannot ignore."

Brynne felt Zael's blood run a bit colder in his veins. Hers did, too, her veins freezing over in dread as she glanced at Tamisia and saw her drop her gaze to her lap as Nethilos continued to speak.

"You lied to me, Zael. You lied to this council when you neglected to tell us that you and this Breed female are lovers."

Oh, God. Brynne briefly closed her eyes, her heart sinking.

"We have a witness who reported seeing you together at the cottage," Nethilos went on. "This witness saw her drinking your blood, Zael."

Brynne felt sick. Guilt and alarm flooded her, along with Zael's sharp stab of shock. She felt the clawing sharpness of his dread…and the bite of his rising fury.

"Was it you, Sia?" His demand rumbled with outrage. "Damn it, did you do this?"

She glanced up now, her beautiful face stark as she shook her head. "No. I swear it."

Nethilos rose from his seat. "There will be no alliance. There cannot be, not under the terms you've proposed, Zael. Not while your loyalty appears to be swayed toward the Breed and the Order."

"What are you saying?"

Another of the elders, Baramael, the male with the bicolored eyes, fixed a disapproving look on Zael. "The colony needs insurance that you will act on our behalf—

in our best interests—should the Order one day come to us for our help in standing against Selene."

"And especially if they come to us for our crystal," added Anaphiel. She had seemed the most amenable to the alliance during the first meeting, but now the soft-spoken black Atlantean female looked at Brynne and Zael in obvious mistrust.

"You say insurance," Zael murmured. "What does that mean?"

Nethilos glanced to his colleagues before he spoke. "The council has decided that the only way we can enter this alliance with the Order is under one condition. That is if you agree to remain behind at the colony."

"For how long?"

Zael's question hung in the sudden quiet of the chamber. He looked at Brynne, and she had never felt so anguished or alone. She had pushed him away yesterday, but she hadn't really felt she'd lost him forever until right now.

He knew it too.

His blood hammered with the understanding of what he was being asked to do.

"You mean indefinitely," he replied woodenly. "Stay here at the colony for the rest of my life."

Nethilos inclined his head in a grave nod. "That is this council's decision, Zael. There will be no alliance without your commitment to our terms."

CHAPTER 34

☾

When he arrived in the council chamber that morning, Zael had been prepared to walk away from it all. Away from his people, and away from the only place he considered home.

After Brynne had pushed him out of the cottage yesterday—out of her life, he'd feared—it had forced him to examine his aimless, long-lived existence. More to the point, it had forced him to consider an interminable future without her.

What he had concluded was that a life without her was no life he wanted to endure.

And if that meant following her to the ends of the Earth to convince her of that, he damned well intended to do it.

But he'd been wrong when he said the alliance between the Breed and the colony didn't matter to him. It did. Because without the potential of peace—without the assurance that Selene would not be able to have the war she seemed so determined to ignite—Zael knew that no one he cared for would ever be safe.

Not him. Not the people of the colony. Not the Breed or the Order or anyone else who should be unfortunate enough to stand in the way of the Atlantean queen's vengeance.

And, most important of all, not Brynne.

As he'd paced most of the night in the confines of the home he kept on the island, he understood that above all else, the alliance had to happen. No matter the price.

He sure as hell hadn't anticipated this.

"You can give the council your answer whenever you're ready, Zael."

At Nethilos's proclamation, the rest of the elders stood, then followed him out of the chamber.

Brynne stood motionless as they left. Utterly silent. He wasn't even certain she was breathing.

"Are you okay?" he asked her, his concern focused wholly on her despite the endless ramifications of what had just occurred. "Brynne, talk to me…"

"This is all my fault." Her words were toneless, but the sob she choked back was ragged with emotion. "Zael, I'm so sorry. I told you what we did yesterday was a mistake. Now, I've ruined everything."

"No. Not you. Don't think that. We both were in that bed together."

He wanted to reach out and stroke his thumb over her quivering lips. His fingers itched to sweep away the lone tear that slid down the side of her lovely, guilt-stricken face. But he didn't know if she would want his comfort now.

And until he found a way to fix everything that had just gone wrong, he had no assurances or promises to give her.

As for the council, he didn't need to delay another moment.

He had his answer for them.

He only had to convince them to accept it.

"Stay here," he told Brynne. "I need to find Nethilos and talk to him privately."

At her nod, Zael dashed out of the chamber. He ran to his friend's personal office in the council building, but the elder was nowhere to be seen.

As Zael stepped out, Tamisia nearly crashed into him in the passageway.

He could barely contain his rage. "Get out of my way, Sia. If you know what's good for you, get as far away from me as you can right now."

"Zael, I'm sorry." Her face collapsed in what appeared to be a damned good imitation of remorse. "I didn't know."

He halted, too suspicious to ignore her, no matter how viciously he vibrated with the need to explode. To rage. To punish.

But he couldn't blame anyone for how he felt about Brynne.

He couldn't condemn the council for their decision to disapprove of what he felt for her—even if that decision held the power to destroy his life.

"What didn't you know, Sia?"

She shook her head, misery in her eyes. "Elyon. He came to me last night, outraged after spying on you and Brynne down at the cottage."

Anger boiled through Zael. "He was there? That son of a bitch was there on that beach?" A curse erupted off his tongue. "You're telling me that Elyon was skulking around, peering in windows while Brynne and I made love?"

And while she drank from him.

The most intimate moments they had ever shared together, and Elyon had invaded their sanctity like a goddamned thief. He'd cheapened a private, sacred experience and wielded it as a weapon.

"He's crazy, Zael." Tamisia shivered as she said it. "He's been talking about the two of us returning to the realm together, but I never wanted that. He wouldn't let it go. That's why I asked you to help me leave."

Zael cursed. "You should have told me why, Sia. You should have told someone, damn it."

"I know." Her regret was obvious. As was her fear. "He was furious to see you arrive here with talk of an alliance with the Order. I think he'll do anything to prevent that from happening."

Zael's mind was churning. He reflected back on the sentry who had once been among Selene's most loyal soldiers. Elyon had been an Atlantean patriot before the fall of the realm. Had his loyalty remained secretly intact all this time?

Worse, could that loyalty now turn him against the colony as a whole?

From what Tamisia was saying, the answer seemed obvious.

A cold foreboding settled on Zael as he considered Elyon's betrayal of him. If the sentry was willing to do anything to stop the alliance, then he wouldn't be willing to stand by and let the council thwart him by giving Zael a chance to repair the damage.

"Where's Nethilos?"

Tamisia shook her head. "I don't know. I haven't

seen him since the council adjourned."

"Damn it." Zael started walking again. "If you see him, tell him he could be in danger. Tell him I need to speak to him at once."

She nodded. "I will."

As he strode through the council building, Zael slowed his thoughts down, centering his focus on the energy that lived in every Atlantean. He searched for his friend using his mind and his senses.

He couldn't locate him.

Holy hell.

If his old friend was in possible danger from Elyon, what about the crystal?

The colony kept their power source in the top floor of the building he was in now. Zael teleported there, disappearing in a burst of light, then materializing in the chamber that held the colony's Atlantean crystal.

He got there just in time to find Nethilos lying in a pool of blood on the floor of the chamber. His head was severed from his body, having come to rest next to a gore-streaked, long Atlantean blade. The kind Zael and the rest of his legion comrades used to carry.

Ah, fuck. He recoiled at the grisly sight of his peace-minded friend. The savagery of Nethilos's killing rocked Zael, but he pushed down his horror and pain so he didn't lose his grasp on the lethal fury that boiled up on him.

Because there was Elyon, standing in front of the crystal. The bastard had removed the protective glass cover and was just about to lift the egg-sized, silvery object from its marble pedestal when Zael's booming voice startled him.

"You cowardly fuck. Get away from the crystal."

Elyon wheeled around at the unexpected intrusion. His gaze flicked to the blade he'd so carelessly dropped after he committed his crime.

The razor-sharp blade Zael now held in his hand, ready to strike.

He advanced judiciously on Elyon, forcing him to forfeit his position near the crystal in order to avoid the striking range of Zael's lightning fast sword arm.

Elyon chuckled. "Been a long time since you wielded Atlantean steel, captain."

"Not so long," Zael returned, demonstrating with a jab that nicked the other male's shoulder. "How long have you been planning to take the crystal back to Selene?"

Elyon's blond brows rose. "You knew?"

"Not until I spoke to Tamisia a moment ago."

"Tamisia." Elyon sneered as he said her name. "I've been trying to convince her to come with me, back to the realm. She wouldn't do it. Beautiful, that one, but she has no sense."

"She had sense enough to turn you down."

He scoffed. "I would've made her come around. I could have persuaded her. But then here you come, back to the island after years away. Talking about defying Selene. Talking about allying with the Order, for fuck's sake. I can't let that happen, Zael."

"It's happening," Zael assured him. "I won't rest until it does."

Elyon shook his head. "We never should've defected from the realm. Living in hiding on this rock, all of us isolated from the rest of world and forbidden to come or go." He chuckled brittly. "Well, all of us except for you, Zael. And now here you are, asking us to put our fate in Breed hands? Never. We should go back to Selene before we trust any of the Breed. We're better off with the devil we know."

The male was getting agitated, and that meant he would soon be unpredictable. Zael edged him farther away from the pedestal that held the crystal, keeping him distracted with short bites of the blade. Finally, he had Elyon pushed toward the center of the chamber, Zael standing between his opponent and the crystal.

But Elyon wasn't finished berating him. He glanced briefly down at Nethilos. "I tried to convince him, but he refused to listen. Why would he? I'm a lowly soldier, only fit for guarding the gates, not breathing the rarefied air of the council chamber. Again, unlike you." Now he grinned, his gaze too avid to be fully sane. "What makes you so damned special? Nothing. Tamisia was no better than Nethilos. With her, I was good enough to fuck, but not good enough to be heard. Not good enough to obey. Well, no more."

Light exploded from Elyon's hands. Even though Zael braced for the impact, the sudden blast of power crashed into him like a freight train. The other warrior had always been strong, but this immense force was something different.

Bloody hell.

The crystal, Zael realized.

Elyon hadn't had the chance to remove it before Zael interrupted him, but he had been close enough to touch it.

And the power he'd siphoned off that brief contact now gave him the strength of ten Atlantean warriors.

The force of Elyon's light blew Zael off his feet, sent him hurtling across the chamber. He lost his grasp on the blade as he slammed into the stone wall of the chamber, bones shattering on impact. White-hot pain exploded all through him.

Elyon's laughter was madness as he raised his hands in front of him and prepared to unleash another punishing blast on Zael.

CHAPTER 35

H e was in agony.
     Brynne felt Zael's sudden, unbearable burst of pain echo through her blood as if it were her own bones breaking, her own skull ringing from a sudden, savage assault.

"Oh, no." A jolt of panic—of marrow-deep terror—gripped her. "Zael."

Her bond to him told her where he was.

She followed the beacon of that connection, moving through the council building and up the stairwell at the fastest speed her Breed genetics would allow.

"Zael!"

She smelled blood even before she reached the top floor of the structure.

So much blood.

The barred door to the chamber was no match for her otherworldly strength. It flew off its hinges as she smashed inside the room.

Streaks of blinding light collided between Zael and

his attacker, the blond sentry she recognized from her arrival on the island. Elyon's face was twisted into a mask of rage as he battled Zael. The sentry's eyes were wild, his expression murderous.

Zael roared when he spotted her. "Brynne, get out of here!"

In that split-second of distraction, Elyon unleashed another blast of power at Zael from the centers of his glowing palms. The bolt arced like lightning, hitting Zael square in the chest. He flew backward on a shout of agony, held down by the force of Elyon's blast.

Brynne screamed—not only because of her shared link to Zael, but out of fury for his attacker. Her bellow tore from somewhere deep inside her, morphing into an unearthly, alien sound as her transformation overtook her.

Her vision flooding with amber rage, she leaped on Elyon. She took him down, her black talons sinking into flesh and bone as she tore at him, tumbling the larger male onto the floor.

She was animal in her violence, but the Atlantean's strength was immense.

Powerful light exploded in her chest and skull.

Elyon threw her off him and got to his feet. He glared at her as she tried to shake off her pained daze, his wounds already starting to heal.

"You stupid Breed bitch," he seethed at her. "Now, you die too."

He raised his hand, a fireball of energy swirling in its center. Just when he would have unleashed it, Zael came up on one knee on the other side of the room. He had something grasped in his closed fist. His other hand was engulfed in light—light he now blasted on Elyon.

Instead of going after Brynne, the sentry swung the full breadth of his power on Zael in defense. Their light clashed and held, its colliding force illuminating the chamber with the heat and brightness of ten suns.

Brynne saw her chance to act. A long blade of blood-stained steel lay just out of her grasp. She lunged for it, then came up swinging.

The sword connected at the base of Elyon's skull. The Atlantean's head went flying.

More energy poured out of him now, bursting from his flailing hands and his severed neck. The body crumpled to the floor, Elyon's immortal life—and his destructive light—extinguished forever.

"Brynne." Zael was at her side in that next instant.

She could still feel his physical pain—broken bones and light-seared organs that were slowly healing, thanks to his Atlantean genetics. She could also feel his relief as he wrapped one hand around her nape and pulling her against him as he brushed his mouth over hers in a fierce kiss.

Part of her wanted to resist his nearness—if only because she wasn't sure she could trust herself under the yoke of her transformation. Although she didn't feel her sanity slip as it did all the other times she succumbed to blood thirst or fury, she recognized the beast within her.

Her blood pounded ferociously in her temples, her vision swamped with amber and still thrumming with the power of her rage. She was Ancient now. Still seething and unearthly.

Hideous.

Yet Zael had looked at her with pure affection. With love.

She tasted no fear in his kiss—not for what she was,

anyway. Only the fear that they might have lost each other today.

And the soul-deep relief that they had both come through the fight intact.

Together.

"Oh, Zael," she gasped against his parted lips. "I was so scared."

"I know, love." He kissed her again and again, as if he couldn't bear to stop. "It's okay now. It's all over."

Brynne's relief was so overwhelming, she didn't realize they were no longer alone in the chamber.

Not until she felt Zael's pulse spike with renewed alarm.

They broke their kiss, both of them glancing toward the smashed, open door of the room where several Atlantean elders and a dozen or more colony inhabitants now stood.

At the front of the group were Elyon's sentry comrades. No longer unarmed as they had been when Brynne and Zael first arrived at the island, but each holding a long blade like the gore-streaked one that Brynne still grasped absently at her side.

Every person standing there looked at Brynne and Zael in accusation.

In silent, horrified condemnation.

~ ~ ~

"Put the crystal down, Zael." Baramael's dual-colored eyes were narrowed on him in a lethal glower as he ground out the command. "Tell your woman to drop the blade."

"It's not what you think."

He knew what it looked like—the most respected of the elders and one of the colony's trusted sentries, both beheaded and lying in growing pools of blood. Him standing there, holding the crystal in one hand while his other hand held tenderly onto Brynne, whose own fingers were wrapped around the grip of a gore-streaked Atlantean sword.

"You heard him, Zael." This threat came from Vaenor, the sentry who had served with Zael and Elyon in the legion. The dark-haired soldier took an aggressive step forward, his blade at the ready. "Put the crystal down."

"Not until you hear me out, all of you."

Zael let go of Brynne only so he could cautiously reposition himself in front of her, in case anyone rushed to any worse conclusions about what they were seeing there now.

Because as stricken as their expressions were as they registered the scene of carnage near their feet, it hardly compared to the shock he saw written on every Atlantean's face as they tried to get a closer look at Brynne.

She was fully transformed, as she had been the night he'd found her in that Georgetown alley.

Her fangs were enormous, her eyes heated orbs of molten amber. Every inch of her pale skin was now covered in a tangle of *dermaglyphs*. Even her face bore the Ancient skin markings, all of them seething with dark colors. Zael didn't need to glance at her hand where it curved loosely around the grip of the Atlantean blade to know that the tips of her fingers were crowned in sharp black talons.

She was uniquely Brynne.

Formidable.

Glorious.

He had never felt so proud to be standing with her.

Nor more in love.

"Holy shit," someone whispered from within the stunned crowd.

"She's something more than Breed," another voice muttered. "Just look at her."

"Yes," Zael said. "Look at her. Thank her, because Brynne just helped save this colony today. If not for her, Elyon would already be standing in front of Selene handing over this crystal."

Baramael eyed him warily. "What are you talking about?"

"Elyon killed Nethilos. I found them both up here, but I was too late to save him." His glance drifted to the carnage near his feet. His bile rose at the sight of his friend's brutalized body. He felt only disgust when he looked at the sentry who had betrayed him. Betrayed everyone in the colony. "Elyon had been plotting to leave the colony and return to the realm with the crystal. The prospect of an alliance with the Order would have ruined all of his plans."

Vaenor grunted. "A convenient explanation when Zael is holding the crystal and the only other two witnesses are dead at his feet."

Rumblings of agreement—of suspicion and doubt for both Zael and Brynne—traveled the crowd.

"It's all true." Tamisia stepped through the gathered throng. "Everything Zael just said is the truth."

The other elders who stood at the front gaped at her in disbelief.

"What is this about?" Baramael demanded.

Tamisia recounted what she had told Zael about Elyon—how he'd been obsessed for some time with defecting and had been attempting to coerce her into going with him. She explained how she had grown wary of him, but that she hadn't realized he would be willing to kill, nor had she ever dreamed he might attempt to steal the colony's crystal for his own gain.

The other elders and the rest of the assembled crowd gaped at her. Soon the animosity and mistrust that had been focused on Zael and Brynne began to shift to Tamisia.

Baramael's bicolored eyes flared with disapproval. "You've known of Elyon's disloyalty to the colony, yet never told anyone?"

"I was afraid of him," she murmured quietly.

"Your fear cost Nethilos his life," Haroth, the other male elder sharply reminded her. The black Atlantean raked a big hand over his short mohawk. "This cannot stand, Tamisia."

"I know." She nodded, tears sliding down her cheeks. "I'm so sorry."

Baramael nodded grimly to the sentries, and they slowly began to guide the spectators out of the chamber. When it was just the elders remaining, he stepped up to Tamisia. "Your actions killed a good man, a friend to us all. That is a loss we can never repair. However, if not for Zael and Brynne stopping Elyon, your silence could have jeopardized this entire colony one day. You leave us no choice but to banish you, Sia."

A sob choked out of her. "Nethilos was my friend too. I don't expect any of you to ever forgive me. I know I will never forgive myself."

"At least we still have the crystal," one of the female

elders gently pointed out. "At least Elyon was thwarted in his betrayal of us."

Zael nodded, agreeing in sober contemplation. "And you still have the alliance. If the colony wants it."

From within Haroth's dark-skinned face, his pale green eyes flicked from Brynne to Zael. "None of this changes the council's condition on the alliance with the Order. What Brynne did here today is admirable—we are all in her debt—but that doesn't change the fact that she's Breed."

Baramael nodded. "If anything, seeing the devotion you share for each other only fortifies the council's concern that unless the colony has a permanent advocate in this alliance, the odds may always swing in favor of the Order."

Zael inclined his head in understanding, even if it wasn't the answer he wanted to hear. He hadn't expected the council to reverse their decision.

Hell, if he were one of the elected elders responsible for the security and governing of the colony, he'd make the same demand.

"Come," Baramael said solemnly. "We can talk more later. Right now, we need to see to our fallen friend and this council needs to offer comfort to his widow and child."

CHAPTER 36

They buried Nethilos at sundown, on the island's highest hill.

Brynne had stood beside Zael and offered her condolences to Diandra and Neriah, both of whom were despondent over the loss of the good and gentle man who'd been so beloved to all in the colony, but especially to his family.

Brynne had felt Zael's grief, too, but he had remained steady and stoic throughout the wrenching goodbyes and the final moments that his friend's remains were laid to rest in the sole grave ever to be dug on the immortals' island haven.

As the gathering dissolved and most of the colony began to return to their homes, the four elders strode to where Zael and Brynne stood on the hill near a grove of fragrant lemon trees. Zael's arm around her shoulders flexed, bringing her closer to him as the two men and two women approached.

Baramael inclined his head in greeting. "It was good

of you to speak at the gravesite, Zael. Nethilos would have been humbled by your praises. It was clear that his wife and daughter took a great deal of comfort in your memories of him."

Zael nodded soberly. "He was a good man. One of the best I've known."

"Indeed. He was a valued member of our council as well. We won't have an easy time finding someone to take his seat on the dais with us."

"No, I don't imagine it will be," Zael said. "And what about Tamisia?"

Baramael and the others exchanged a look. "She will be banished from the colony at first light."

"Unfortunately," added Haroth, "she has left us little choice."

Brynne couldn't deny the pang of sorrow she felt for the Atlantean female. Tamisia had been negligent in looking out for the colony's best interests, especially in her role as elder, but her remorse had been painfully evident. She would have to live with the guilt of her unwilling role in Nethilos's death for the rest of her immortal life, which was a punishment that would probably weigh on her more than anything else.

"If she can make repairs somehow, will you let her back in one day?"

The elders all looked at Brynne, but it was Nathiri, the light-haired female with the silver eyes, who spoke first. "Redemption can be a very long and arduous road. It will be up to Tamisia to find her way back, if that's what she truly wants."

Baramael's unsettling green-blue gaze slid to Zael. "Have you thought any more about what you will do?"

"I have," Zael answered, his tone serious.

Brynne looked at him in question. They had only talked briefly about the condition the council had imposed on the alliance, neither one of them seeming ready to discuss the potential of a future spent apart when they had come so close to losing each other for good earlier today.

He gazed at her, and the affection she saw there helped to ease some of her anxiety.

Some, but not all.

She could feel how deeply he cared for her, but she couldn't read his mind.

She pressed her lips flat, afraid to ask the question. "What will you do, Zael?"

"The council has determined that the alliance depends on my remaining here at the colony," he replied solemnly. "So, that is what I'm prepared to do."

Brynne couldn't breathe for a moment. She didn't know what to hope for. After all, the council had put him in an untenable position. But hearing that he would remain behind at the colony with his people opened up an empty spot in her breast that ached with the loss already.

Zael glanced back to the elders. "I'm not about to let the alliance fall apart now. Not after my friend has lost his life because of it. And not after Elyon's long-festering duplicity only drives home the fact that the colony must be vigilant—within and without the veil that shields us."

He was right and Brynne knew it. She could feel how committed he was to his people and their security.

And to this magical place.

Baramael's narrow stare studied him. "So, you fully intend to accept our terms?"

"Yes. I will make the colony my permanent home,

271

just as you've insisted. But I have a condition of my own."

As he spoke, his gaze caught hers again. She saw the tender look in those cerulean blue depths. She felt the expanding warmth of his affection... His love.

"Tell me," he asked the elders, although his eyes never left Brynne's. "Has the colony ever denied sanctuary to a mated couple?"

For a long moment, there was only silence. But then Baramael slowly shook his head. "No, we have never."

Zael's smile tugged at the corner of his shrewd and sensual mouth. "Then can I expect that you won't start now?"

Happiness and hope climbed up the back of Brynne's throat as the four elders spoke quietly among themselves. But there was a trace of doubt too. None of this changed the fact that she was an outsider in this place. More than an outsider, she was made from the worst enemy these people had ever known.

And yet Zael was suggesting he would take her as his mate.

He was actually pressing these four elders to accept her as one of their own, and allow Zael and her to live together here, at the colony.

"Zael... We can't. Do I really have to tell you all of the reasons why this is impossib—"

He silenced her with a kiss. "Do you love me, Brynne?"

"God, yes. More than anything."

"And I love you," he told her intently. "I love all of you, Brynne. Every last cell. And I'm not about to live a single day—on this island or anywhere else—if I can't do it with you at my side."

His vow tore something loose in her chest. It was her heart, she realized. It sailed skyward as he drew her to him and kissed her deeply, without a care for the several pairs of Atlantean eyes that watched them.

Finally, someone cleared their throat.

He and Brynne turned to face the sober gazes of the elders.

Baramael spoke for the group. "This is a most unusual request, Ekizael. However, these are most unusual times." Over the male's one blue eye, his black brow arched. "And you have fallen in love with a most unusual woman."

Zael grinned, drawing her close. "Yes, I have."

A smile tugged at Baramael's mouth as well. "We owe you a debt for what you did today, Brynne. Not only the four of us, but the entire colony. So, it's the agreement of this council that it would be our privilege to have you a part of this community."

"Thank you," she murmured, humbled by their acceptance. She'd never dreamed she would find that here.

She had never dreamed she'd find the kind of love and passion and contentment that Zael had brought into her life.

His fingers laced with hers as he drew her gaze back to him. "You haven't given me your answer yet, Brynne. Can you love me enough to stay?" His eyes searched hers, solemn, earnest. "Can you love me enough to be my mate and spend your lifetime here at my side?"

"Can I love you enough?" Joy swamped her. All of the emotion she felt swelling inside her—both her own and Zael's—was too much for her to contain. It spilled over in the tears that streaked down her cheeks. "Zael, I love you enough for a thousand lifetimes. You are my home and my heart. My everything."

"Forever," he murmured, his deep voice rough with feeling too.

As his mouth slanted sweetly over hers, she wrapped her arms around him and surrendered completely to the moment, to the man who was all she would ever need.

All the uncertainty and fear that had lived in her for so long evaporated under the warmth and strength of Zael's kiss. Of his love.

In his arms, she had no doubts.

She belonged to him—body, blood, heart, and soul.

Irreversibly.

Eternally.

He broke their kiss on a sensual groan. Swiveling his head toward the elders as if in afterthought, he smirked. "If the council will excuse me, I'd like to take my beautiful mate home now."

He barely gave them a chance to agree.

Brynne laughed as he scooped her up into his arms. His lips brushed her ear as he lowered his voice to a whisper meant for her alone.

"I want to show you my home, love. *Our* home. And our bed."

CHAPTER 37

He had never brought a woman into his private home on the island.

As he carried Brynne inside the white stucco cottage on the same high hill where Nethilos had been laid to rest, Zael had never felt a greater sense that he had—at last—arrived where he belonged.

With Brynne as his mate, he would always be home.

"It's beautiful," she said as he brought her into the open-air residence with its wide garden terrace that overlooked endless turquoise waters. She sighed in unabashed awe, her dark green eyes lit with wonderment. "Aren't you going to give me the grand tour?"

"Oh, yes," he said, his voice rough with desire. "We'll start the tour in the bedroom."

"That would be my first choice too." She smiled, licking her lips in a way that made his blood run hot and arrow straight to his cock. "After the bedroom, then where will you take me?"

He smiled, thinking of all the erotic possibilities. "Everywhere and every way," he promised with a kiss, already hard and eager to have her beneath him.

A soft evening breeze rolled off the waves below and sifted through the flowering bushes outside the bedroom's open wall of glass. The air was filled with the fragrance of salt and citrus and sweet sea roses, although it couldn't compare to the scent of Brynne's arousal as he laid her on the white cotton sheets of the bed and began to undress her.

He explored her skin with his mouth and hands as he unwrapped her for his hungry eyes. He didn't think his desire could grow any more intense, but as he watched her transform beneath his fingers and tongue, he knew he would never see anything hotter than Brynne when she was fully Breed. When she was writhing and moaning for him, her body surrendered to him completely.

Solely his.

"You're mine now," he told her, stripping out of his clothing and then kissing his way back up her naked body. "Forever, Brynne."

"Yes." Her gasp lengthened into a slow, pleasured sigh as he sank into her heat. "Oh God, Zael. I feel you in my blood. I feel your light in me...in my veins, everywhere. It's so powerful."

Hearing that made him smile with pure male possessiveness. Knowing that a part of him lived inside her now only made his desire for her spike and deepen, along with his devotion.

"I felt your blood and your light when I fought Elyon too." She reached up, cupping his face in tender hands. "It centered me, Zael. It kept me sane, even at my worst. I felt your blood and your light in me, and I wasn't afraid. Not of anything. Not even myself. *You* do that for me, Zael. You and your blood. And your love."

The thought that he could bring her comfort or grounding humbled him, honored him more than his words could ever express to her. Brynne's love was an honor to him, and he looked forward to spending his life proving to her that he could deserve her.

"So long as I draw breath," he promised her fiercely, "you will never know fear or darkness again. Only love, Brynne. Our love."

"Yes," she answered, arching up to meet his deep thrust. "Zael, yes…"

They moved together in a perfect friction, skin on skin, touching, kissing, caressing. Zael couldn't look away from the emotion he saw in her smoldering gaze. The love he saw there staggered him. It humbled him like nothing ever had before.

He wanted to feel that love inside him.

Through blood and bond.

He wanted it so fiercely, it became a drumming in his veins.

In his heart.

Slowing his tempo, he reached up to stroke her beautiful face. His thumb swept over her parted lips, his eyes rooted on the pretty white points of her fangs.

"I want to feel your blood inside me, love."

Her soft, indrawn breath seemed uncertain, as if she still didn't quite believe that he could mean it. Before she had a chance to voice a single doubt, he lifted her chin and held her burning gaze.

"I've never been more sure of anything in my life." He kissed her, unrushed and meaningful, letting his tongue trace the razor-sharp tips. "Let me taste you, Brynne."

When she hesitated, he took her hand in his and brought her wrist up to her mouth.

"You've given me your love," he said, still amazed that she had. "Now, give me your bond."

Brynne swallowed, her eyes never leaving his. She gently bit her wrist, then withdrew her fangs from her tender flesh and turned her wrist toward him.

He closed his mouth around the bleeding punctures, sealing his lips over the wound.

The first sip slammed into his senses, hard and powerful. He wasn't expecting to feel the need it stirred within him, the deepening thirst for her.

He groaned with pleasure—with amazement—at the erotic taste and staggering force of her blood. He felt it surge into him like a wave of heat and energy, even more invigorating than the light that lived in him as an Atlantean.

His erection turned to granite with each draw from her vein. His desire ignited into a need that shocked him. One that demanded to be fulfilled.

He moaned, his hips flexing on their own, his cock pushing deeper, more urgently inside her. He could hardly hold on to his lust now. Like his love for her, his need was too strong.

It owned him, just as this woman did.

She gently pulled her wrist from his mouth and sealed the wounds with a little swipe of her pink, wet tongue. Her face was resplendent with desire and emotion, and the flush of her escalating release.

"Mine," Zael growled.

Her answering smile nearly undid him.

"Mine," she said, drawing him down for her passionate kiss.

He didn't think his connection to her could be any stronger, but then he began to feel his pleasure mounting, doubling. The love he felt was growing, too, intensifying into something so profound he struggled to hold it all inside him.

It was Brynne.

He could feel her now, in his heart, in his blood.

"Yes," she whispered, nodding. "Forever, Zael."

She wrapped her arms and legs around him, holding him close as their bodies fell into an urgent, perfectly matched rhythm. They climaxed together, her cry joined with his hoarse shout. His orgasm would have been explosive enough by itself, but twined with the pleasure of hers it was staggering, the most intense rush of sensation he'd ever known.

And it wasn't enough to sate him.

Zael rolled her onto her side to start another round of lovemaking.

It was a damned good thing they would have an eternity together, because the love and thirst he felt for this woman—his blood-bonded mate—knew no end.

CHAPTER 38

At dawn that next day, Brynne and Zael awoke to find the four colony elders on the doorstep of the cottage. They had arrived with a special request—and a gift for the newly mated couple.

They brought them down to the beach, to where the sailboat she and Zael had arrived on was moored and waiting at the end of the island's stone dock.

"You agreed to live at the colony," Baramael announced. "However, we have decided to amend the terms of our agreement."

"What do you mean?" Zael asked, sounding as surprised as Brynne felt.

"The four of us met again last night to discuss the proposed alliance with the Order. This morning, we met with the rest of the colony and explained everything that happened these past couple of days—including the role you and Brynne played in protecting our crystal." Baramael put his hand on Zael's shoulder. "The colony agrees unanimously that you and Brynne should have the freedom to stay here with us and to return to the outside as you choose."

Brynne swallowed, looking to Zael in shock and confusion. She felt the same reaction in him, through their bond.

"Come and go as we choose?" Zael asked cautiously. "This is...most unexpected."

"Consider it our gift to you," Anaphiel said, smiling warmly at both of them.

Haroth nodded. "With our trust. You've both earned it."

"You have the trust of the whole colony," Nethiri added, the female elder's silver eyes shining with kindness.

"The freedom doesn't come entirely without some responsibility," Baramael said, his bicolored gaze moving between Brynne and Zael. "To be specific, the council would like you both to be emissaries of the colony in our new alliance with the Order."

Brynne could hardly contain her gasp. As prepared as she was to remain on the island with Zael for the rest of her life, there had been a part of her that yearned to see her sister again, if only to say goodbye. But what the elders were offering was something far better. A chance to keep Tavia and the rest of the Order in her life as partners in the alliance.

"Yes, of course," Zael accepted, bringing Brynne under his arm.

"It would be our honor," she told the elders. "Thank you for this very welcome gift."

"It's well-earned," Baramael said. He smiled, and it was a revelation to see the stern Atlantean's face soften with his warm regard.

"You also mentioned a special request," Zael prompted the dark-haired elder.

"Yes. There is the matter of Tamisia."

Brynne hoped the council had also softened toward their colleague's fall from grace. "Have you reconsidered your position with her as well?"

"No," Baramael replied soberly. "That we cannot do. Her banishment still stands. However, as she's never been away from the colony to see where to teleport, she will need help leaving."

He indicated the waiting sailboat.

"Of course," Zael said, understanding at once. "Brynne and I can take her to the mainland."

Baramael nodded. "She will be pleased to hear that. We will inform her to prepare for the journey as soon as you and Brynne are ready to depart."

"As for her banishment," Zael said, "adjusting to life on the outside may not be easy for her. Will the council allow us to ensure Tamisia has somewhere to go once she's away from the colony? Someone to help look out for her, if she needs assistance?"

They all agreed, and not long afterward, Brynne and Zael found themselves on the sailboat with Tamisia, heading back for Athens.

The blonde Atlantean remained in the cabin below for most of their journey. But by nightfall, as the craggy shoreline of the mainland drew nearer, Tamisia emerged to join them on the deck.

Her lovely face was still miserable with contrition. "You didn't have to do this for me. Neither one of you."

"We wanted to," Brynne assured her, feeling no animosity for the woman, only sympathy. "Lazaro Archer will see that you have somewhere safe to stay in

Rome until you're settled. We didn't want you to be all alone."

Zael had made the arrangements after telepathically connecting with Jordana to explain the situation. As the Order's command center in Rome was the closest, Lazaro and his Breedmate, Melena, now waited to meet the boat personally in Athens when they arrived at the docks.

On shore, the black-haired Gen One Breed male stepped out of a large SUV with the curvaceous redhead who shared his bond. There was another Breed male with them. Massive, intimidating, there was no question the scowling male with the shaved head and *glyph*-covered arms was a warrior.

Lazaro and Melena introduced themselves, both of them pleased to hear that the alliance with the colony had been accepted. If Jordana had told them the circumstances of Tamisia's ousting from the colony, neither of them gave any indication to make her feel uneasy.

Unfortunately, the same could not be said for the behemoth who stood behind them. Unfriendly didn't even begin to describe his forbidding demeanor. But Lazaro and his Breedmate seemed to trust the male implicitly.

"Trygg will see you to the car, Tamisia," Lazaro informed her. "Melena and I will be along momentarily."

"Thank you," she said, then turned to Zael and Brynne, remorse glistening in her sky-blue eyes. "I don't know how to repay you."

Zael touched her shoulder and gently shook his head. "There is no need. Take care of yourself, and maybe one day the three of us will meet again."

"I would like that very much." She smiled at Brynne. "I wish you both every happiness."

Brynne clutched her hand and gave it a tender squeeze. "The same to you, Sia."

She headed off, looking more than a little anxious as she followed the big warrior back to the waiting vehicle.

Lazaro ran a hand through his ebony hair. "I hope your friend doesn't scare easily. I would've brought one of my other men along, but I've lost one of my team to family obligations and a new Breedmate, and another is gearing up for a covert mission. Trygg's not much of a people person."

Zael grunted. "Don't worry about Sia. She's never met a male she couldn't charm."

"She's never met Trygg," Melena said, smiling wryly. She glanced at Brynne. "Congratulations to you and Zael on your mating. I'm sorry—I'm trying not to stare, but it's difficult. It's not every day that Lazaro and I get a chance to meet a daywalker or an Atlantean."

The Rome commander's mouth quirked. "Not to mention how rare it is to meet the diplomatic envoys for the Atlantean colony."

"Thank you for the well wishes," Brynne replied. "As for our diplomatic role, I imagine Zael and I will be seeing much more of you both."

"And the Order in general," Zael added. "This alliance is a partnership between our people, but I hope you and the rest of the warriors understand that beyond any formal agreement, you also have my friendship. And my service, should you need it—whether that's in battle against Selene or any other threat we have to contend with."

"That is most appreciated," Lazaro answered. "Unfortunately, it seems Opus Nostrum isn't about to give us any rest. It will be a damned good day when we finally take the bastards out."

"Let's hope it's soon," Brynne said. "If there's anything Zael and I can do to help make that happen, the Order needs only to ask."

"You honor us well," Lazaro replied with a formal bow of his head.

The phrase was tradition within the Order, one of the highest praises bestowed on its brethren. That he said it now, to Brynne and her Atlantean mate, was a compliment they both would aspire to be worthy of from this day forward.

The Rome commander gestured toward the vehicle Tamisia had entered. "And you have our word that we'll make sure your friend gets whatever she requires while she's with us."

"Thank you both," Zael said as the two men shook hands.

Melena pulled Brynne into a brief hug. "I so enjoyed meeting you."

"The pleasure is mine," she replied, smiling as she drew back from Lazaro's mate. "May I ask you a personal favor?"

"Of course, anything."

"When you speak with the Order again, please tell my sister I am well, and that I hope to see her soon."

"But not too soon," Zael interjected, a grin tugging at his mouth. "Brynne and I have a blood bond to celebrate. I plan to keep her all to myself for as long as I possibly can."

They said their goodbyes, watching as the SUV rolled away into the gathering night.

Zael's eyes glimmered as he took Brynne's hand and led her back onto the sailboat. She couldn't wait to be back on the island. Back in her Atlantean mate's arms, and back in his bed.

Their bed.

In the home they would make together.

And, if they were so blessed, in the home where they would one day start a family of their own. The wish took root so firmly, it swept her breath away.

Because it wasn't only her wish, she realized.

She felt that same hope shining in Zael's heart too.

It was in his blood, in the bond that now connected their hearts and their futures.

He pulled her into his embrace, his mouth coming down on hers in a kiss so passionate and filled with emotion that it shook her to her marrow.

"Yes, I want it, too," he murmured against her lips. "I want it all with you, Brynne. Forever."

And when he pressed her down onto the deck with him to lie beneath the blanket of stars, she knew to the depths of her soul that she was already holding the future in her arms.

She was for the first time in her life—and forever—right where she belonged.

~ * ~

ABOUT THE AUTHOR

LARA ADRIAN is a New York Times and #1 international best-selling author, with nearly 4 million books in print and digital worldwide and translations licensed to more than 20 countries. Her books regularly appear in the top spots of all the major bestseller lists including the New York Times, USA Today, Publishers Weekly, Amazon.com, Barnes & Noble, etc. Reviewers have called Lara's books "addictively readable" (Chicago Tribune), "extraordinary" (Fresh Fiction), and "one of the consistently best" (Romance Novel News).

Writing as **TINA ST. JOHN**, her historical romances have won numerous awards including the National Readers Choice; Romantic Times Magazine Reviewer's Choice; Booksellers Best; and many others. She was twice named a Finalist in Romance Writers of America's RITA Awards, for Best Historical Romance (White Lion's Lady) and Best Paranormal Romance (Heart of the Hunter). More recently, the German translation of Heart of the Hunter debuted on Der Spiegel bestseller list.

Visit the author's website and sign up for new release announcements at www.LaraAdrian.com.

Find Lara on Facebook at
www.facebook.com/LaraAdrianBooks

Never miss a new book from Lara Adrian!

Sign up for the email newsletter at
www.LaraAdrian.com

Or type this URL into your web browser:
http://bit.ly/LaraAdrianNews

Be the first to get notified of Lara's new releases, plus be eligible for special subscribers-only exclusive content and giveaways that you won't find anywhere else.

Bonus!
When you confirm your subscription, you'll get an email with instructions for requesting free bookmarks and other fun goodies, while supplies last.

Sign up today!

Look for the next story in the
Midnight Breed vampire romance series

Midnight Untamed

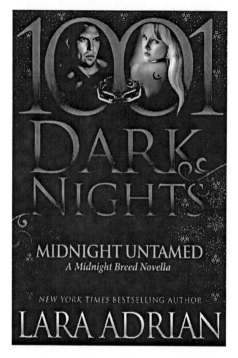

Available October 11, 2016

Available in ebook and trade paperback

For more information on the series and
upcoming releases, visit:

www.LaraAdrian.com

Thirsty for more Midnight Breed?

Read the complete series!

. . . and more to come!

Presenting a fun and relaxing new way to enjoy the Midnight Breed series!

The Midnight Breed Series Coloring Book

Featuring 21 coloring pages of original art and illustrations inspired by Lara Adrian's characters, book quotes and story world. With a variety of pages ranging from simple designs to intricate patterns, this book will keep you entertained for hours!

AVAILABLE NOW

If you enjoy sizzling contemporary romance,
don't miss this hot new release from Lara Adrian!

For 100 Days

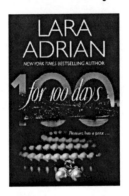

The 100 Series: Book 1

*"I wish I could give this more than 5 stars! Lara Adrian not only dips
her toe into this genre with flare, she will take it over . . . I have found my
new addiction, this series."* --The Sub Club Books

**Available now in ebook, trade paperback and
unabridged audiobook.**

COMING SOON:

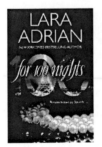 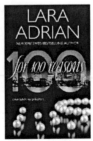

More romance and adventure from Lara Adrian!

Phoenix Code Series
(Paranormal Romantic Suspense)

"A fast-paced thrill ride." –Fresh Fiction

Masters of Seduction Series
(Paranormal Romance)

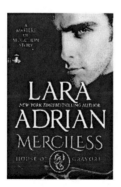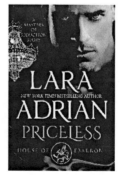

"Thrilling, action-packed and super sexy." –Literal Addiction

Connect with Lara online at:

www.LaraAdrian.com

www.facebook.com/LaraAdrianBooks

www.goodreads.com/lara_adrian

www.twitter.com/lara_adrian

www.instagram.com/laraadrianbooks

www.pinterest.com/LaraAdrian

CPSIA information can be obtained
at www.ICGtesting.com
Printed in the USA
LVOW11s2303131216
517166LV00001B/167/P